ALAN J HILL was born in St Helens in the north-west of England in 1961 before moving to Hampton where he has lived since 1993 with his wife Deborah. He has four grown-up children and hopes that this, his first novel, is the first of many. The sequel, Underworld and Overland, will be published early in 2010.

TREMAIN
BOOK ONE

The Seven Faiths

BOOK ONE

The Seven Faiths

ALAN J HILL

ATHENA PRESS
LONDON

TREMAIN BOOK ONE
The Seven Faiths
Copyright © Alan J Hill 2009

All Rights Reserved

ISBN 978 1 84748 647 9

First published 2009 by
ATHENA PRESS
Queen's House, 2 Holly Road
Twickenham TW1 4EG
United Kingdom

Printed for Athena Press

For Lisa, Richard, Amy and Adam.
Never stop believing.
Deb, the next one's for you.

Contents

Part One
Jost

Part Two
Ontrades

Part Three
Seathon

Part Four
The Landsplitter

Part One
Jost

Dreams

Sheldrak let loose the arrow with a swish that was heard too late for the large, shambling grey creature feeding on the other side of the clearing. The grey bedago came crashing to the ground. Six foot in height with a long snout, the sprawled animal looked like a cross between a small grizzly bear and a large, unfortunate badger. The arrow was embedded deep in the shoulder blade, down to the fine white feathers at the base of the shaft, and the thick fur was already matting with blood.

The young man responsible for the creature's misfortune stood glistening in the sharp morning sun that filtered through the thick foliage of the forest walls. Lithe, with dark brown tanned skin, short-cropped fair hair bleached by the forest sun, he stood with his heart pounding in his young chest. He was fifteen years old and on his first solo hunting expedition and had ventured all of three miles from his village to 'hunt, kill and skin an animal greater in size than himself'.

He smiled as he remembered what his best friend Divad had suggested: 'I think I'll go out into the meadow and kill Father's old cow.' Somehow he didn't think Divad was overly interested in making the Seven Faiths of Strepsay.

The beast was down but Sheldrak could not tell if the heavy movement of the chest meant the bedago was in shock or readying itself to fight his new enemy to the death. As if reading the animal's mind, Sheldrak lowered the second arrow he had instinctively fitted to his bow and paused to consider the word 'enemy'. Since when, and how, was he the enemy of this poor bedago? He wasn't even going to eat it, just take the skin back to the village as proof. Proof of what? That he could shoot an arrow into something the size of a small outhouse from a distance of five paces? He was doing it again, questioning the teachings that had gone for centuries before him and his family were living in the village of Jost, in the province of Irga.

Bravery was one of the Seven Faiths and if he was to become the first elder in his family then he had to prove his. But at this moment he didn't feel very brave. He felt mean and a little like a coward. A coward who, when faced with real danger, wasn't too sure how he might react. He might not know yet but he would do soon as his life was about to take a large step into the unknown.

The bedago was not unconscious at all but very much aware of its surroundings. With a speed associated with the shout for last drinks at the local inn, it sprung on to its back legs and pulled itself to its full height, which to Sheldrak now looked to be over twelve foot. Sheldrak was surprised to find he had reloaded but now found similar reflexes sending the arrow off into the trees. The creature roared. Sheldrak called on all his training, looked the beast in the eyes, dropped his bow and arrow, called out a local expletive – 'Jak!' – and turned and ran.

This act, to a neutral observer, could have been construed as sheer panic and, as Sheldrak ran, jumped and skipped over branches and small streams, he was trying to tell himself that it wasn't. He quite simply did not want to kill the magnificent grey animal but, in the same breath (or lack of breath), he wasn't prepared to relinquish his hold on life either. In the circumstances, which he had provoked, this seemed to be the best solution – for both parties to walk away. Damage limitation! Unfortunately for Sheldrak the bedago was a lot faster than he had expected. The race was on and, to the winner, life.

The surrounding area was well known to Sheldrak but in

his panic he wasn't sure in which direction he was running. The sun was directly in front of him, streaming into his face and making it difficult to see where his next step would fall. He turned to his left so that the sun no longer shone into his eyes, slowing him down long enough for an almighty swipe of a paw to narrowly miss his foot.

'Strepsay jak!' he shouted. The creature was so close, saliva from its muzzle fell on to his leg. He needed to get into open ground where he believed he could outrun the animal.

He jumped a fallen branch on the forest floor, swerved around a large oak tree and saw a small break in the undergrowth ahead of him. He was drawing clear. He relaxed but stepped out into fresh air. It wasn't a clearing at all but a steep decline and, like a small infant taking his first step to find that tomorrow would be first-step day, he tumbled forward down the scree. His hands flew out in front of him, but it was his head that hit the ground first. His legs quickly caught up with the rest of his slim body as he rolled over and over, sending arrows spilling and twirling like the spindles of a cartwheel.

Seconds behind him the bedago was sliding down the hill in a fast and controlled manner. The hare had made a big mistake and this tortoise had more than finishing first on its mind. Sheldrak needed to regain his feet quickly. As he continued to tumble, lights went on and off. He wasn't sure if it was the sunlight flashing as he rolled, or if he had really hit himself hard and the flashing was inside his head. He came to a stop at the bottom of the hill and instinct once again took over as he pistoned his legs firmly into the ground. Springing to his feet and opening his eyes, he looked like a deep-sea diver coming up for oxygen. Claws raked his back and he could feel the blood welling into the newly formed cracks in his skin.

He pushed his legs forcefully, feeling something tear in

his calf, then blackness as he turned into the low branches of an elm. Had he hit the branch when sprinting, it would have taken the top of his skull clean off. He passed into unconsciousness, blood seeping from his head. The animal approached and the last thing Sheldrak saw was the bedago licking his blood from the ground at the base of the tree. The cat has the cream, he thought as he mercifully left all thought behind…

He was in a cave. Sat on the floor, he had no sense of location, with the walls too far away to be seen. He could hear running water. Falling water, dripping. He shivered. The dampness of the wet stone he sat on seeped into his bones. It was the sort of cold that had permanence to it and even the rich, deep coat he wore did nothing to make him feel warm. The noises surrounded his shivering body and the acoustics of the cave confused his senses so that he could not work out from which direction the flowing water came.

He stood. There were other noises in here. Something slapped gently against the wet floor like the sound of a fresh fish hitting the deck of a boat. He was not alone, and fear slid slowly over his body like a dawn mist. The fear grew and he realised that he was terrified. This wasn't normal fear but a sort that made his head throb with pain and his legs buckle as he fell to his knees.

'I've died and gone to hell,' he thought. A pale grey shadow moved in front of him, then to his right, and finally flitted swiftly behind him.

A voice whispered into his ear, 'I have you.'

Sheldrak's bladder nearly released, such was the emptiness of the voice. If a black widow spider could speak before it ate its prey then this would be the sound. Sheldrak turned to meet his destiny and found himself in the middle of a beautiful green meadow with thick waves of grass flowing across and down the dales to greet him.

He turned and in all directions the green met the blue of the sky with no interruption. Something at the edge of his vision twinkled. A star during the day, he thought, realising all fear had left his body as if the bright sun had burned the dawn mist away.

Another glitter and then another. He spun around slowly, getting faster and faster, his eyes searching for what now looked like seven diamonds spaced around him evenly at shoulder height and drawing ever closer to his spinning body. He stretched his arms out and put his head back as though on a ride at the country fayre. The lights approached him and he laughed out loud with delight.

He saw as the lights drew closer that they were not lights, but bright flames. In the centre of each lick of white was a clear centre with a blue pupil the colour of the deepest ocean. He screamed with pleasure and then abruptly stopped spinning.

From all sides of him the deep green grass was being enveloped by poppies rushing towards him from all sides, as though a great dam had burst and released a sea of foaming red. The seven flames blinked out as the poppies streaked towards him. He once again felt fear. His last recollection was the sun going out as though someone had licked his fingers and extinguished a candle. Sheldrak knew that this was the light of the world and it would never shine again.

He awoke. He actually spoke the word 'Alive' before lifting his head and seeing, sat opposite him, the bedago, looking at him quizzically.

'Animal, I have no fight left in me,' he croaked before passing out once more.

The second time he came back to his senses the sun had almost passed over and he knew that if he didn't try to get moving his injuries would begin to cramp up to such an extent that walking would become difficult, and then impossible. His bow and arrows were strewn somewhere back up that bloody hill and a night unarmed in this forest was a test too far with his body this battered.

The Bravery Faith of Strepsay could wait until he didn't feel as though a small army had just used his head for club practice. He looked up and saw that his foe was still with him. The bedago watched him with keen interest and with what looked to Sheldrak like strange curiosity. He hoped it wasn't the kind of curiosity that resulted in spiders getting their legs torn off by young boys.

The ferocity of the situation had filtered away as surely as the fading sunlight. Sheldrak dragged himself to his feet. The beast lowered its head, raised it again, then turned and lumbered into the undergrowth.

'My Faith,' whispered Sheldrak as he tried to keep his tired body from falling once more. Did that beast bow to me? It couldn't have. I must have got hit harder than I thought. Why did it not kill me while I was out? Kill me – it seemed to be watching over me, protecting me. These thoughts flew through his mind but, like a tiny humming-bird looking for nectar among the flowers of the woods, never settled quite long enough to take weight.

The three miles back to Jost were going to feel like thirty. His calf muscle pulled, screaming at him to stop with every step. His back was clotted and clogged with dried blood. It stung under his light tunic but this was the least of his pains. When he raised his hand to the front of his head he realised that the gash would need help from a healer. Thick, congealed blood with large clots in it was stuck to his hair and down the side of his face and someone had let hornets loose inside his head while he had half-slept.

He walked a couple of leagues out of his way to go to a small stream and bathed his face, then lay full length in the water letting it wash away the dirt and dried blood attached to his back and head. This caused his scalp wound to bleed slightly again but pressure with some large leaves soon got it to re-clot. His head still ached but the pain had moved to the outside and was now hammering on his skull, trying to get back in.

He could normally run the three miles home in twenty minutes but the journey today took him an hour and a half, and the last thirty minutes were spent in darkness as he limped back to the main gate of Jost, his home village.

He was greeted by a shout from the guard. 'By my elders, who is it out there in the dark, travelling with no light?'

'By my elders, it is I, Sheldrak of Jost, son of Whinst and Azores.'

'Sheldrak, where have you been? Your parents have been looking for you. You were due back long before sunset.'

'Unfortunately, Jason, nobody bothered to tell the bedago what time dinner was. I'll get home straight away. If you see Father or Mother let them know I'm OK and on my way to the cottage.'

The village housed over 400 people of Irgania, who resided in small stone cottages which, if viewed from above, were built in ever widening circles around the main street. The main street was the heart of the village, housing all the trading centres, the smithy, the church, a couple of inns, (the Duck at one end and the Jolly Farmer the other), and the pride of the village, the Old Hall. It was made totally of wood and used for all important meetings, functions, betrothals and any other reason for a good old get-together.

Sheldrak's home was two rows behind the church on the

opposite side of Main Street from where he had entered the village. After what he had been through, this last couple of furlongs was proving the toughest. He limped down the side of the church, past the graves (never a comfort in the dark) and was approaching his cottage when something grey moved in the periphery of his vision. He turned but could see nothing in the darkness.

Ignoring the pain in his leg, he broke into a gentle trot. Spooked once again he ran up his garden path and bashed open the front door of the cottage.

'Hello, Mother. No need to worry, I'm fine,' were his last words of the day as he passed out for the third time, falling at his startled mother's feet.

Later that night after his father had come home and carried Sheldrak to his cot, the dream returned.

Village Life

Sheldrak woke late the next morning. He knew it by the angle of the sun dripping over the top of his shutters and falling on to his linen cot covers. The dream again. What did it mean? The colours were so vivid: green, blue, red and grey. Was that the same grey he thought he'd seen as he walked past the graves last night or was that also part of this horrible nightmare? Only if you'd been dreaming while awake, spoke up the rational part of his head.

'About time too, you lazy bugger,' came a voice from his right.

'Jak.' Sheldrak's heart missed a beat as he started to wonder if he would live to see his seventeenth year. 'Divad, how long have you been sat there?'

'Oh, fine. No thanks for sitting up all night with you. Just "How long have you been there?" '

Sheldrak realised how abrupt he had sounded to his best friend, Divad. 'Sorry, Vad, I didn't mean to sound ungrateful. So how long have you babysat me?'

Divad was one of the few people in the village to own a timepiece and never wasted an opportunity to pull it out on its chain. He looked long and hard at it, held his fingers out in front of him, did some tough mental arithmetic which looked as if he were trying to pass something the size of a loaf of bread, and then proudly said, 'I got here about two minutes ago, but you are the talk of the village.'

Sheldrak groaned loudly and slumped back on to his pillow.

'Faith,' he breathed. Vad was an absolute loon but thankfully he never failed to cheer up Sheldrak with his idiocy and absolute disregard for anything that was considered important. 'What do you mean I'm the talk of the village? I only went hunting. In fact I didn't even go hunting, I was training for Strepsay.'

'Yes, but you went training for Bravery and ended up practising Humility instead,' Divad responded.

'Shut up, loon. At least I take this seriously. I will be the first member of my family to become an elder.'

'If you live long enough to become an elder.' The voice was that of his mother, Azores. 'Sheldrak, don't forget another of the Faiths is the one of Wisdom, and if yesterday is anything to go by that is the one that you need to concentrate on most.'

Azores was a small woman, who had lived her full thirty-eight years in the village as the loyal wife of Whinst. The hard years putting enough food on the table for the three of them had taken their toll. She was homely, but the eyes retained enough of a sparkle to brighten up her husband's day and a smile that could keep the cottage lit well into the darkest night.

'Divad, out. You can come by after lessons to see how Sheldrak is. If he is feeling well enough you two can go for a walk. Sheldrak, no riding, hunting or climbing. You are not even going to break into a trot for a couple of days. On your way, Divad, and please tell Methon for me that Shel won't be in until I give the word. Your mentor won't be very pleased with you, Sheldrak, but that is another lesson I hope you have learnt from your escapade.'

Divad left for his daily lessons and Azores soon filled the vacant chair by Sheldrak's cot.

'Right, son, I want an explanation.'

It took Sheldrak about fifteen minutes to run through the adventure of the previous day. For some reason that he was not aware of, he omitted the dream that he had now had twice, and instead concentrated on the reality. Azores showed genuine surprise and horror when Sheldrak relayed the part about being knocked out for so long and being at the mercy of the bedago.

'And it didn't touch you at all? What about those scratches on your back? When did that happen?'

'Honestly, Mother, that happened when I was running away. I guess it didn't attack out of some form of decency or respect for an enemy. I don't really know.'

Azores knew her son well and was under the impression that he was holding something back, but if she didn't push too hard she knew that eventually Sheldrak would tell her what was bothering him. Until such time that Shel could sort out his jumbled thoughts he was only going to share them with one person. He might be a loon, but by Faith, Divad was a loyal loon, and Sheldrak could trust him with his life. Faith forbid it would come to that.

At four Sheldrak was woken from a light sleep by the banging on the front door of the cottage of what must have been a small army. He guessed who it was and was already climbing out of his cot when Divad burst into the room.

'All right, my friend, I have obviously shamed you into actually moving today. Come on, quick, get dressed and we'll walk down to the tree house and you can tell me all about your fun yesterday.'

Sheldrak dressed, but not quickly at all. This is how he imagined dressing after thirty years as an elder, not as a young man of fifteen. He hoped the walk would help to stretch his aching muscles. His head wouldn't benefit from walking but the soothing liniment Azores had applied under the thick towelling dressing was easing the pain from the nine stitches his Father had closed the wound with.

His mother fussed a little more, instructing him as to what he could and could not do today (but perhaps tomorrow or the day after). He and Divad set off at a leisurely pace through the copse at the back of the cottage, turning north at the boundary wall and into the north meadow, which this year was not being used for one of the crops that the village relied upon for their existence.

As Sheldrak had decided that climbing the tree was, as his mother had already pointed out to him, 'for tomorrow', they both flopped into the long grass, hidden from view, and chatted as teenagers worlds over did. Only they understand that there is nothing better than talking, laughing, sharing, with someone who even at that tender age becomes so close that he or she becomes an extension of your own personality. They lay there, as they had on many sunny afternoons, cementing into place a friendship that would last for ever. At least, that's what they thought.

Sheldrak told his story again, but this time including the dream, which he had experienced for the third time during his fitful sleep that morning. He always told Divad the truth, knowing that he would receive in return an honest, if at times humorous, opinion.

Divad gave his joke interpretation of the dream: 'Well, the cave and old Greybones is obviously your fear of not performing well in the Strepsay Faiths. This is due to you turning bravery into cowardice by running away from the bedago, which you should be killing. Then you knock yourself out before your enemy has a chance of touching you. Always a good move that, hurt yourself before the opposition can.

'Secondly, the grass represents how you now intend to spend your life. As a lazy farmer who lets the grass get too long and spins about in it instead of cutting it. The seven lights are the Seven Faiths of Strepsay that you now have as much chance of achieving as I do, and they are put out by the red poppies which represent something that I don't have a clue about because I am now very bored.'

Sheldrak roared laughing. Divad had once again managed to put things in perspective for him. But once they had both finished laughing Sheldrak said, 'I know that you don't have exactly the same beliefs as I do and you think that interpreting the dream is nonsense, but to have the same dream three times in a row makes me think there is something more behind it. I just wish I knew what!'

It was then that Divad came up with an idea that would change both their lives for ever. 'Don't laugh at me now because I am going to be serious for once. You know Greeg, the old sayer who lives in the broken-down hut on the east boundary wall?'

'Yes, of course. Every child in the village is warned not to go anywhere near Greeg's hut.'

'Well, I've been told that years ago he used to tell your future, read hands, tell unwed mothers' parents who the father was and tell you the meaning of your dreams. All for the price of a few beers.'

'But,' said Shel, 'that was before he got blamed for those missing children about ten years ago. Nobody speaks to him any more; in fact he hasn't been seen for five years.'

'Sheldrak, please listen me out. I have never talked this long without trying to crack a funny. My mother says he still exists. She occasionally sees a light on in the winter months when she returns from the fields. Greeg can tell you what you need to know, if you are sure you want to find out.'

'Vad, I know you mean well, but how can we make him see me? As you just said, nobody goes near him since the rumours of the missing children, and I'm sure as Faith that if I turn up out of the blue and ask nicely he'll say, "Certainly, young Sheldrak. Pull yourself up a missing baby and make yourself comfortable!" '

It was Divad's turn to shriek with laughter. It was so funny because it was unlike Sheldrak to say something so outrageous.

When Divad calmed down he returned to his theory.

'Greeg still lives within the boundary walls of Jost. He must abide by the village rules the same as you or I or face expulsion. In four weeks' time it's the Great Race. The winner of the Great Race is granted one request by the village elder, provided it doesn't break any laws. All you have to do, Shel, is win the race, request a sitting with Greeg as your prize, get the dream translated into something you understand and then we all live happ—'

'Don't say it, Divad. Don't tempt Faith. We both know that, since either of us can remember, Arkel has won the five-mile run. I'm strong and I'm now old enough to enter, but in the history of Jost no one has ever won it at the first time of asking.'

'Then it is time, Sheldrak, that you started to make history. Let's go and see Methon. He'll tell us whether or not it's possible.'

The Training

Methon's large quarters lay to the north-east of Main Street, two or three leagues from the Jolly Farmer, which Methon liked to frequent every couple of days for a few ales. He was considered high up in the village pecking order as he was one of the ten or twelve mentors the village employed. The number of mentors was dependant upon how many children were living there at any one time. Hence he got the larger premises, but with them came the responsibility.

The people of the village of Jost believed in the principle that, as children got older, they needed to spend more time with their mentors. Also, as the child got closer to becoming an adult, class sizes got smaller, and set times for learning decreased. Sheldrak and Divad had reached the age, at least according to Methon, whereby they saw him as much as they wanted. Sheldrak had waited for this age all of his life, only to find out that now he wasn't forced, he actually utilised Methon's time far more than he ever had as an infant.

The doors to the learning quarters were open and Shel and Vad strolled in, shouting Methon's name as they did. The words rolled around the thick wooden beams before bouncing back to them quickly, as quickly as Methon had appeared out of the book room at the rear of the class.

'Young gentlefolk,' he cried, 'and one who limps because he knows more at fifteen summers than many do at forty.'

'Good Faith. Is there some form of telepathy in this village? I'm sure that if someone sneezes on the east wall, the guard on the west wall shouts bless you!'

'If you were to think for a second, Master Sheldrak, you

would remember that you were due to see me at sun-up this very day, but Master Divad sent your apologies with a story you have just confirmed by carrying that leg as though you had a log of wood attached to it.

'So how can I help you fine gentlemen?'

It didn't take very long for Sheldrak to relay his tale once again, omitting the reason for needing to see old Greeg. In all honesty he had been considering an attempt on the Great Race this summer so it did not come as any shock to Methon that he expressed himself so. Only the reasons why, and Sheldrak's proposed request of the village elder should he win, appeared curious.

Methon as always let the young men talk until they ran out of things to say. Divad had built up such a thirst that he sat there like an old dog that had been chasing rabbits in the sun for an hour and was desperate for a cold bowl of water.

'Sheldrak, you know that I will train you. I would be telling an untruth if I said I didn't expect this request, but it seems strange to me that yesterday you get mauled and today you decide to run. I see the hard look in your eyes that tells me you will do this with or without my help and so I will aid you. You must do exactly as I say for the next four weeks or I will withdraw my aid. And I ask one thing of you – that if you win and get the chance to see Greeg, you tell me first why you have to see him.

'I know you will have heard old stories about the hermit's alleged powers but not all that he will tell you will be true. It is for your Wisdom Faith to come to the fore. Remember the Seven Faiths of Strepsay and know truth from falsehood. Now you two, come and chant the Faiths with me.'

At Methon's request the three of them bowed low their heads and chanted in sequence:

Love… Honour… Bravery… Loyalty… Humility… Wisdom… Sacrifice…

'And now the second cycle.'

Bravery... Love... Honour... Humility... Wisdom...
Sacrifice... Loyalty...

'Never forget,' Methon whispered, 'behind every Faith the
second cycle lies. Now, Sheldrak, I don't want to see you
for three days, after which you must be here at sun-up every
morning from then until the day of the race. If you are to
beat that wily old dog Arkel then we have much work to do.
I will give you a rub for the calf which you must apply many
times a day for the next three days, and that should also give
you enough time to clear your head and let that gash heal

enough for you to start some light running. Now away with you and enjoy what is left of your childhood, for I feel that Strepsay will force itself upon you far earlier than Faith intended.'

Three days went past in a blur for Sheldrak. The rub worked small wonders on his leg and he helped his father in the fields on the third day, such was the healing power of the balm.

'Methon knows a little too much for his own good,' was Sheldrak's mother's verdict, but she had never totally agreed with Methon's ways. Luckily for Sheldrak, Methon had been his father's mentor and so a wink from him had been enough for Shel to close his mouth and not enter into yet another debate about mentors.

On the fourth day he stood in the early morning gloom at the door to Methon's living quarters like a shadow hiding out of existence before the sun brings it to life. The door burst outwards as the rays of dawn peeped over the horizon like strands of bright-coloured yarn.

'Good morning, fine sir,' said the ramrod-straight Methon. Sheldrak was always amazed how a man of his years ('He must be really old if he was my father's mentor,') could stand so straight and tall. Six foot at least, with a shock of thick grey hair and the loose-limbed look that some men seem able to carry all their lives.

'Today I shall bring the brains and you will bring the strength and stamina of your young years. Between us we have all the attributes we require, but we need to squeeze enough of them into one body to give us a chance of success. Did you manage to shake off that loon of a friend of yours?'

'Yes, but he's really unhappy at being left out of this.'

'Sheldrak, is Divad running in the race? No. Well, that's the last we need to say about that. Come, today we will walk the course and I will tell you how you will run on the day. But first a present for you.'

He handed Sheldrak a pair of very strange footwear items. They looked like boots a deep-sea diver might wear, but to Sheldrak they were the strangest pair of shoes he had ever seen.

'Put them on, Sheldrak. They will go over those running moccasins you wear. This is metal dug out of the ground in a land far away from here, called Mina. The smithy on Main knocked them into shape for me. Now try to walk quickly for me over to that far tree.'

Sheldrak landed on the ground with such a thump that it probably got a few villagers up out of their cots that morning.

'Bloody Faith,' Sheldrak let slip. 'Sorry, Methon. These are more difficult to move in than I thought.' He picked himself up and clumped away to the tree, turned slowly and clumped his way back.

'You already have an advantage over the other thirty runners. They will turn up on the day knowing their limitations. But, my young friend, you will glide like a small water fly over the surface of a pond, hardly touching the ground, and that is just the first advantage you will have. Come, let us walk.'

The course of the race ran alongside the eastern boundary of the village in a shape that was like a long, squashed sausage. The start was a flat field, previously used for growing wheat and other grain crops, that ran in a gentle slope down to a small pine forest. On either side of the field was an eight-foot hedge and, as the entrance to the pines got closer, the two hedges drew into each other providing a natural funnel.

The young and old walked side by side towards the gap and it became obvious that the two of them could only just slip through at the widest point of their shoulders. The villagers called this place the Giant's Cup, as the ground fell away steeply on entering the pine trees. From a distance it must have looked as though Sheldrak and Methon had swapped bodies, with Methon standing proud and tall like one of the pines while Sheldrak stooped like a weeping willow, leaning into a winter wind.

The path then wound its way in and out of the trees, sometimes wide enough for two or three but quickly dropping back to a width that would accommodate only one. During the walking of this part of the course Methon pointed out places where Sheldrak could expect to overtake or be overtaken. There were more than three weeks to go but already Shel could feel the first rumbling of excitement deep in his tummy, which would gradually build to an unbearable level on the day of the race.

Faith, if he could feel it now, could his nerve hold on the day? He reminded himself of the dream, which he had experienced again the night before, awakening in a cold sweat as the blackout of the sun became chilling in its execution. He sensed that time was running out.

After about a mile they approached Dread's Dyke. Dread's Dyke was a twelve-foot-wide rip in the earth. No records or memories existed of a time before this channel. It looked as though something had tried to rip a hole in the very fabric of existence and it was here that Arkel normally won the race.

By arriving here first and nimbly trotting along the two-foot-wide beam over the ravine, he beat the bottleneck created by the surging runners behind him. The time then spent waiting for one's turn to cross the beam was directly dependent upon the bravery of each runner to get across the makeshift bridge. It was written in village lore that the depth of the ravine was such that if you dropped a stone to see how deep it was, the race would be over by the time it landed.

After the Dyke came the Steppes, hewn out of pure granite. The runners climbed in a semicircle, each step being more than a foot in height and so varied in depth that on occasion you had to stand on your toes to negotiate them – a hundred stones rising over 100 feet and turning the runners 180 degrees for the mile sprint back down the east boundary wall. The final rise brought you right back to the start. After this you ran around the pole and headed off again to complete another two-and-a-half-mile circuit.

'My dear Sheldrak, it is known in some quarters as the Great Five and not the Great Race. Surely you remember this from years gone?'

'Of course I do, sir, but watching as a child with naught but a desperate desire to take part is a far cry from standing here now at the top of the Steppes and wondering if I will ever get air into my lungs again.'

'Do not worry. At this stage you are doing remarkably well just to walk to the top of here with your shiny new footwear. You will fly up here without them. Let us now make our way back to my quarters, where we will discuss how you will put yourself in the best possible position to win this race.'

In the shade of Methon's cookery, with his boots flung into the closet and a large cup of blackcurrant juice in his hand, Sheldrak had recovered his composure, and his grim determination to succeed had returned.

Sheldrak broke the silence. 'What will you have me do to win Methon?'

Methon considered his answer. 'What are you prepared to do? Pray tell me, what did you see today? Surely you have worked out some tactics of your own.'

'Indeed I have. I intend to sprint flat out from the start, get in front at the Cup and stay there for the rest of the race.'

'I see,' replied Methon. 'At least I now know that you really do need me. Listen well and we shall try to be just a little more astute than "sprint flat out".' The young man raised his head and listened, as intent as a young sheepdog waiting for the whistle of his master.

Later that day after running in short sharp bursts for three miles up and down Billing Hill, boots reflecting the late afternoon sun, Sheldrak lay in his favourite spot in the long, deep grass of the meadow with Divad by his side.

'…and that is how I am going to make village history.'

'Huh, remember me? I am your best friend. Or at least I was before Methon became the almighty mentor of the Great Race. He doesn't look as though he could run for last drinks in the Farmer.'

Divad joked, but if Sheldrak had listened not only to the words but also to the hurt hiding behind the jester's mask he might have realised his best friend was missing him far more than he thought.

'I'm sorry, Divad, but for the next three weeks my routine is going to take up so much time. I still have my normal lessons to work through as well as many daily runs, all with these bloody metal shackles on. I have arm and body exercises to do. And every other day I have to run up Billing Hill, which should ready me for the Steppes, and then I have to balance on a beam one foot wide for at least fifteen minutes every day. No one is allowed on the actual course for the next three weeks so we have to stimulate – no, what did Methon say? – "simulate the race conditions".'

'I know, Shel. Nobody wants you to win more than I do but I'm already tired of being on my own and it's been three days, not three weeks.'

'Don't be stupid, Vad. Anyway, I have to go home now, I have an early start tomorrow. By my elders, I'll see you when I can over the next few days.' He ran off in the direction of the church steeple.

Divad lay back down on the grass, staring up into the sun

as long as he could before a trickle of moisture left the corner of his eye and rolled down his cheek.

'Bloody sun,' he said to himself. He could not keep his thoughts inside for much longer, for he too was experiencing strange dreams. When he awoke in the night, damp with fear, he felt so tired, as though he had been involved in some test of strength. One that he was sure he was losing.

The Great Race

Divad had found the three weeks of training harder to endure than had his best friend. The metal boots than Sheldrak was clumping around in were nothing in comparison to the mental boots that poor Divad had to experience. The dreams troubling Divad had arrived at exactly the wrong time for him, as he had chosen not to burden Shel with the added pressure of his own problems until after the Great Race was over. Divad's mother had noticed a difference in him that the preoccupied Sheldrak had missed altogether.

Divad had all but stopped eating. His normal exuberant self was retracting as surely as a turtle pulling back its head into its shell. He was pale, quiet and solitary. He blamed the 'jak Great Race' for his change of character and thought that talk of Shel's nightmares had started his own.

He dreamed every night without fail. If he didn't know it was only a dream he would have been sure that the very essence of his soul was being sucked out of his body. Absolute nonsense of course, but there was only one person he could confide in and old clanky legs just did not want to know.

Essdark sat silently in his cave. He nearly had him. One or two efforts more. The Spawn Sheldrak had forgotten about his best friend so Essdark had to seize the opportunity. He had to get the younger, stupid one while he was weak and vulnerable. He pulled the grey cowl closer around his body, a body so emaciated that the skin stretched across the bones like the webbing between the toes of a fat toad. His hollowed eyes were black, with red pupils that shone in the dark like a predator of the night. So thin were the lips that his mouth looked as if a knife had ripped a gash in his face. He no longer fed as other mortals. For over 100 years he had thrived on nothing more than fear, pain and power.

Stupid oaf thinks he's dreaming. He'll be dreaming soon of nothing but emptiness. But taking him was proving more difficult than he had imagined as the stupid one had a strong life force. He would need to rest for a long time once he had him, but did he care? Pah! He had all the time in… Well, all the time in any world he chose to inhabit. He knew that the Spawn, the Chosen One, had been born nearly sixteen years ago and he had shown himself briefly, teasing. The war was about to commence. He could afford to lose one or two battles along the way but he needed the sword, the sword that had been hewn at the beginning of time, the sword that could split the world asunder or bring it together.

Good or evil? It had always been this way. For thousands of years the world had waited. Who would win? He knew there was a stronger power and he had to play by some strange rules, but the winner won more than a game. He wasn't even sure what he was any more. But he knew he was strong and he had many servants out there, willing to do his bidding for their pleasure as pawns in his macabre game of destruction.

He would take the stupid one and set the trap accordingly. In the meantime he would take pleasure from the natural order of things that gave him his strength.

Somewhere a small child starved. Elsewhere an old man was set upon by thieves and beaten. Tomorrow a race would be run and someone might just fall to their death. He did hope so.

On the morning of the race Sheldrak's body clock woke him as the cock crowed for the first time. He rose, washed with cold water fresh from the well, ate a small light breakfast of dried bread and goats' milk and walked over to Divad's to get some moral support for the day ahead. Divad opened the door to his cottage.

'Morning sleepy he—' For the first time Shel noticed that there was something really wrong with Divad.

'For the love of Faith, Vad, what is wrong with you?' Sheldrak's shock and concern distorted his young face and for a second he looked as he would as a middle-aged man.

If Shel had looked like that for a second, Divad's middle-aged look was more permanent. He tried a smile, which faded from his face as a tree fades when cut and placed in a pot. His eyes were almost opaque and his skin had taken on the look of week-old dough that never reached a hot oven. He must have lost twenty pounds and his nightgown hung even looser than normal on his bowed body.

'I'm so scared, Shel,' he said as a tear crept from the corner of his eye and made its lonely way down the side of his cheek. 'You don't think I have the death sickness, do you?'

Sheldrak felt the pain of guilt rip into his chest surely as if someone had stuck him with a knife.

'Faith, I am so sorry, Vad. Of course you don't have the sickness. If you did, the whole village would be ill by now. This is something else, something that Greeg can help us with. You go back to rest and I will win this race, but I won't see Greeg, you will. My stupid dreams can wait. Faith will lead us. If I am to have no greater part to play in this life than that of a farmer then I shall live as proudly as my father has. I must help you first. I cannot forget the Faiths of Loyalty, Honour and of course Love if I aspire to one day becoming an elder.'

Divad's mother came out of the house and helped Sheldrak carry Divad back inside. After they had laid him back in his cot and he had fallen into an uneasy sleep, she spoke quietly to Sheldrak.

'We are a simple family with no knowledge of what goes on in the wider lands. Divad's older sister has married and moved on into the next county and, as you know, Shel, Divad's father, Seth, is no longer with us.'

She lifted her head, strong, proud and with a look on her face that cried defiance. 'I will come down to the race this afternoon and cheer you on as Divad would have done if he had been well. I know you will do all you can. Now go and prepare well and I will tend to Divad until the time for running is near.'

Sheldrak faced his best friend's mother and tried to think of some words of comfort, but none came. He was still shocked both with how Vad looked and with the force of the self-contempt he felt.

'By my elders,' was all he could manage and, with a long, deep bow, he turned away.

By four that afternoon he stood at the starting line with the other thirty-eight hopefuls, all waiting to try to wrest the title from Arkel. Arkel, as last year's winner, had pole position lined up directly with the middle of the distant dark green V-shape, and he shook his arms and legs loosely to make sure he didn't cramp up. The charge for the bottleneck was about to commence.

Virtually everyone from the village was there. Sheldrak saw his mother and father arm in arm about thirty yards away from him, restrained by the taut fretted rope which had been slung along the poles on either side of the starting line. He also looked for the mother of his sick friend but could not see her in the crowd. Methon saw him looking about and pointed to his own head and then pointed directly at Sheldrak, mouthing the words, 'Get your head together.'

Sheldrak thought of his instructions for the first part of the race. Methon had decided that it was no use competing with Arkel at the start, as losing face before this crowd meant he would fight to his last breath not to lose the initiative so early.

The words of Methon came back to Sheldrak, 'Arkel will lead going into the pines and will want to get to Dread's Dyke first. Stay with him but behind him. Watch what happens when someone tries to overtake him in close proximity. He will not have it. He will be insulted, especially if he is within sight of the crowds. Try to get to the Dyke in second place, because if you don't you will be caught in the pack and have to wait to cross. If this happens, you are already beaten.'

Sheldrak sucked in great gusts of air, his chest rising and falling like the bellows of a fire, but the fire he stoked was the fire in his heart. He must be strong. To him came an image of Divad, trying to stand up but falling, and he quickly erased it from his mind as a drawing wiped from a child's blackboard. If he were to help Divad he had to forget about him for the next thirty minutes.

The village elder mounted the stairs at the side of the racers and solemnly announced, 'Men and women of the village, by my elders.' Every man, woman and child answered in unison, 'By my elders.'

'This year we have thirty-eight proud men, from the youngest who is fifteen to the eldest who is forty-four. Arkel, our champion from last year, is here once again to defend his previous wins and Tredores, second for two out of the past three years, is once more here trying to win my favour.

'Gentlemen, I will count to three and then will release the village flag to commence. One, two...'

Sheldrak blinked the sweat out of his eyes.

'Three!' The flag fell. Even as the elder was losing his

grip on the flag Arkel had gone and most of the rest were left standing, but not Tredores and Sheldrak. Methon's first advice came back to Shel. 'Don't watch the flag, watch Arkel. When he goes, you go. No one has ever called him back for starting early and no one ever will. This will leave you behind Arkel but ahead of the rest.'

As the gang of men charged off into the distance, Methon smiled to himself because his first tactic had worked. What he didn't know was that his most important one would not!

At the same time as the elder shouted three, Essdark pulled back his cowl, uncovering a head full of wispy straggly hair. He leaned his head so far back that his neck was almost at a right angle to the rest of his body.

He started to chant, 'Χον τρολ ημ, χον τρολ ημ. Ηε ισ μιυε. Ηε ισ μιυε. Τακε ηισ σουλ. Τακε ηισ σουλ. Μακε ημ μιν ε, μακε ημ μιν ε.'

The words meant nothing to any normal human. Hundreds of miles away, some night animals cowered and whimpered. The chant was emitted in a growling, screeching wail that would have stood anyone's hackles straight to attention. Essdark started to sway but his feet never moved. Backwards, forwards he swayed as the screeching got louder and louder.

Divad twitched silently in the cottage. His eyes opened suddenly as though a pin had been thrust into him, but his mind stayed closed. The eyes took on a dull look as though they were looking through a bowl of dirty dishwater. He sat up, trancelike, rose, and walked unsteadily towards the door. He left his mother's smallholding and staggered in the direction of the race.

Sheldrak was in third place, heart and legs pumping to his own rhythm. He wasn't sure what tune the rhythm came from but now he didn't wear his metal feet he felt as though he could run for ever. The runners were approaching the entrance to the Cup when a long, thin youth not much older than Shel made a quick burst for the front. The crowd's voice roared as one and he went into second place, drawing alongside Arkel.

An elbow flew out from Arkel's side, hitting the youth straight in his midriff, instantly doubling him up and dropping him in front of Tredores and Sheldrak. They immediately hurdled the youth and moved into the pines just behind the favourite. The runners behind must have fared slightly worse, as Sheldrak heard the cursing and shouting coming from behind him as runners tumbled.

Forget what's behind me, he thought, I have to get in front of Tredores before the Dyke.

His mind switched to his training sessions and the side-stepping he had been doing over and over, but with dummies instead of people. He knew that there were only two places on this path through the pines where he could overtake someone, but everyone else also knew of them and they prepared to broaden their shoulders.

Methon and Sheldrak thought that they had found a third and it was just around the next bend. Shel was about to find out if they were right.

It was all about timing, and Sheldrak had to trust his memory of this area of the pines. The pace had slowed after the initial sprint to the front and Arkel picked his way along the dark green, wooded path, the sun flashing in and out of the shadows of the tall trees. The three of them dropped to a steady but hard trot. On their left, just off the edge of the path hidden in a cluster of thorns, was a large rock sticking out of the bushes. It was over three men high and sloped back towards the track from its peak at about seventy degrees to the ground.

Shel breathed deeply and sprinted at the back of Tredores, looking as though he were going to run straight into him and knock the two of them flying on to the forest floor. At the last second before impact he threw his whole body weight sideways. Not letting up the pace, he hit the large rock with his right foot, he then took his next stride and his left foot hit the rock before he pushed off it with all his might and picked his stride straight back up were he had left it on the forest floor.

There was one large difference, he was in second place, and he laughed out loud. Tredores nearly ran into a small tree as he gasped, convinced that Shel had just flown past him almost horizontal to the ground.

Arkel permitted himself a look over his shoulder as he approached the Dyke – and did Sheldrak see a small look of admiration from the seven-times winner? He wasn't sure and he certainly did not have time to speculate further as Arkel was already running over the bridge without even breaking stride.

'Jak!' said Shel. He would have to keep his wits about him crossing this. He slowed down gently to about half pace and purposefully stepped out on to the impossibly thin board, which creaked appreciatively as he made his way across. Much slower than Arkel but, unknown to him, faster than virtually everyone else, he got over and began to climb the Steppes.

The cave glowed with a gentle green light, like ivy fresh with morning dew, but then the green took on rippling movements like very gentle waves on a beach. The walls of the cave looked alive. Creatures ran over them, some so small that they couldn't be detected, others the size of a small dog or large rat. These were no normal animals or insects but were abominations of nature.

There was a large, fat spider but with no legs and a small claw that came out of the front of its head and grabbed the ground, dragging the body behind it before starting the sequence again.

Something that looked like a small rabbit hopped across the wall before turning and looking at Essdark, who was swaying and screeching in the centre of the cave. Except it couldn't look, for where its eyes should have been there was nothing but two holes that drilled into the head and oozed with pus the same colour as the cave walls.

Hundreds of these poor, sad creatures ebbed and flowed around the wailing Essdark.

The noise emitted from the raggedy, thin man swelled in volume, becoming a rant as spittle flew from his mouth. His eyes rolled into his head leaving only the black corneas showing. If he hadn't looked quite sane before, he now looked like a demon preparing for death.

Divad stumbled down Main Street. He had some semblance of memory. He knew where he had to go but he didn't know why. Where was his mother? What was this buzzing in his head? Why did he keep dreaming about these strange, sad animals that should never have been allowed to live? He fell, ripping the skin off his knees and tearing a hole in his nightgown, but didn't feel any pain. Only Sheldrak could help him but if it wasn't soon this buzzing in his head would take over and his thoughts would not be his own.

Shel had picked up some of the ground he had lost at the Dyke by striding out the way Methon had showed him over the long run down and then back up the hill to the starting line. He wasn't sure whether Arkel was conserving his energy and lulling him into a trap. The Steppes had been hard for them both but neither lost nor gained, and as they finished the first round with two-and-a-half miles to go, Arkel led by ten yards on Shel, who was twenty yards ahead of Tredores.

After him, forty yards away, was a group of six or seven runners. The rest were also-rans or had stopped and given up. The crowds roared their approval as Arkel gave a cheeky wave as he turned around the pole and sped off down to the Giant's Cup for the second time.

Shel's lungs were now fit for bursting. He knew there would be a time in the race when he had to dig deep and this was it. He hoped for his second breath as he pushed to get within five yards of Arkel as they entered the pines. This time, as Arkel approached the boulder in the thorns he swerved towards it, making it impossible for Shel to complete his 'running up the wall' trick, as it became known in future years. It didn't really matter as Sheldrak only one had trick left and was about to cash the chips in on his final hand.

Arkel left the pines, ran towards the Dyke and took a stride on to the plank. He could hear Sheldrak close behind him and tensed as he awaited another footfall on to the thin bridge. None came. The next thing Arkel knew was a swoosh as Shel went flying past and landed on the far bank. The younger man had jumped the Dyke. Arkel looked aghast, took his eye off the rickety bridge, missed his footing and fell into the ravine.

Divad stopped at the top of Billing Hill, looking down on the race below. He looked like in inmate from the county asylum who had escaped a week before and had been sleeping rough ever since. His eyes had the look of a man sleepwalking to his death. Nobody noticed him, they were too intent on the events in front of them to see the sad figure walking, stumbling and falling down the hill behind.

Essdark stopped swaying. The walls momentarily lost their glow. Someone might die in that race, he thought as he resumed his chanting. He had him; it was almost killing Essdark, but the fool was to be his.

Arkel fell forward and grabbed the far bank of the ravine, but the earth was loose. By all the Faiths, he was going to fall to his death. Shel was already on his way up the Steppes when he heard the cry behind him and turned to see what had happened. Arkel shouted, 'For the Faith of Love, help me.'

Sheldrak thought of his Faith of Sacrifice. Was this to be it? His friend's life for that of Arkel? Or the other way around? He had no time to think, but he knew he could not let this man die. He ran back to the Dyke, thrusting out an arm to Arkel and pulling and struggling for what seemed like an hour (but was seconds) and dragged him on to the bank. In the meantime, Tredores had run over the plank and taken the lead.

Arkel looked at Shel and said, 'By my elders, I owe you my life. Come, I will pace you and together we will catch him, but mark, I cannot let you win. Once we both catch Tredores the race is back on for all three. Now come, we must go.'

Arkel moved rapidly up the steep chunks of granite that Tredores had climbed thirty seconds ago. At this stage of the race it was a great deal of time to make up but this was the situation that, two years earlier, Arkel had found himself in. Then, he had managed to break the younger Tredores with less than fifty yards to the finishing line. He knew he could do it again, not just for him but also for this remarkable young man whom he believed he owed at least a chance to win, if not a great deal more. He also knew that in his own heart he would never be able to stand aside and allow someone to pass him to win the race. He also believed in Strepsay, and Bravery and Honour were uppermost in his own ideals of how life should be lived. Pushing over some young fool who was trying to pass you in front of the crowds was one thing, but to give up his very belief for living was another. As this thought passed through his mind he realised that he would step into the Dyke before losing deliberately and pushed up the Steppes with renewed vigour.

Sheldrak was struggling. He continued to keep up with Arkel as he got to the top of the Steppes and started on the long journey of the last mile. Thank Faith it was all down-hill apart from the last few hundred yards. Ahead of them both, Tredores was tiring, but Shel knew that Tredores was not going to be his problem. It would be the man pacing him whom he could have left hanging over the edge of the Dyke.

He remembered the joke that Divad had told him about the frustrations of a one-armed man with an itchy arse hanging off a cliff. He nearly laughed out loud there and then, but for the fact that he felt as if he was sucking red-hot coals into his lungs instead of air.

'Stay with me, we are catching him. Get right behind me and lengthen your stride like I do. Shelter yourself from the wind behind me and we will catch him.'

The crowd could now see the battle that was underway as the two runners, who were so close together that from a distance they looked like one, hauled back the lone man in front. That was how it seemed, not the two behind catching but as though the single man was a giant trout on a hook being pulled back to the two fishermen on the shore.

With only 300 yards to go, all three men were in a line.

The masses of people lining either side of the finish screamed for their particular favourite, but Shel was spent. It seemed to happen all at once, but his legs suddenly became those of the farmer's scarecrow in the field as the ground went from a downhill slope to flat and then into a rise.

For Shel it might just well have been the side of the Dyke. The race was over for him. The two older men pulled away and then Arkel kicked into the lead. It was all Shel could do from falling off his feet and all he could think about was poor Divad...

...who was now pushing his way through the people at the rear of the ropes. They pulled away from him, as people will do when the power of the unknown takes over. They all knew Divad, but in this condition, his eyes rolled into his head showing only whites, just as...

...Essdark's eyes showed only black. The running Spawn was in great pain, he thought. Good, but not as much as he was about to feel. He stopped swaying. The glow faded to a very pale green and the creatures disappeared off the walls. He stood upright, not moving, and with an almighty scream pulled Divad's mind into his own and trapped him in the depths of his skull. Essdark shuddered when...

...from somewhere inside Sheldrak's mind a voice said, 'Do not be afraid. I am one of the Seven and my name is Isthmus. I am going to push your body to the limit, which is far more than you can with your feeble mind. Relax as I take over.'

Sheldrak's body shook as his legs pumped again but he was a puppet in a child's game. He quickly caught Tredores, who looked amazed to see Shel coming back, but not as amazed as Shel himself, whose legs were a blur in comparison with those of the two men running with him. His chest seemed to swell in front of him. His arms pumped strongly with the recognition that with fifty yards to go he had drawn level with Arkel, whose eyes popped out of his head like a squashed bullfrog's.

Isthmus spoke again. 'Do not panic now, for you are going to win. This is still your body and if your will were not so strong it would matter not what I could do.'

With those words Sheldrak was pushed strongly from behind, carrying him over the line in first place with Arkel the width of a body behind him. It was said years later that the cry from Sheldrak was heard in the next county. The voice in Shel's head said, 'And now I go,' as the boy collapsed in a heap to the ground, only to look up in horror as Divad fell out of the crowd with a scream that commanded immediate silence from all who heard it. Divad's mother ran out of the supporters and grabbed her son around his shoulders, lifting him into a sitting position.

Divad opened his eyes and spoke in a voice which was not his own. 'I have you,' screeched the creature that had once been Divad.

Sheldrak could not stop the darkness that came to him and he accepted it as a friend, escaping the madness of the waking world.

Greeg

It was mid-morning on the day following the Great Race and Sheldrak was sat with his parents in the small dining area of their cottage. Whinst, Shel's father, had not gone to work that day, the only time that Shel could ever remember his father not going into the fields on a work day. They sat around the table contemplating the events of the previous twenty-four hours.

According to his mother, Azores, Shel had been out for only seconds before the muted acceptance of the crowd stirred him again. Muted, because poor unfortunate Divad had hushed the ignition of any normal celebration like kindling dampened and then drenched by an unexpected shower of rain.

Shel walked himself home with his mother while his father and other men of the village carried Divad home. Later that day Shel would go to see him, as soon as the elder had arranged the meeting with Greeg. He prayed Divad would show signs of recovery. A shiver ran down Sheldrak's back as he thought this, because he knew that the words Divad had used were the exact ones used by the grey-cowled creature in his own dream.

Whinst, who never used words when he could convey his thoughts with an expressive silence, spoke to his wife and son. 'I have no idea what the events of yesterday mean, Sheldrak, but I have a real fear for your safety. In a couple of weeks' time you will reach the first stages of manhood, sixteen, and I truly believe you are ready for it. Nevertheless, there are far stronger powers at force here than those of a sixteen-year-old man.'

'Do you mean what happened to Divad, Father, or my own dreams?'

'Both.' His father lapsed back into his normal mode of communication.

Azores looked at the men in her life and again wondered at the similarities in their looks. Same hair, physique, eyes and mouth. Shel had already started to attract the attentions of most of the girls in the village and didn't need much prompting. Whinst, on the other hand... Azores was only too aware of who had made most of the moves between her and Whinst.

She spoke for them all in the way only a woman can, cutting through all the speculation of what was and what may be.

'It's as simple as this. Divad looks as though he is dying and seems to know of something that happened in Shel's dream. As Shel told him about it he could have been hallucinating, but I heard that voice he used and something that didn't belong in that young man's body had forced its way in.

'Shel won the race for one purpose, and that was to get to see Greeg. Divad is in no condition to do so, therefore I see no better way forward than for Shel to go as per his original plan. Something tells me it has been written this way and we have no control over the writer.'

She looked straight at Sheldrak and held his gaze in hers. 'I believe, son, that until you understand the dream you will not be able to help poor Divad, hence that must be your course of action. You took that as your prize yesterday when you spoke to the elder and he will have already have spoken to Greeg, if I am not mistaken.'

The room went silent as the men took in the wise words of wife and mother respectively. The love in the cottage had never been as strong as it was at that moment. Unfortunately it was the last time that they would ever sit around that table together.

Later that day, Sheldrak walked down the path to Divad's home, taking with him some wild roses he had picked for Helen, Divad's mother. He did not have to knock when he got there as Helen was sitting outside in her rocking chair.

'By my elders,' she barely whispered as he closed the gate behind him.

'By my elders,' he replied, his voice croaking on 'elders', betraying his anxiety. As he spoke, the village healer came out of the cottage and summoned Helen back inside with him. Sheldrak stood waiting, not sure if he should stay or go. He had turned to leave when the physician left, bowing quickly in Shel's general direction. He left as one who has come to call as a favour but found it to be a favour impossible to complete.

'Come and sit with Divad a while and talk to him. The healer said he might be able to hear you.'

Shel walked into the room, which was unnaturally dark because of the curtained window. The first thing his senses picked up was the rancid stench coming from the spent husk lying in the cot. Up to two days ago it had been the most vibrant, noisy boy in the village. Shel gasped and then stifled the sob welling up in his throat. For the sake of Helen he had to hide his horror.

Divad lay, eyes open, staring upwards at the ceiling. His breath came in gasps akin to those of someone who had just finished the Great Race. A pool of spittle and drool lay on his pillow. His skin was almost translucent and the dark veins showed up under his skin. If Sheldrak had come across such a creature lying out in the forest he would have killed it with an arrow without thinking twice. He told himself again, this is my best friend, and then he wept.

Helen had left the room so that Shel could talk alone with Divad, but it was fully ten minutes before he could lift his face back up and look again at Vad lying on his cot.

'I swear on every Faith, on Strepsay and the honour of my

father, Whinst, that I will find out how to help you, my friend, or I shall die not knowing.' He struck his breast three times and then leaned over and kissed Divad on the forehead. He spoke no more and left the room and the cottage before, remembering his Faith, he turned to Helen and said, 'The next time I see you I will have the cure for Divad. Remember my words and let them be a comfort to you in your pain.'

Helen handed a small wooden carving to Shel and said, 'This is a carving of Divad that his father made for him many years ago, but you can still see the likeness of him. I don't know what you think you can do, Sheldrak, but I believe that you believe and today that is as much as my sick heart will allow.'

With tears now streaming down his young face and his shoulders trembling with the pressure of holding back the grief, he sobbed, 'By my elders,' and turned and ran until he was out of sight.

His appointment with Greeg was at sunset. Initially, as expected by everyone that knew, Greeg had totally refused the elder permission, until the elder had pointed out that Greeg would be escorted to the edge of the county and never allowed to return under the threat of death. Greeg had conceded but told the elder to, 'Go and eat jak,' which under any circumstances, anywhere in the known universe, is not considered overly pleasant.

Expecting no welcome and with the change of weather that suited his mood entirely – a thunderstorm – Sheldrak arrived at the hovel that Greeg called home. The little wooden shack could only have been held together with cobwebs and mould. Everywhere you looked there were bits of different woods knocked on and hammered in. The only sign of life was in the lazy draughts of smoke that oozed out of the hole in the broken roof. Sheldrak couldn't decide whether the fire had been placed to make use of the hole or if the hole was there by design.

Water pattered down around him, splattering the dust of the floor on to the bottoms of his legs. The door opened before he had the chance to announce his arrival. He couldn't see anyone in the dusk of the cottage, and called out, 'Greeg, by my elders!'

'Stick your elders up your arse,' replied an old, resonant but firm voice.

This was going to be an experience Shel wasn't likely to forget in a hurry, but one that would become very useful to him later on that year.

'Shut the bloody door, you idiot, and sit down by the fire where my poor eyesight can see you.'

Sheldrak moved towards the small fire surrounded by earthen bricks lit in the centre of what he now recognised as a one-room house. A figure shambled out of the gloom and sat next to Shel on the only other available surface that he could see. He had left the real chair for the host and he was sat on an old wooden crate that, from the smell, had once carried some root vegetable about twenty summers ago.

Greeg was a bundle of rags with a head sticking out of one end, two of the most filth-encrusted hands Shel had ever seen in the middle, and things at the other end that must be feet but didn't warrant consideration. The head was also covered in grime so that the whites of the eyes glowed eerily out of the surrounding darkness. A grey growth of beard was stuck to chin, one of those beards that never got any further than looking just like a lazy week of not shaving. The final feature that Shel noticed was enough nose hair sprouting out of either nostril that he fully expected birds to take flight from them.

'Tell me your damn dream, then I'll make up some rubbish and you can sod off,' said the friendly little man.

Sheldrak held back his real thoughts and told Greeg his dream from the start in the cave through to the sun going out at the finish. As he retold his story he perceived a change in Greeg. The old man didn't even look as if he were listening when he started, but by the time he got to the poppies, Greeg was sat forward like a hunting dog pulling on the chain and waiting for the 'fetch' from its master. At the finish Sheldrak also told Greeg about Divad and the change in the boy, plus the words he had used before collapsing – the very words from Shel's dream, but in someone else's voice.

'OK, I admit you have me interested,' said Greeg. 'This could be the one,' he added to himself.

'The dream itself is quite straightforward, but remember that this is my interpretation of it. It is not the truth. Some of it may happen, some of it may already have happened and some of it I might just make up for a bloody laugh. None of it is for sure and the future is still out there waiting to be changed.'

Without pausing for breath he launched into his version of what Sheldrak's dream meant.

'The grey cowled one is Essdark, Lord of Death, killer of children, he who walks in people's nightmares. He comes in many guises and is also known as Millghrew or, in female form, Isintress. It is written that he once took a woman and has a son roaming the lands, but I have never heard of him if it is true.

'He wants you. You either have something he wants or he fears you. Since time began the myths state that one day a brave man will come from a humble background and oppose him. Is it you? I know not. If you do oppose him, what will be the outcome? Only the great being who plays with us all like pawns knows the answer to that.'

The fire flickered as a breeze moved between them and away into the dark recesses of the hut. Shel had heard of Essdark. The other names were new to him, but the magnitude of this chilled his blood.

Greeg continued, 'If you choose to oppose him you will

be one of seven representing the Seven Faiths of Strepsay and each one will have their own path to follow. The six others will come to you as surely as moths to a candle, but be warned; as I said earlier, no outcome is sure. The poppies mean that some of you live through your ordeals and some of you do not. You are the centre around which good flows, but he is strong. The sun going out was his warning to you. Think about it. Who brings the laughter to your life? Who is your sun, your light? Who is the centre around which your village life turns?'

Sheldrak's jaw dropped. 'Divad?'

'And you never saw it coming. I hope for your sake you do not represent Wisdom, or you may as well stay here with me.'

Greeg cackled at his own joke but for Sheldrak all levity had left with the chill breeze that had stirred at the very name of Essdark.

Shel was full of questions. 'Please tell me what I must do. Where do I go? How do I help Divad? Do I leave Jost?'

Two bony arms thrust forward out of the bundle of rags and grabbed Sheldrak, making him fall backwards, but the hands were far stronger than they looked and held Sheldrak in his position on the crate.

Small balls of blue static electricity flew from the ends of Greeg's beard and rags, alighting on Shel, giving small shocks which made every hair on his body stand on end. A torrent of words streamed from the foul cave that was Greeg's toothless mouth and fell into the void between them,

'You must follow the sword. The city of Ontrades awaits you. You are not alone. You have met the first of the six. By my Faith, you are the one.' These last words were shouted so loudly that Shel winced.

'You must seek the lost city of Tremain. Essdark will try to rebuild it and you must oppose him. He goes back to the beginning of time, his evil resurfacing every few years. Plagues, wars, famine, murder. The worlds must choose good or evil, right or wrong, life or eternal death.'

Greeg's voice was getting higher and higher and the blood in Sheldrak's arms was having difficulty in reaching his fingers as Greeg tightened his grip.

'Follow the sword of Strepsay. On a full moon lay it on bare earth and it will turn and point you true. True to Faith and Strepsay. True to your heart. But straight to Essdark and Tremain.'

Greeg left go of Shel and took a few moments before he looked up at him.

'I never believed it would happen, but that must be the reason I have been allowed to live for so long. You are the one, known to him as the Spawn. But I have something for you. If it does not open then I am mistaken.'

He placed his hands into the fire and, whispering some enchantments, pulled from the hot embers what looked like a small glass case. He handed it straight to Sheldrak and said, 'It will open only for the right person.'

Sheldrak turned the case in his hands. It was no more than six inches in length but as he held it, it began to glow, becoming longer and slightly wider. The glass shattered but no shards exploded around them. The glass melted like snowflakes landing on warm skin.

In his hands Shel held the most ornate sword he had ever seen and would ever see: a broad blade carved with strange symbols and a thick helm with one word engraved in golden metal, *Truth*.

He held in front of him, the Sword of Destiny, the sword of Strepsay, and his future and that of the world.

'It has an ancient name, known only to a few. In our tongue it is known as "Northstar" and will be your guide on the journeys ahead. You must leave immediately. Take only what you can carry on a small mule to help you onwards.

We both know you are not alone. Who is the first of the six?'

Sheldrak wondered at the knowledge this old grubby man had, both of the past and that which he could only have picked from searching Sheldrak's mind with his own. He spoke, not lifting his eyes for fear that Greeg could look so deep into him that his soul would be laid open for the world to see.

'He called himself – at least I think it was a he – Isthmus. He came to me during the race but since then I have heard nothing. I think he is a spirit, a poor creature who must have some unfinished business with the living and therefore cannot join the true resting place of the dead. It had the ability to take over my body.'

Now Sheldrak looked up. In all honesty he had been wondering to himself if he had cheated and therefore had won with no honour. This came out now in the sheepish look of embarrassment he gave Greeg.

'Do not worry, it was meant to be. It was still your body that won the race. If you had not been capable, the spirit could not have done any more than you could have done, but I do think it brings a whole new meaning to the phrase, "It was his spirit that won it for him." '

Greeg once again chuckled at his own funny before saying in a loud, authoritative voice, 'That is it. You have claimed your prize and I cannot do any more for you. You must go home and prepare to leave. If you will take my advice you will leave in the morning, rain or no rain. The longer you delay, the harder you will find it to go. Farewell, or as I like to say, bugger off.'

Sheldrak stood hiding Northstar as well as he could in his clothing, faced Greeg and exclaimed, 'By my elders!' He walked out of the hut, realising that he would never see Greeg again.

Farewell

Sheldrak strolled slowly home, the substance of the ornate sword weighing heavily on his leg but not as heavily as on his mind. The rain continued to fall as he walked, but the pattering on the leaves of the trees didn't distract him from his main concern. How was he going to tell his mother? He believed his father had already prepared himself for the announcement, understanding that they were a small chapter of a much greater story.

Azores would not care whose story or what chapter they belonged in, she would be totally against him leaving on his own, especially so soon after the race and with two weeks to go before his sixteenth birthday. He prepared his argument mentally, hoping that they would not part with ill feeling. He knew he had to leave and the last thing he needed was to set off on his journey downhearted.

He got home in time for the evening meal; his parents, even though they were desperate to find out how the sitting with Greeg had been, were attuned to his requirement to be quiet. As they ate the lapin stew, Azores and Whinst chit-chatted about the crops, the heavy rainfall of the day, the excitement of yesterday's race, how it was the first time in the history of their family that they had a village champion. Then their thoughts turned to Divad and finally Sheldrak joined the conversation.

'I went to see him today. If he is not dead he may as well be. The only good thing is that I think I know where he is and what I must do to rescue him.'

Azores questioned his reasoning. 'What do you mean, "where he is"? He is still lying ill in Helen's cottage. He doesn't need rescuing; he needs help from a powerful healer.'

'Mother, you are wrong.' And with his silence now broken, Sheldrak told them everything that Greeg had told him.

After twenty minutes of what turned into a question-and-answer session, which Whinst sat on the outside of, Sheldrak came to a finish with, 'So that is my dilemma, parents. Either I am some sort of folk hero that has been waiting to happen or the whole story is a bunch of nonsense, but either way I cannot sit in this village every day watching the greatest friend anyone could ever wish for die. At least I will be doing something.'

Azores rose, banging the table as she did and knocking plates to the cottage floor. 'I'm sorry, I cannot accept this. My son, Shel, the saviour of the known lands? The boy suckled by my very breast to battle Essdark, Lord of Death? I need more proof than the ramblings of an old hermit.'

'Well what about this, Mother?'

The beautiful sword fell with a heavy dull thud on to the table. As Shel touched it, it glimmered and glowed with an inner light. Every time he looked at it he saw something new, either a carving he had missed earlier or a different metal within the depths of the blade that shone with a new colour under different light.

'This sword, Mother, came from a glass box that was no more than six inches in length.'

'It's impossible, Shel. You must have been hallucinating, or he gave you a drug or something.' Azores's pleas were getting increasingly frantic. Sheldrak thought that this was going in totally the opposite way from how he wanted. Another voice in the room whispered, 'And are all three of you hallucinating now, I ask?'

All three members of the family turned towards the cottage door to see who had entered without announcement, but no one was there.

Then a twinkle of light was followed by another, and then too many to count, and the light took on a shape, the shape of a young man. The man was very fair with narrow, almond-shaped eyes and a pixie face. The facial features were so pretty that they would not have looked out of place on a young girl.

'Please do not be afraid, for I am Isthmus, a spirit, and I have been chosen to accompany you, Sheldrak, on our quest. Now, Azores and Whinst, believe, for I am as real as either of you and proof that all your esteemed son says is true.'

Whinst had stood up during the appearance of the spirit and now stood next to his wife with a protective arm around her. Funnily enough they both looked as though they had seen a ghost.

It was Sheldrak who spoke first. 'I recognise your voice but I am not sure if I hear you with my ears or with my mind.'

'I can communicate with you however I please or which-ever way suits you. Look at your mother and father. They do not know I speak now. But now they do.'

'Now they do what?' stammered Azores.

Isthmus spoke for all to hear. 'I did not want to show myself to you at this early stage, but I have also been selected. Do not ask me how I know, as I am no more certain than Sheldrak. I will leave you, but tomorrow, early on our journey, we must talk, Sheldrak, as I hope we will be friends for a long time.'

With these words the tiny lights that made up any solidity that the spirit might have had faded one by one until the three people were once again looking at a solid wooden door. The voice of the spirit continued to echo in their minds and had the sound of honey dripping from fresh bread.

Azores slumped into the hard chair at the tableside. 'So it

is done and chosen. Everyone in the land expects and accepts that my fifteen-year-old son is to walk off into Faith knows where and fight some mythical devil, some being that has frightened children and adults alike for centuries.' Only this time her voice had a resigned sound to it that had previously been missing.

For once, Whinst spoke. 'Son, we both love you dearly and I will come to terms with you leaving, but for your mother it will take much longer. As the head of the family I give you my blessing. Azores?'

Her eyes were downcast but she raised them and said, 'By my elders and against my better judgement, I too give you my blessing.'

She walked over to Shel and threw her arms around him, clasping him tight to her heaving chest. It was to be; on the very next morning Sheldrak, son of Whinst, was to leave the family cottage, depart the village and set out into the lands to search for Tremain.

It was written that six would join him in his adventures but not all would return. Even those who survived knew not what land awaited them. Would it be a land ruled by light and truth or by death and blackness? A fifteen-year-old boy was about to find out.

The next morning Sheldrak mounted the furze his father had given him to ride. A furze was a tough, hardy creature, smaller than a horse but bigger than a pony and known for its ability to cover tough and rocky terrain on small rations. This one was called Randeed and had worked for Whinst for years in the fields and also as a steed when he had to journey out to markets to buy seed and trade his crops.

It had coarse, white hair in the winter months but now had its short, black summer coat. It stood almost as high as Sheldrak and looked like a large Shetland pony with one exception. Its hooves were very wide and flat, with tough leathery skin and four toes or fingers. Indeed, this might be a beast of burden, but it could also pick a flower and pop it into its mouth if it so desired.

Sheldrak had packed enough dried food and water to last him a couple of weeks, after which he had seed that his father had spared for him to trade. After that he was on his own. He also had Northstar tucked away in his bundle alongside the carving of Divad. Methon had come to see Sheldrak leave; his work had been complete and Shel had won the race. Methon was not to leave with Shel. His adventuring days had long since passed.

Shel was heading for the city of Ontrades, 200 miles north into the onrushing winter and resulting cold. If he travelled twenty miles a day the food that Shel had packed should be more than enough. For a moment he wondered if spirits ate, and if they did, what, but then his mother was at his side making final adjustments and comments more to comfort herself that anyone else.

Randeed shook her head and neighed. She could sense that the time for leaving had arrived and wanted to move on. Taking Sheldrak on a journey to somewhere new must be better than trotting around a field all day. Whinst held similar thoughts before striking his breast three times and saying, 'Faith be with you, my son. By my elders.'

Sheldrak spoke for the last time and repeated, 'By my elders,' before slapping Randeed on the rump and trotting out of the village.

He wondered to himself, 'What age will I be when I return?' before some part of his mind that he wished had remained silent replied, 'if you ever do!'

Part Two
Ontrades

Hemm

Hemm had lived his whole life as a loyal member of the Ontrades society and, for the past twenty years, as a proud soldier of the Inner Guard. He had met his wife Marggitte during his training and, as befitted two members of the Inner Guard, had given up all rights to have children. They had each other and their loyalty to the state and therefore had little need for any other stimulus in their lives. It was Marggitte's decision, as she was the child bearer, and she had the ability to conceive taken away by one of the city's top healers. Sometimes 'healer' was an unfortunate choice of word.

Hemm now stood on his night watch, guarding the tomb of the last emperor. If he were the only person left standing in this city as it was attacked by hordes of wild men, he would not leave his post. If no replacement came for him then the rules of the Inners were simple. He stood at his post until he died.

The whole of the community was built around the military. The hierarchy of the city was founded on traditional grounds. The Emperor and his immediate family ruled the city along with the twelve Elders. The Elder with the most power also doubled his responsibility as Capatain of the Inner Guard. After that were the rank and file soldiers, split into divisions of twelve. The most senior rank was capatain, followed by second, corp, serge and finally the foot soldier or horseman.

It was a sprawling city of over 20,000 inhabitants, most of whom were home-grown men and women of Ontrades. There were also pockets of immigrants, wanderers from the flatlands, sailors and dock handlers from the port of Seathon on the river Landsplitter, a small community of giants from Arbrain in the deep south, and a handful of cave dwellers from the Bluetop Mountains which majestically guarded the rear of the city.

The community was built on the Strepsay Faith of Honour. Out of the 20,000 inhabitants, 12,000 of them were in the ranks of the military but a mere 300 attained the honour of the Inner Guard. Only the best of the best made it into the Inners and there was no need of rank among these elite. Every one of the 300 reported directly to the Capatain, one of the Elders.

Their duty was built into them over many years of training. Some of the families had been in the Inners for generations, others were the first family members. Every man or woman born within the walls of the city had an equal chance to succeed. There was no favouritism, only elitism through an ability to shoot an arrow through the eye of a hawk at 300 paces; through fighting skills to overcome ten others wielding swords when you had naught but a stave; and finally through a will to put the honour of the guard above everything else that your life stood for.

Hemm had come from a poor family. One of seven brothers and five sisters, he learnt from a very early age that life was going to be slightly harder for him than for most others. His father had been a ghrunt, a foot soldier who earned the basic military pay, and therefore his mother, when not having children, had to work in a bakery. It was years later that Hemm realised that if his mother had worked cleaning the stables then they might not have had something as nutritious as stale, unsold bread to eat for supper.

From a young age he learnt to fight. He fought with his older brothers for the right to get a seat at the table (he was twelve before he sat down for his first meal and that was because he had found a flagon of milk that some poor unfortunate soldier had dropped. He turned it over to his mother and for his reward he got his eldest brother's chair). He fought with his childhood enemies, defending the reputation of his poor family and more importantly he fought in the cadets. He was taught to be a warrior before he knew if he had a cause to fight for.

He was good. Whether it was hand-to-hand, with a stave or club, on a horse with a spear or lance, shooting an arrow in the air or swinging a broad blade, he very rarely lost. His father saw the skills his youngest son had in the playground and soon singled him out for special treatment – an extra piece of meat now and again, a trip to the barracks to see how the regular soldiers lived, and lessons upon lessons.

Hemm would never forget the time he was fourteen and was sent by his mother to pull his father from the nearest inn, the Sweaty Serge (It was just called the Serge; the 'sweaty' followed because of its reputation as a high-class, clean-drinking establishment.).

Hemm wandered into the dark interior of the inn. The large mirror behind the bar reflected a line of heads mostly covered in the helmets of footmen. Sawdust covered the floor and sure enough it hadn't got its nickname for nothing, although it was difficult to differentiate between the hops and sweat.

'Hemm, me young pride and joy,' came a shout from the end of the bar furthest away from the door. It was easier for his father to see his silhouette against the light through the door than it was to look into the dark with the brightness behind him.

His father had drunk one ale for each member of his twelve that night and swayed over to Hemm, knocking three flagons of good ale splashing over the floor and upsetting three very tired young horsemen who had been out riding the city walls all day and did not want some staggering old bugger ruining the first pint. Now, under normal circumstances nothing would have happened. Hemm's father, also called Hemm, would have bought the three men a drink each, apologised and gone home for a supper of bread and fruit.

Tonight was not normal. Hemm Senior had been on latrine duty all week. He had also spent the last trade he had on his final flagon of strong ale and our three young men had decided that their arses were so sore from riding that this 'bastard waster' was going to get a kicking. One of them had a particularly nasty streak and was going to 'break a few bones, just to teach him a lesson'.

The final ingredient to this volatile mix was Hemm Junior, now six-two and still growing. He was not about to let anyone kick his father, no matter what he had done.

'Sorry lads, Dad's had one or two more than he should. I have no trade to give you but I promise I will return in a couple of days and pay for the spilled ale.'

'Jak,' came back the age-old retort. 'We'll take it out of him.' And with that the closest one to Hemm Senior threw a roundhouse right, catching him flush on the cheekbone and knocking him cold with the first punch.

Hemm Junior moved into the centre of the three, his arms held away from him ready, bobbing nimbly on the balls of his feet.

'That's the last old man you three will hit for a while,' he whispered before moving into action.

Hemm lifted his elbow and dug it hard into the midriff of the boy on his left, who was not much older than he was. He dropped to the floor, gasping for breath. Hemm knew that these next two would not be as easily felled, especially the one with the big beer belly who had hit his unsuspecting father. He feinted to hit the man on his right, who had a particularly nasty scar down the side of his face, but at the last minute threw his foot out instead, catching Beer Belly on his knee and forcing him to fall forward.

Scarface, who was pulling away from a blow that never came, saw his chance and charged at Hemm, hitting him around the middle and forcing them both to the floor.

'Hold him there,' said Beer Belly, rising from his knees. 'Let's see how jakface likes this.' He aimed a kick at Hemm's face but Hemm was already rolling, using the momentum of Scarface's charge to turn them and getting his attacker to take the kick at the base of his spine. Yelping like a young pup whose paw had been stamped on, Scarface released Hemm, who jumped to his feet.

Don't want to stay down there too long, thought Hemm. Youngster had also climbed back to his feet along with Scar and stood on either side of Belly, breathing hard. This had all happened in the space of twenty seconds and they were right back to where they had started, except that Hemm was hardly breathing.

Hemm flung himself forward into a press-up position and, rotating his body like a gymnast on a pommel horse, turned his body 360 degrees, parallel to the floor, using his legs as clubs and sweeping all three of the antagonists crashing to the ground. Scar hit his head hard and Hemm, back on his feet again, could see that he had had enough. He moved towards Youngster and, using the base of his palm, rammed it hard into his temple, leaving him lying unconscious in the damp sawdust.

Beer Belly had decided that this whirling, fighting mad-man child needed teaching a real lesson of life and he pulled a long-bladed knife from underneath his grubby tunic. Sawdust fell out of his dark, lank hair into his dirty beard and he looked as though he had the worst case of dandruff ever seen.

Hemm could not believe how the situation had got so out of hand. Only three minutes earlier the worst he could have expected was an argument between Mum and Dad about Dad being drunk again. Now a soldier who had at least 100 pounds on him was trying to climb over his two fallen mates, holding a knife as big as a small county in order to split him from arsehole to midsummer.

Hemm decided to take this particular argument outside. He backed quickly away, keeping at least a two-man gap between Belly and his chest. The sunlight hit his back as he moved from the shadow of the inn. Jumping, he grabbed the door lintel and kicked with enough force from his swing to hear a very satisfactory crunch from the nose in the beard. The sawdust dandruff was now joined with thick clots of strawberry blood.

Leaving go of the door, Hemm grabbed Belly's knife-carrying hand and with one deft twist applied enough pressure that either the bone would give way or the knife would hit the floor. A pleasing thud meant the knife had gone and for the first time Hemm relaxed. Belly hit him with a swinging left that should have broken Hemm's jaw, but he did manage to move away enough so that the blow didn't land cleanly. It certainly reminded Hemm that this was not yet over.

Two seconds later it was. A large pewter mug hit the back of Belly's head, dropping him back into the sawdust for a third and final time, leaving a lurching Hemm Senior leaning against the frame with a mug handle in his hand.

'Cheers, son. I sorted that messh out for you. That should have warmed me up fu the tougher tashk ahead. Your muvver,' said Hemm senior with a roguish, lopsided grin and the start of what was going to be a stupendous black eye. 'Come on, lesh get home before any of these buggersh get up.'

The following day, word quickly went through the rank and file about the demon fighter known as Hemm Junior and, before Hemm had a chance to worry about a spell in the brig, he had been summoned to the home of one of the members of the Inner Guard. The guard wanted to discuss training Hemm with the possibility of him becoming an Inner.

Hemm made the grade and used his skills to come to the aid of his family. The Inner Guard received far more trade credits than ordinary soldiers and horsemen, and through his hard work Hemm helped his father drink himself into an early grave.

The duties of the Inner Guard were many but predominately revolved around the protection of the Emperor, his family and the twelve Elders. The city had many enemies as it was located by the only pass through the Bluetop Mountains. All traders had to pay for the right to pass under the shadow of the Citadel, the tallest tower in any of the lands, to gain access to the city from the mountains or out of the city to trade with the wild men of the North.

In the past Ontrades had entered into many battles with various tribes and peoples who wanted to take over the right to the mountain pass, but to date all had failed. Battles had been mostly won, one or two lost also, but the Ontradeans had always kept the upper hand. The Morg community, who controlled the major throughway from the East to the West of the Landsplitter, had similar control in their area of the lands but, never satisfied with what they ruled, were bringing together the greatest army ever, to launch another assault upon the citizens of Ontrades.

Hemm stood on duty as guard to the tomb of the last emperor, who had died some fifteen years earlier. Hemm was proud of all the duties and tasks that he performed as part of the Inner Guard, but this one even he admitted was only ceremonial. Even he knew that nobody wanted to invade the tomb of one of their previous leaders but there were stones and gold and famous weapons that the unscrupulous could make many trades with if they ever got the chance. Today they would have to get past Hemm and it would certainly take many men to do that in his protected position.

The city nestled in the foothills with the menacing heights of the Bluetops as its backcloth. Most of the city had been built hundreds of lifetimes ago into the sides of the mountains, so most of the roads and passageways in the city had an 'uphill' and a 'downhill'. As the city flattened out at the bottom of the mountains the many barracks and army quarters were built. Then, further upwards through the city, family homes were situated, sometimes wedged into the niches and crannies of the mountain rock walls.

The border of the city was a boundary wall twenty feet in height and wide enough for one man to walk behind the balustrades built for protection against enemy arrows.

In the far north-east of the city lay the heavily guarded tunnel that indicated the beginning of the mountain pass through which any safe journey over the Bluetops was required to start. This was the trading centre of the city. Once a month peoples from hundreds of miles around came here to trade their wares. Many wild men from the mountains came and sometimes even groups of giants from as far away as Arbrain would travel the 500-or-more miles to undertake business.

The monthly trade day was very important to the wealth and prosperity of the city but, as years had gone by, with reducing respect for the Faiths it had become increasingly difficult to maintain law and order. Unfortunately for the Ontradeans, fighting and skirmishes were now common-place on trade day and even the occasional murder didn't frighten the potential buyers and sellers away.

Apart from the monthly trade day, markets ran perpetu-ally, daily all summer long and, dependant upon the cold and snow, also for many of the days in winter. This part of the city was known as 'the Pass' and if anyone needed anything, legal or otherwise, then you could bet your last trade on finding it at the Pass.

The Pass was the second highest part of the city, and the Citadel was the first. It was a perfect white tower and housed the homes of the regal family in its uppermost rooms and those of the Elders in the bottom half. It was certainly a tower, but one so big that it had five or six rooms on every level and an iron staircase running up through the centre with landings on every floor, the rooms leading off these. Every floor had a member of the Inner Guard present at all times and a long narrow passageway at the foot of the tower always had two Inners on duty.

The only other route that led away from the passageway was the one that led down to the tombs and to where Hemm now stood. He had been there for seven hours with no food, drink or communication with anyone else. In one hour he would be relieved by another Inner and he would return sixteen hours later to take his post again. Duties lasted for one month before he would be moved on to another, and he received one month a year without duties when he was free to leave the city and go wherever he wished in the lands.

There was not one historical example of a member of the Inners ever leaving his post. The punishment for such a crime quite simply did not exist, as there had never been the need. If ever the need arose (Faith forbid), the unwritten law was death. There would be no course of challenge; a decision made by the Elders had no challenge, not even by the Emperor himself.

It was eight in the morning when Hemm was relieved. He nodded solemnly and struck his chest three times as Biarn replaced him. Every member of the Inners knew each other intimately and there was no need for special pass-words or identity charms. They would know if it was not one of their own.

'By my elders,' they stated in unison as Hemm moved from his position and Biarn took it.

Hemm walked home knowing that Marggitte would have just started her eight-hour station and then she would come home and they would spend eight hours together before Hemm went back on duty. They both chose to sleep alone when their partner was working; that way they would have eight hours together every day for 'recreation'. Hemm, on many occasions, thought this was a strange choice of word as the only thing they definitely couldn't do was 're-create'.

Their time off together was spent riding, shooting, walking and of course making love. This they did with such passion, almost as if they tried to make up for their inability to have children by the physical expression of their love.

Hemm quietly and quickly undressed and lay on his double cot and immediately fell into a dream-free sleep. He had no anxieties and had worked hard to achieve everything he wanted in life. He was respected in the city as being hard but fair. He had never used his position in the Inners to take advantage of the less fortunate. He only used his tremendous fighting skills for good or in defence of his city and everything it stood for. He had a wonderful, beautiful and passionate wife who shared his strong beliefs about what was right and wrong in this violent land they lived in. He had come from a poor background but shared his good fortune with the rest of his siblings, ensuring at least that they never went hungry.

He had earned the right to a peaceful sleep but little did he know his peace was about to be stolen from him.

Isthmus

Three days and nights had passed since Shel had left behind the tranquillity of village life for the routines of a journeyman. He slept where he could find shelter, eating carefully from his provisions even though he should have more than enough to last him to Ontrades. It was as though he knew that there were harder times ahead and he might as well get used to it now.

He was also feeling homesick, missing not only his best friend but also the normality of getting up in the morning, completing his chores and learning from Methon, and the simplicity of sitting around a table with his family. Randeed was enjoying her new freedom and had found carrying Shel for twenty miles a day a delight as opposed to a burden.

The route Shel was taking was to follow the Dapple stream, which wound its way through the neighbouring villages to the north of Jost and eventually led into the Redlands forest. At least this way he would encounter people on his journey and not have to rely upon talking to a furze or, as he reminded himself, a spirit.

Every now and again words would pop into his mind, and at first he thought it was the ruminations of his own thinking until he recognised the light, airy tones of Isthmus. Even so, it was disconcerting and felt to Shel as if he were going a little mad.

He was camped in a farmer's field, with permission of course, in the northernmost town of the county, a little place called Red. He found that he could acquire what he needed if he was friendly and gave a story which was almost the truth, about how he was on a mission of mercy to

Ontrades, where he was hoping to find a healer who could help his very sick friend who had fallen ill with something that no one in the village of Jost had ever seen before.

This explanation always came out in one breath, as if pausing to think too long would cause him to stumble over the words and make him sound false.

This was a twisted version of the truth but one that Shel found easier than telling these good people a story how he had to battle evil to save the lands from eternal darkness. No, he would save that story for a time when he had more conviction in it himself and he didn't feel quite so alone.

In the morning he would leave Red and embark on the part of the journey that was bothering him. He didn't actually know how deep Redlands Forest was but was hoping to get out on the other side before the sun set on tomorrow. He was a little more at ease in the open than he was in the confines of a forest.

He chose to speak aloud to see if Isthmus would come to him. There was little light as the moon was quartered and the sky was cloudy after the rain of the last three days. In the flickers of the tongues of campfire Shel squeaked, 'Hello, Isthmus.' He cleared his throat and tried again. 'Hello!' This time he shouted. 'By the sweet Faith of Love,' he muttered, 'I sound like the village loon asking for a slice of the moon,' quoting from the children's verse.

'Except the village loon normally has more conviction,' sang Isthmus as the spirit appeared in a sitting position on the opposite side of the fire from Shel.

'Bugger,' said Sheldrak, 'I don't know how many times you are going to do that before I get used to it, but I have to admit it's good to see you again. I thought you would be with me all the time when you said you were one of the Seven and coming with me to Ontrades.'

Isthmus smiled. 'If only it were that easy, my brave friend. I have limitations to my power. Sometimes I feel strong and other times I cannot even come to your mind. Making myself visible to you is a drain, but now that I know you prefer to see me I shall try to visit more often.'

'I don't really understand, Isthmus. What is your place on this journey? Why are you here, and from where is it that you visit me?'

'Some things I know not, but the only reasons that spirits walk the earth is because of their refusal to believe their body has died or because of their defiance to cross over into another world. I know my body has gone but I am here by choice. At some stage we will come face to face with Millghrew and at that time I can be a great help to you in your quest to defeat him.'

Isthmus asked, 'Let me see the Sword of Destiny, or if you prefer, Northstar.'

Shel stood up and walked over to his pack, pulling from it the sword bundled up in old rags. When he unfolded the rags the weapon instantly grabbed the light of the fire and cast it back in a dazzling display of multicoloured radiance.

'My Faith, it's not lost any of its beauty,' exclaimed Isthmus. 'I too used to carry the blade you hold in your hand and many moons ago it was I, Isthmus, who travelled the land as one of the Seven in search of Millghrew.'

Shel spoke back, 'Millghrew, Essdark, same person?'

'I don't think you could ever say "person" when referring to the Grey One but, yes, we speak of the same creature whatever name we wish to use. I am here to help you because I have travelled these paths before, in another land with different people but with the same quest, to put to rest once and for all the Lord of Death. Last time we failed and now I walk the land between the living and the spirits until the chance to meet and avenge what has gone before. One day, Shel, I will tell you my story, for it is part of yours, but now is not the time. That day is in the future, when you are ready.

'I tire now, but this chat has helped me. When I go it's as though to sleep but a sleep in which other spirit creatures exist also. It is a terrible place, Shel, for not all spirits wish to do good as I do. There are things in here with me that could drive you to kill rather than see them for a second time. Men have taken the lives of their own children and then killed themselves after experiencing the evil spirits that refuse to pass over.

'This is the only way I can build strength to come back to you, perhaps for one hour in every day if you wish to see me. But it is much easier to talk to you in your head if you can get used to it. As the days turn we will work out what is best for us both.

'I start to fade. By my elders...' And Isthmus was gone.

'Wait!' shouted Shel, but to no avail. An hour later, as Shel was curled up in his blanket by the fire he thought, 'I do wish he hadn't finished with the talk of bad spirits,' and then he passed into an uneasy sleep. He dreamed of a land in which he was the only one alive and everyone else floated a foot off the ground. Everywhere, spirits like Isthmus drifted like kites in the wind but at the edge of his vision something grey was floating; grey, and bigger than everything else.

The next morning he woke tired. His eyes seemed sore as if he had spent all night rubbing them instead of sleeping, and dark circles had formed beneath them.

Wonderful, he thought, I am only three days out of Jost and already unable to cope. He unfairly admonished himself because, although he knew he hadn't slept well he could not remember a thing about his dream. Under the circumstances this was for the good, as dwelling on the meaning of another dream would only initiate yet another uneasy sleep the following night.

He ate a good breakfast of fresh bread and cheese as

supplied by the farmer upon whose land he camped, and washed it down with strong herbal tea. The leaves had been given to him by Methon and, as he had suggested at the time, provided Shel with quite a lift. His limbs, stiff with the damp ground, were refreshed within moments of quaffing the brew.

'Come on, Randeed, let's get moving. I want to be out of the Redlands Forest by nightfall.'

Randeed whinnied as if in agreement and a few minutes later the camp was cleared, everything packed on to the creature, including Sheldrak, and their trek north recommenced. It was a sticky, balmy morning and it wasn't long before the pair of them were sweating profusely in the damp, misty heat.

It was going to be a long, hard day and Shel longed for company, real company, people who were there for more than an hour a day. If the second of the Seven was Isthmus and he was the first, then when would he pull the third to him and how would he know? One thing was certain, he hoped it wasn't in Ontrades, or he had another seven days of talking to his furze. My Faith, he thought, the quest might be over in the first ten days if I don't get company soon.

The morning dragged but after an hour or more the trees of the Redlands came into view. They took a course close to the tiny spring they had been tracking. As they got to the forest entrance Shel filled all his water bottles with fresh water and then he and Randeed drank their fill. The water sparkled and chattered to them as it danced over the rocks and then into the dark shade of the forest cool.

The forest was beautiful but so dense that in places it looked as if some giant green stonemason had laid a wooden wall. The variety of trees was great, with large sturdy oaks, horse chestnuts, beech and elm. These trees were bigger than the normal-sized trees that Shel was used to seeing back home and the soil was an incredible deep, black loam. If there is a place in these lands, thought Shel, where the gods put their garden, then it must be here.

A magnificent willow, fully twenty paces in diameter, stood as a sentinel to the forest and the stream bubbled away behind it. Shel noticed immediately as he dismounted from Randeed that the noise of the stream became muffled like the singing at a party that is far away; you can hear the music but you cannot recognise the song. So the dark greens of the woodlands hid the song of the stream. Not only did the bubbling die away to an occasional gurgle, but also the stream itself became almost impossible to follow. It veered left and right sharply and dropped away into steep narrow valleys before reappearing 100 paces away to the left or right.

'This is jak,' said Sheldrak aloud. Only then did he realise that the forest was not only quiet but so quiet that his words had been absorbed into the greenery like dregs from a used teacup mopped up by a dishcloth. He could not hear any birdsong or the normal scurrying in the undergrowth that he might expect. He decided he didn't want to hear any rumblings in the undergrowth after all, but wanted to get through the ten miles of forest that prowled before him like a cornered beast.

'Isthmus, I don't now how high your energy level is but I would really like to hear your tinkling voice as a replacement for the tinkle of the stream.'

'Do not worry, my friend, I am with you.' The voice was not heard by Randeed for it was in Shel's head only and that was fine by Shel. Voices in his head was better than no voices at all.

'By my elders, Isthmus,' and once more the quiet of the forest was disturbed by Shel's dulcet tones. From far away the lone cry of a hawk or eagle split the eerie silence but then was heard no more.

'Try to speak to me in your head as I do with you. You do not need to speak aloud. Say the words in your head.'

'Like this,' Sheldrak thought.

'Yes, that is perfect. You will soon find that you can shout or whisper or argue, whichever you feel, exactly as you would with your speaking voice.'

Sheldrak stopped and turned to Randeed, who was nuzzling his palm for comfort. Had the animal sensed the presence of Isthmus or was something other than the spirit bothering her?

'How do I stop you listening to my innermost thoughts? Will I ever have any privacy again?'

'Of course you will. I cannot hear anything you do not want me to and, Sheldrak, please do not insult me, for neither would I even if I could.'

'By my elders,' stammered Sheldrak (if it was possible to stammer with a thought), 'you have my sincere pardons.'

'Ha, ha,' chuckled the spirit, for the first time that Shel could recall, 'I have embarrassed you. It is of no concern. I too forget I am just a spirit, how can I be insulted? No one else can know, just you and I.'

'But what happens when the others are pulled to us, am I to deceive them? That does not seem to be the Faith for which we stand.'

'There will come a time on our journey when I must become known to others, but until I choose, we will keep Isthmus as a secret between you and me.'

Sheldrak then asked a question he had been longing to ask since winning the Great Race, which seemed so long ago but was only five days.

'Can you move into anyone's body and make them do things they ordinarily could not?'

'Of course not, Shel, I only did what you allowed me to do. I can never move against the wishes of my host. You wanted to win the race. Your body, although you did not think so at the time, was capable of winning. All I did was push it that little bit harder. You won the race, Sheldrak. All the training you did with your strange boots and Methon's guidance won it for you, not I. Now come, we must move. We can talk as we walk, for I will not last in your head for the full ten miles, but I can guide you most of the way.'

The morning passed into afternoon and not once during the struggle through the trees did Shel spot any sunlight. Shel imagined that if he could ever walk on the bottom of the sea it would feel like this. The dark green sky was occasionally lighter with the promise of blue, and pushing through the undergrowth was like pushing against the flow of tidal waters. It was slow progress but luckily (either from a previous life or in the spirit world) Isthmus knew his way through the maze of tree, bush and shrub.

The Dapple stream had disappeared into mud and slime and on a couple of occasions Sheldrak went down with a thump on the seat of his leggings. How disconcerting it was to fall and then to hear a giggle of laughter from inside his own head – and he swore that Randeed had a smile glowing across her horsy features.

The land began to rise and the undergrowth thinned slightly as they trekked up the big hill that lay approximately two thirds of the way into the forest. For the first time in over eight hours Shel glimpsed the sky and his heart sank. The sun had almost crossed and he knew he either spent the night within the forest or pushed hard and finished the day's trek in the dark with the added risk of losing his way.

'Isthmus, what is your counsel?'

The reply in his mind was very faint and Isthmus sounded out of breath, if that were possible.

'Push on, Shel, as fast as you can. You don't want to be in here too long after twilight.' And with that Isthmus was snatched away, as a pet on a lead being pulled angrily home by its master.

'By my Faith, why did Isthmus not tell me earlier that the Redlands were dangerous after dark?' Shel spoke aloud once more.

This time it was his own inner voice that spoke back to him: Don't pretend you didn't know. You haven't seen a living thing all day, with the exception of the trees.'

The thought made him shudder. He had a premonition of the trees pulling their roots out of the ground as he slept and slowly slipping them around his legs, chest and throat until he became part of the forest. For ever!

'Come on, Randeed, we can cover this last three miles down the slope in no time.'

Randeed whimpered in reply. Something had upset the furze from the second she had set foot under the covering of green, but now she was getting more and more spooked. Could she tell that the soothing presence of Isthmus had gone?

If she was spooked then, she certainly was two minutes later when a howl went up into the night air that made every hair on the furze's body leap in protest.

'Wolf,' said Shel to himself (he hoped). 'It came from somewhere behind us.' Another cry split the night air like a streak of lightning illuminating a cloud-darkened sky. That one came from in front and to the left, the direction that Shel and Randeed were heading. Instinctively they moved away to the right. Shel loosed his bow from his back. Randeed stopped.

Come on, girl, don't stop now, Shel thought as they stumbled down the slope and into a clearing. Three yips stopped them dead. The animal cries came from directly in front of them. The yellow eyes that peered out at them from the gloom of the twilight ahead had an intelligence in them that was at once terrifying and fascinating. The lupine ran at them. Much bigger and quicker than a normal wolf, it leapt in an instant as Shel was struggling to fit an arrow. The arrow fell from his sweaty hands and he grabbed at North-star, hidden beneath his tunic.

He pulled, but it caught on his belt and he looked up into certain death as the yellow eyes met his at no more than three feet away.

It couldn't end like this, could it? was his last thought before the lupine sailed over his head and hit the smaller grey wolf that Shel hadn't seen and which was about to sink its fangs into the small of his back.

Sheldrak had no time to think as two more grey wolves crept into the clearing, followed by a third and fourth. Shel pulled another arrow and this time the arrow flew as sure as his mother's love, tearing out the throat of the lead wolf. From behind him snarls and growls filled his ears, but he could not afford to turn his back on what lay ahead.

Randeed decided that she may as well die fighting, and gripped the nearest tail with one of her four-fingered feet and flung with all her might. The furze was a lot bigger than the grey wolf and tossed it like a soft rag into the bark of a sturdy oak. The thud and following crack meant that something had broken, and Shel turned his attention to the two remaining wolves.

'By the sweet Faith.' His lips moved as another wolf slunk out of the bushes. He was still one against three and if he shot another arrow he would surely take one but the other two would be turning him into a red pulp. He felt something brush against him and the next moment the large lupine stood by his side. He didn't know what he had done to deserve this help but wasn't about to question it.

The lupine drew level and then without pausing launched itself into the midst of the remaining three, blood already covering its muzzle from what remained of the first wolf. Shel picked up his sword from where he had let it fall and with the golden runes sparkling on the blade, leapt to the side of the very brave or foolhardy lupine. Shel thought, if we beat these three do I then have to fight the lupine?

One of the greys had singled Sheldrak out and crouched low on its haunches. Its lips were pulled back to reveal sharp incisors still red from the blood of the previous kill and with bits of flesh hanging from its back teeth. Shel held Northstar out in front of him and they circled, keeping a respectful distance. On the other side of the clearing the lupine was struggling, with a grey on either side taking turns to run in and bite and retreat. The intelligence of these creatures was disturbing.

Shel feinted forward, stopped dead and dropped to one knee. The wolf, expecting the attack, sprung forward into the air, only to find Shel gone and under it. Northstar struck upwards, splitting the wolf from the neck down through its underbelly to its hindquarters and dropping its steaming, foul innards on to the head of Shel. He lifted and emitted a roar that awoke Azores from her sleep back in Jost and left her wondering what had woken her.

He was covered from head to foot in bloody, stinking offal. The two remaining live wolves took one look at this new, screaming creature, turned tail and scurried off into the dark depths of the forest cover.

Shel stood silent, looking at the large lupine that had helped him. Had it helped him or had it just got caught up in a fight for its own existence.

The lupine looked at Shel with its rheumy yellow eyes and said, 'All right mate, I'm Shade. I believe you're Sheldrak!'

Marggitte

Marggitte was on early duty. She was one of the sixteen women who had aspired to the level of the Inner Guard and therefore was stood outside the Princess Ararra's quarters at the top of the Citadel. The princess was the ten-year-old daughter of the emperor and was the most closely guarded treasure of the whole of Ontrades. The poor child was never allowed out of the white tower, not since her older sister had been badly hurt in a riding accident.

The older princess now sat in another of the Citadel's many chambers, never moving, never speaking. Strephanie had hit her head hard that day. The thunderous hooves of the stallion had then trampled over her back. The combination had left her without movement or speech.

As far as Emperor Daynor and his wife Ester were concerned, one paralysed child without the faculties to feed herself was enough for one regal family. Since that day the younger daughter of the two royal children had never been allowed away from the guard of an Inner and never allowed out of the Citadel. So now Marggitte stood, knowing that this was the most important of all the duties she undertook.

As Margg was one of the few women in the Inners, (despairingly, Ontrades was the same as any modern society, incredibly sexist), she regularly got the child-minding duty ahead of her male counterparts, but she overlooked the insult and instead chose to enjoy her time with Ararra. This also was one of the few duties where speaking, moving and play were allowed. The Inner's role was one of a minder and during the early watch, eight 'til sixteen, Ararra was at her most lively.

Marggitte had known the child since birth and, as was customary within the royals, the empress spent less time with her own child than she did with the elders; hence Margg had a very strong relationship with the young princess. Marggitte was one of two sisters and her father had been a corp in the infantry and had become famous in the city in his younger days for his riding skills. Now he had matured and retired but was incredibly proud of his daughter, who had improved on his rank by becoming an Inner.

Marggitte had been in a position of relative luxury as a child, with her father such a revered rider and a corp as well. She hadn't wanted for much and, in direct contrast to Hemm, had never needed to fight for anything. She may have never needed to fight, but, by all the Faiths, that never stopped her.

Margg was the original tomboy and went out of her way to provoke the boys to such an extent that they would lose their tempers with her and, next thing they knew, they would be flat on their backs seeing stars, day or night.

For a time, until she built her reputation, because boys would not hit her she had an obvious advantage, but her father had taught her well and it wasn't long before the young men stopped pulling their punches. They could still rarely hit her, but now it was not through fear of hurting a girl.

She soon moved through her military classes with ease. Her father, having the position in the ranks that he did, soon positioned her to join the Inners as one of the few women graduates.

It was during her training that she met Hemm. Margg had been in training for two weeks when they met; he had been training for two years and was already destined for great things. Even when he was at the age of sixteen it was a foregone conclusion that he would graduate into the Inners, and him a kid with no military pedigree.

'His father is a pisshead,' was the sad story that moved around the camp as quickly as the pox in a brothel and with just as devastating results. The chip on Hemm's shoulder was big enough to be a second head.

Marggitte had only entered into real bouts of unarmed combat with her father. Never had she taken on a real champion before and yet here she was, two weeks into her Inner training, face to face with one of the best reputations in the camp: Hemm, son of Hemm the pisshead.

She took to the thick reed matting that the practice fights were held on and looked down into the dark brown eyes of her foe. She was over six foot in height and her long blonde hair was tied up in a bun. She was not traditionally beautiful but had the sharp, handsome features you would normally associate with a pretty young boy. Her shoulders were wide and strong and Hemm, looking up at her, actually afforded himself a smile.

Big mistake. Margg saw this look as a sign of condescension and flew at Hemm with all the fury of a women not scorned, but one who had decided she never would be. Hemm used her weight, size and inexperience to good effect, deftly stepping out of the way, and with a gentle trip he sent Marggitte sprawling on to the matting.

The crowd of young men cheered until the training serge shut them up with one look that would have taken the polish off the table. Margg jumped to her feet. Anger spilled out of her like blood from a gutted calf and she raged again at Hemm. Once more she ended up on her arse.

'Jak!' she screamed. She could not remember being more annoyed. This time her attack was a little more controlled but equally as aggressive. Hemm fended, left parry, right parry, blocked kick with his instep, double parry, but Margg's attack continued to roll on, backing Hemm up until he was against the chest of the first man in the crowd surrounding the mat.

Marggitte was shouting with every single blow she was raining in on Hemm's head and body, and still he blocked every one. Then from nowhere he struck out, ramming his hand hard into the chest bone of the young girl, sending her spinning around and down again.

Panting, her hair now loose about her bowed head, she gasped for breath and Hemm realised he had hurt her. Bending down he offered his hand as the crowd nodded their consent; this fight had gone too far. But Margg wasn't finished yet and instead of taking the proffered hand of help she pulled on it with all her might, at the same time driving her head into Hemm's midriff.

Even though Hemm had genuinely been offering his hand as help he never lost his concentration for a second. Jumping into the air he avoided the head butt and instead locked the head of the blonde whirlwind between his legs. Falling back on to the mat, he pulled her head back in a leg lock that she would never have got out of if they had still been fighting today.

'OK, that's enough, Hemm, let loose,' came the gruff voice of the serge. Hemm obeyed the order and, as Marggitte stood up, face red and fiery, he looked deep into her eyes. Now here was a woman, he thought. Margg looked back with respect. He was the only man who had ever treated her as an equal, no holds barred, one versus one. Now here was a man.

Within two weeks they were in love. Twenty years later their love was stronger than the Bluetop Mountains and the passion had never dimmed.

Arrara had woken earlier and dozed until the time she knew that Margg would be on duty. Then she could pull her into the bedroom to play with her dolls. Margg was the only friend that Arrara had in the world. Of course she had her poor sick sister, but face facts, as her father was fond of saying, she would get more reaction from her rag dolls than she would from Strephanie. She wasn't being nasty, just honest and, 'The truth is the most important thing of all.' She knew that from her nanny and so Margg was her 'bestest' friend.

For Margg it was something more than that. The life decision she had made with Hemm didn't prevent her from wanting to have the chance to pass on her life values to a child, just like any mother or father. The difference was she had to be so careful not to impart any life lessons that were in direct conflict to those of the emperor and his wife.

Royalty had a certain way about them, a strong self-belief of superiority, which in certain circumstances would be harmful. All Marggitte attempted to do was to rub a few of the rougher edges off this self-belief to teach the child a little humility. After all, it was one of the seven Faiths, although one royalty sometimes chose to forget.

The child and adult sat upon the large cot set against the wall furthest from the double doors of the very large sleeping chamber. Apart from the family of rag dolls sat on the cot between the two of them, you would never have known that the room belonged to a ten-year-old girl. It was exceptionally ornate in its decoration: heavy maroon velvet curtains, glistening shields and swords fixed to the walls and thick animal fur coverings on the cot and floor. Where were all the trappings of a child's playroom?

If the emperor and his wife were not careful they would find Arrara as badly hurt as her sister had been from the fall off the horse.

Arrara's one comfort was Marggitte and for at least an hour of every day of her life they had managed to meet. Margg listened to the little girl's problems and to the important things in her life, such as how she could avoid eating spinach or what you should do in the classroom when you trumped and it smelled icky. Margg smiled as she wondered if the two problems were linked. The two had a bond, not that of a mother and daughter but as close to it as Margg was ever going to get.

The double doors to the bedroom opened and the nanny entered. She was an elderly lady with quite set ways about how a young princess should behave and sitting on the bed with one of these 'dirty guard women' was not one of them. She knew the princess and the Inner were good friends and despised Marggitte all the more for it. Good Faith, was that any way for a woman to behave, covered in armour, wielding a sword? Taking away the one reason women were put on this earth?

'Out,' she screamed. It was almost as much of the daily ritual as washing her face.

'Out, before I call the emperor. Go and stand on your guard. Go on. Get out.' The words came out like drops of venom spat from a snake's jaws. She meant well, it was just that her meaning well was most other people's wishing ill.

Marggitte had for years controlled her anger in the face of such provocation, and she turned to Princess Arrara. Offering a deep, solemn bow she said, 'My Princess, by my elders.' And striking her ample breast three times she turned and left the room.

For the next seven hours she stayed on guard while food was brought back and forth, lessons were had, two other friends, handpicked by Nanny, also made a visit. Arrara's mother and father spent a good five minutes with their daughter. Marggitte lived for her honour, but on days such as this she certainly had her doubts.

Nanny had a real name, a name not known to many but, ironically, in the ancient tongue one which meant joyful. Her name was Joice. In the same way that Marggitte had her code of honour and loyalty to the Inners, Joice believed she too had devoted her life with honour and dignity to the emperor's family.

She was a sprightly seventy-three years old and had

many years of service left in her yet. Her three children had long since gone and she didn't know if they lived in the city still. In fact, she didn't even know if they lived at all. It mattered not to her, as she had Arrara, whose need for discipline, since that nasty accident with her sister, kept a nanny as firm as she was in a job. Joice wouldn't bow to the whimpering of a snivelling little girl.

Faith, if she didn't need Arrara alive she could have pitched her out of the window years ago. Her husband had outlived his usefulness and, Faith bless his soul, he had got a little too close to a window after a copious amount of ale. Accidents do happen.

She looked after the younger princess and looked after her well. She was never allowed out of the Citadel, rarely let out of her room, and Joice played the game perfectly, allowing others minimum access to the princess. These buffoons who called themselves the Inners, especially Marggitte, could be relied upon to keep the rules. One thing they never did was break any bloody rules. Oh no, death before dishonour.

'Jak,' she said to anyone who bothered to listen to her. She must stop upsetting herself this way. It was happening more and more as she got older. Were some of the accidents she had arranged in the past coming back to haunt her? Well, let them come, all of them; I'll rip their eyes out with my teeth and spit them in the lane. These thoughts were tumbling through her head as she tumbled down the lanes to the part of the city known as the Pass. If you wanted it, you could get it here. Her purse, hidden beneath her well-tailored but ultimately grubby clothing, was full of gold trades she had stolen from the Citadel.

The alleyways around here were narrow, twisting and turning at every avenue. If you did not know them you would be lost within seconds. Joice knew them well, as well as the thick, blue veins that ran raised on the back of her hands. It was already dark and the Pass nightlife was creeping out of its daytime sleeping holes. Vagrants, prostitutes, thieves, smugglers, illegal-substance users banned from the city, all had made this their home. It was a trading centre by day, but the night brought traders of a different kind.

She stopped outside a door painted a dirty blue, the colour of a dead man's eyes as his still warm body drifts from present to past, and rapped a code on the door. A large, dark-skinned man answered, swarthy in complexion with scars covering his face. He'd been involved in a scrap or two. He knew Joice and shoved a dirty big hand, palm upwards, out at her. Trades were exchanged with no words and Joice entered the dark of the house.

Squeals of delight came from the rooms scattered about the dirty landing, some sounding closer to pain than pleasure. This is all I live for now, she thought as she crept behind a door to experience the dark pleasures awaiting her.

Essdark knew he had allies in Ontrades but didn't know them all. He was always recruiting but had enough for now to help him with his plans. Armies were forming all over the lands, some to do his bidding consciously while others were naturally malevolent, not converted. It all amounted to the same thing, evil for evil's sake.

There was more at stake this time. This was his last chance. If he lost now then he lost for ever. There would be no coming back again in 500 years with a different name and body. This time he beat the Spawn or lost everything. He had no real doubts he would get the sword and with it the ruling of everything that walked, crawled or grew in these lands, but first he had to entice the Spawn to him. Not the rest of the Seven; they played on his mind but he didn't need them. Together, united, they were powerful and dangerous, but split asunder he could have them and then the sword.

He was in human form today, walking about the labyrinthine tunnels and caves that made up his abode. Soon he would be strong enough to walk about again up top, but for now he would use his mind. He had to undermine what the Spawn was doing, worry him, kill a few of his so-called friends. It was also a time for a show of strength, time for the worlds to see that Essdark was back – and what better way to do that than to infiltrate the Citadel of Ontrades?

I have just the people to do that for me, he thought, and I have an advantage. I know who the Seven will be and I intend to get to them before the Spawn does.

Battles were to be fought, on scales both large and small, but it might be the smaller battles that would win the war.

Hemm lay in his cot. This was by far the best part of their day. He was lying after seven hours' sleep, waiting for the love of his life to walk through the door and into his arms. He heard the door to their quarters open and slam closed and then the door to the room he slept in opened. Instead of Marggitte standing in the doorway stood the largest troll he had ever seen. In its arms it held a large, curved sword, which swished through the air, causing enough of a draught for Hemm's hair to blow back on his head. His arm reached out for his own weapon but the mighty troll's sword chopped down, cutting clean through Hemm's arm at the elbow.

Hemm screamed loud enough to wake the spirits and sat up in the cot, covered in a fine sheen of sweat. There was no one in the room but himself and when he looked down at his arm he was overjoyed to see that it was still the complete article.

'Good Faith,' he uttered, 'where did that come from?'

The door to the sleeping chamber did open and Marggitte entered after her duty at the Citadel to find her beloved sat up in his covers looking as if he had just run a twenty-mile trek in full armour.

'Hemm, by my elders, what is wrong?' she said.

'Nothing, I just had a dream, that's all. Don't worry. Come on, get out of that armour and get yourself washed. I want you cleaned and in this cot in five minutes.'

She kissed him tenderly and duly obliged. Some time later when passions had been sated they lay and talked about the impending wars.

'I heard today,' said Hemm, 'that the Morgs have got together the biggest army of warriors that they have ever mustered. Over 20,000 from all over the lands, and rumours abound that there are more than just Morgs. There is a suggestion that even some giants from Arbrain have gone over to their side and some of the cave dwellers of Mina are also with them.'

'We have nothing to fear,' Margg replied. 'In times gone by we have had to fight when the numbers have not favoured us. We have the best-trained men and women from all the lands.'

Hemm cleared his throat before asking, 'What if it isn't just Morgs? Have you ever seen a troll?'

This question seemed to have special emphasis and Margg raised herself up on to one elbow so that she could see her husband's eyes. 'You know I haven't. Why do you ask?'

Hemm told her of his dream and explained how real it had seemed. 'The creature was here in our chamber. Why did I think that? I have never felt unsafe in our quarters before, ever. The dream just came from nowhere.'

'Darling, if we knew where dreams came from we would

not have to fight in the Inners to earn our keep. But I know what I can do to help you forget it.'

Margg managed to take Hemm's mind completely off his dream.

War Council

On the eighteenth floor of the twenty-four that made up the Citadel the twelve men of the Elders, plus the emperor, sat down to discuss the latest developments of the impending battle and possible war. The counsel room was the only one in the whole building that took an entire floor to itself. The table in the centre of the circular room was oblong and its dark mahogany wood was in direct contrast to its surroundings in both shape and colour. The whitewashed walls of the counsel had very little decoration apart from the evenly spaced red flags of Ontrades, twelve of them in all, hung upon the whiteness like blood showing through a dressing.

At the head of the table sat the emperor, dressed in a simple red tunic, and on either side of him sat six Elders, all dressed in the holy cowls they received on their ordination day. They too were clothed in red but a lighter, fresher red as of a raspberry, and the whole room was brightly lit from the many windows spread around the circular hall. On entering the room one would have thought the gaiety lent itself to a meeting to arrange the midsummer fayre rather than to discuss the dark deeds of war and death.

There was no seniority among the Elders, but when the meeting was a War Council as it was today then Rawt who doubled his role as Capatain of the Inners, and Shint, War Elder, held the casting votes in making decisions. Each member of the council had a role to play in the running of the city but ultimate responsibility lay with Emperor Daynor. The other Elders had various tasks: Travil was in charge of law and order, Mantin, finance, Pual was the Elder for Trading, Nalla, Bedora, Kadric, Gedar, Eventu, Zilmath and Trenc all had their specialist tasks; but Trenc's ability to saye was the one that in times of war became the most valuable.

Today at the behest of Rawt two members of the Inners were placed inside the council room – two of Rawt's most trusted and worthy guards, Enth and Hemm. Hemm had been summoned to Rawt's quarters during the night and told to go back to his room to sleep as he was on special duty today at the War Council. It was the ninth day since Sheldrak had left his village and even as the council began its deliberations a runner was on his way from the southern outpost with news of a strange young man and his pet lupine.

The emperor called for silence and greeted the hushed gathering, 'Members of the highest council in the land, by my elders.'

In unison the chant came back and all thirteen men struck their breasts three times. They sat and waited for the emperor's address.

'As we know, the Morgs have been gathering their forces for many months now and many of our outriders have been lost or have disappeared without word. Shint, my friend, what report have you back from our capatains?'

Shint, an ex-capatain and now the War Elder stood his full six feet. Even at his age, which no one was quite sure of, he stood proud and erect. Still capable of taking on most men in combat, he had one regret: that in becoming an elder he no longer had the chance to draw sword in battle. He was worth so much more as a controller of the battalions of men on the field that no risk could be taken with him. His mind was as sharp as the spear he had carried victoriously into war on hundreds of occasions and no one man was his equal in the tactics of combat.

'I have news, sire, but not news that will cheer the heart.

We now have lost over 100 outriders and the Morgs have assembled over 20,000 in the flatlands to the east of the city. I believe that they are but two days' ride away. My scouts bring news from far south on the plateaus that the cavemen of the Mina Mountains are gathering and our trusted friends the giants of Arbrain may soon be called upon to defend themselves.

'I now bring news that will chill the hearts of you all. Rumours abound that the reason for this gathering of our enemies is that the Grey One walks again.'

A cloud passed across the sun, darkening the room for naught but a second before shining again, but it did not go unnoticed by the council.

The emperor was quick to continue, not wishing for the council to be distracted. 'Trenc, have you seen anything with your second sight which could have any bearing on this matter?'

Trenc was the oldest member of the council and had until now looked to be dozing peacefully in his chair. By Faith, the other members knew that he never missed anything of importance and could retell word for word everything that had been said weeks later when the other Elders had forgotten. He tried to get to his feet but a wave of the hand from the emperor permitted him to remain sitting.

'I have seen plenty,' he said in a voice that belittled his frailty, 'some which I know to be true and some which I am unsure about. I will talk and let the council make of it what they will.

'This battle, which will undoubtedly happen, is about greater deeds than just trading or ownership of this city. Essdark, Juunes, Millghrew, which ever vile name he chooses to go by or we choose to use for him, is indeed strong again. I cannot see if he walks yet for he is far stronger than all of us together, but there is someone now as I speak drawing near who is chosen.'

Rawt jumped to his feet. 'Do you mean *the* Chosen One? The one that the scriptures foretell will destroy the evil that is Essdark?'

Trenc raised his voice. 'You are a good man, Rawt, but you at times have the impetuousness of youth. Know your learnings – the scriptures never said the Chosen One would rid us of Essdark, but they did say he would confront him. I think that time draws near. The leader of the Seven comes to the city and he is one of three. When he leaves he will be one of five, but his time here will be troubled and the battle ahead is but a part of it.

'We must all be on our guard. There is evil among us, infiltrating the higher ranks of the city, but my sight is cloudy. Someone among us has the protection of the Grey.'

Rawt again was quickest to react. 'Then we shall find him, whoever he is. We must use our best Inners to find this traitor.'

The emperor held his hand up and silence reigned. 'I hear what you say, Rawt, and I will leave that matter with you.'

Rawt bowed deep and low.

'For the rest of us we must think of the best way to protect our city and people. Shint, you must set your mind to the battle, for I think it will be fought within five days if what you say about the gatherings in the flatlands is true. It would not be wise to ride hard for two days and then fight when tired. I think we have five days, maximum.

'Trenc, you have the hardest task of all, for with all the visitors in and out of the city you must try and recognise the Chosen, if that is possible.'

'Now, Shint, give the council a full report on your men and where you have them stationed.'

Hemm listened to every word, remembering as much as he could to take back to his cot. He knew he would share this with Marggitte; he had to share it. This was their time.

This was all they had lived for: honour and truth, he thought as the council discussed events for many hours more.

Marggitte and Princess Arrara were playing a game of chequers when Joice came storming into the room. Even for her this attack was particularly acidic.

'Get away from her!' she shrieked, leaving both Margg and Arrara wondering which one of the two of them the nanny was screaming at.

'You are her guard. Not her mentor, not her tutor and definitely not her nanny.'

Arrara, for once, spoke up for herself. 'But Nanny, my father and Rawt have both agreed that because I cannot leave my room that Margg's help is good for—'

Before the child could finish her sentence Joice had raised her hand high to slap the girl. Cutting her off with reflexes at least three times as fast, Marggitte grabbed the old woman's arm and held it firm. Their eyes locked and for a moment Marggitte saw fear, but it was soon replaced by anger.

'Take your hand off me now or you will find your place in the Inners gone for ever and as for your husband, well, his dirty paws won't be groping you again.'

It wasn't what was said that upset Margg but the hatred that it was said with. This was a woman who looked after the only able heir to the dynasty of Ontrades and she looked and sounded completely mad.

Marggitte decided that a tactful retreat was the only option. 'Arrara, I will be stationed directly outside the door and one word from you will have me in this room. Joice, as for you, if you choose to harm the princess in any way, even one slap, I have the right to kill you dead on the spot. Listen well, for there is not a person in this city who would doubt the word of an Inner, not even the Elders themselves.'

Marggitte let go of the nanny's arm and walked from the room, giving the princess a comforting smile as she left. Joice, determined to have the last word, shouted after her, 'You stupid woman. You are taking on someone far greater than I and by your stupid Faith, no mercy will be shown at the moment of reckoning.'

This last statement was not fully understood by Marggitte, but she had already decided that the princess was not safe and intended reporting the situation to Rawt. Something was going to have to be done about the nanny from the Underworld, as Marggitte had decided to call her.

In Arrara's room Joice's mood changed, with her final words still echoing off the broad shoulders of Margg as she left. Joice knew she could not frighten the child any more. That last show of anger had been stupid and she didn't want to upset him. He had promised her much more of what she could get in the Pass. Stronger, so that the pleasure would be unbearable. Joice might even lose consciousness. How much pleasure would that be?

She turned to the young girl whose startled eyes could not hide the fear dwelling deep inside her.

'I'm sorry, Princess,' she said, 'it's just my jealous streak coming out. You know how much I love to play games with you. You need not worry, for I will never hit you. It was simply a reaction that I managed to stop in time. Come, it will be time for your lessons soon, let me ready your hair.'

Arrara may have been only ten years old but she was not taken in by the dramatic mood swings of the old woman. Her behaviour had been weird and strange lately and she'd started to smell a lot, a bit like an old dress that's been left in a cupboard for a very long time. The princess decided there and then that she would start to be a little more careful around Nanny in the future. It remained to be seen if that would be good enough to save her life.

As they were both on duty at the same time that day,

Hemm and Marggitte lay in their cot together for both lovemaking and sleep that night. It was an unusual occurrence. As Marggitte had said on walking through the door, 'I thought my luck had changed, my love, only to find it was you lying in the bed.'

Hemm had taken this joke in the manner it had been given and had thrown Marggitte to the cot before she had chance to think about anything else. Now they lay in each other's arms, their bare bodies still glowing with the exertions of their love.

They shared the day's stories. The Chosen One was on his way. He would leave with two more than he came. Armies were forming for wars bigger than all of them. Essdark's name was whispered for fear something was going to leap from under the cot and kill them where they slept. The nanny from the Underworld – this description made Hemm laugh out loud. Was the princess safe? These thoughts were rolling around in their heads as they eventually moved into restless sleep. Hemm's last thought before tiredness took him was to wonder what part would they play in all of this. As long as they had each other and their honour, what did it matter?

It was going to matter a great deal.

Shade

It was day eight after leaving Jost, and Ontrades was two days away. The War Council was being set up for the following day. Sheldrak believed that he had picked up the next member of the Seven to challenge the Grey One, Essdark, and all the other names by which he was known. Shel thought the confrontation was far away but he had many hurdles to get over if he was going to get there. Plus this new companion, the talking lupine, Shade, was as crazy as any loon he had ever met.

The creature ran back and forth with no sense of the direction they were heading. Although it was bewitched – why else could it talk? – the animal spoke absolute jak. He lay panting on the other side of the campfire, while Isthmus had vanished for the evening. The spirit didn't particularly like the company of Shade as on more than one occasion the lupine asked Shel to whom he was talking when Isthmus was in Shel's head.

Shel was coming to the conclusion that it was he who had gone mad as he spent his day alternating between talking to a spirit in his head (who, when feeling tired, buggered off) and chatting to a talking wolf.

'If this is a dream, then I'll write it and sell my story,' he said out loud.

'Only nobody will believe it,' Shade answered. 'Sell what story? Sell, sell, no, buy, buy.' He laughed, which came out human but then changed into the coughing bark of a large dog. 'Someone get that bloody phone,' he added. He realised that Shel was looking at him and said, 'All right mate, how are you? Can't get used to being a lupine. Doesn't seem right not being able to wipe your own arse.'

He then proceeded to try to use his front paw to reach behind him and promptly fell flat on his snout. Sheldrak couldn't help himself but laugh at the plight of the poor creature. If it was a man in a lupine body, no wonder the wretched soul was going mad.

Shade said, 'It's OK for you, laughing, I can't even answer the phone.'

'What's a phone?' Shel replied.

'What do you mean, "What's a phone?" And you think I'm daft? Sorry, forgot, no phones here. So, Shel, when do we eat this bad guy, then we can all go home? Where are the rest of 'em? Shouldn't there be seven of us? Got anything to eat, I'm starving? Come on, let's go. No, get some rest first. I've been running all day. It's fine for you but my arms are aching off. No arms, talking shit, sorry, jak. You talk jak, I talk shit. What do we know? Jakshit!'

Shel listened to all this with a bewildered look on his face. When Shade shouted 'Jakshit' the animal howled and howled as a human, then as a lupine and back to a human until the tears rolled down its fur. Shel was laughing also, but he didn't know what he was laughing at and all the while Shade just kept saying, 'Jakshit, jakshit, we don't know jakshit.'

He had been with Shade for three days and nights (although Shade crept off in the deepest night to do wolverine-type things) and Shel wasn't any closer to understanding how he had come to be a man in wolf's clothing, or lupine's clothing to be absolutely correct. The sad man had been driven totally mad by his dilemma and tonight for the third time Shel was going to try to get closer to him.

Isthmus had refused to show himself to Shade. He told Shel that he could not help him with the animal so for the time being would remain hidden. This was in spite of the fact that Shade looked totally puzzled when Shel and Isthmus were 'talking' and it was obvious that the animal instincts could sense another presence. All Isthmus would offer was that Shade was not of this world and that they would attract an awful lot of attention in Ontrades if he could not be persuaded to be quiet. Shel thought that if that turned out to be true, then it was Faith.

They were his thoughts as he looked at the barking, laughing, loopy lupine who had the keenest yellow eyes he had ever seen.

'So, Shade, tell me once again, how did you come to be here?'

'Shel, I'm sick of this story. I got up, went to work, went to the sandwich shop on the corner for lunch. Next thing I know I'm a lupine in a forest looking for a young kid called Sheldrak. Get that phone, mate.'

Shel only got part of this. 'What is a sandwich, Shade?'

'Well, that depends, doesn't it? Brown bread, white bread, ciabatta, tuna with or without mayo, easy on the black pepper, ham, cheese, French stick, cucumber and lettuce, sir? That's a bloody sandwich. Can you hear something ringing?' Shel said it more to himself than Shade,

'So you went for food and became a wolf?'

'Not a wolf, I can sort them buggers out. No, I'm a lupine. But don't ask me how I know this. Then the bus hit me. That's it, the bus hit me. Christ, don't tell me I'm dead? Heaven or hell? That is the question. To be or not to be, a wolf or a lupine? Well, if this is heaven, thank God I'm not in hell.'

Some lucidity came into Shade's speech. 'Sheldrak, I don't understand either. I have been in this body for over a month, trapped in these woods, waiting for someone called Sheldrak to come along. Only you can help me.'

'Help you with what?'

'To get me back to where I belong. I know certain things about this place, and the Seven, and some grey guy – he's the baddie, I know that much. You and I can help each other. Now I have to go and answer the phone. I'll see you later.'

Shade turned and ran into the night. Two seconds later he was back. 'Do you want mayo on that rabbit?'

Shel nodded; it seemed the best answer to give.

The next morning brought a light drizzle of rain blown from the peaks of the Bluetop Mountains that could be seen looming up ahead. Today they would reach the southern outpost and tomorrow they would reach Ontrades. Sheldrak knew he would not be able to keep Shade quiet, although the previous night's chat had changed the man/lupine, for he was quieter and not as wild as he had been. Randeed had taken an immediate dislike to Shade, especially when he was ranting, but the furze had started to get used to him and was less jumpy today.

Isthmus came into Shel's head. 'Good morning, my friend. By my elders. Have you persuaded our new traveller to keep quiet? Because if you have not we will cause quite a stir.'

'By my elders, Isthmus. No, I have not, but as you can tell he is not quite as frisky today as he has been. I think last night he recognised the predicament he is in. He thought he might have died, which is very disconcerting, because if he did die in his world and came to ours, where will we go when we die? Back to where Shade came from?'

'By my Faith, Shel, he is not dead. But he is with us for a reason and that will become evident to us on our quest. He has already saved your life once, so perhaps that's what he is, a bodyguard.'

'But he thinks I can help him get out of this animal body he is trapped in and I know not how.'

'And perhaps you can, Sheldrak. Faith will find a way if it is the truth.

'Tonight, Sheldrak, you will sleep in the barracks of the southern outpost, but it is also a full moon. You must get away and test the sword, Northstar. Do not forget, it is your guide. Now I will go. Try to talk to the animal. It really would be better if you could keep him quiet when we meet the footmen of Ontrades.'

Before Shel could speak, Shade looked up at him from his side and said, 'Can you hear ringing in your head too? I know you are listening to something but to what I have no idea. If you want to answer the phone when you don't know what one is then you've got worse problems than I have.

'Shel, I know I'm a human and I'm not from here. I'm just about holding this together, but there are going to be times when I become a little difficult to understand. I have moments of clarity in my head but they are not very often.

'At first my human side was disgusted with the way I ripped small creatures like voles and rabbits to pieces. I must be dead – perhaps my sandwich didn't agree with me? I'd sue the buggers if I weren't a bloody lupine. Ha hah howwooooooo…'

The voice tailed off into a wolverine howl followed by, 'Don't worry, if we meet anyone else I'll try to shut up but I can't promise.'

The day passed slowly, mainly because the mountains ahead never seemed to be getting any closer. They loomed over proceedings like some giant grey sentinel, always watching. Sheldrak stopped when the sun was at its highest; at least he assumed this was the case, because although the rain had stopped the cloud cover remained thick, adding to the feeling of oppression. They ate a meal of dried bread and cheese and drank spring water they had picked up from the woods, but that had been two days ago and the water was tepid and dull.

Shade had picked himself up a little and had roamed off to do whatever he did to fill his belly and fulfil his needs. Isthmus, on a rare occasion, chose to appear to Shel, as Shade was not around. The faint hovering apparition of a man spoke.

'By my elders. Well done, Shel, you seem to have got through to our four-legged friend. He has more intelligence than I gave him merit for. I was thinking we either had a slow human or a clever wolf, but now, having listened to some of what he has tried to explain, we may be able to help him on our travels. His must be a tortured soul.' Isthmus spoke as though he knew.

'By my elders, is there no way you can warn me that you are going to appear like that? It must be shortening my lifespan every time I see you.'

'In a couple of hours we will hit the south post and you must prepare a story to tell. Something about travelling to seek your fortune will suffice for the soldiers, but when we get to Ontrades I have a belief that lies will be found out. However white they are.'

A howl from somewhere out of the tall grass that stood on either side of the pathway they were following caused the glittering body of Isthmus to fade. Shade came bounding out of the grass to the side of the path were Shel was sat. He leapt upon him, slobbering,

'Come on, Shel, I've got a good feeling about today. I think a little clearer and someone has answered that phone because the ringing has gone. I've just eaten a juicy, plump creature, of the rodent family I believe, and I've found a fresh spring with some coooool water. Get it, cool water. No, you don't. Never mind. Let's get going. Randeed must want some fresh water carrying you around all day. Owwwooooo.'

Accompanied by Gobby the lupine, Shel went and filled the water bottles. He was starting to like Shade as time went on, probably because he reminded him of Divad. He had the same non-stop chattering and the constant need to be wanted, loved and, of course, amusing. Shel's thoughts turned to Divad and he pulled out the carving with which Helen had entrusted him. He kissed it gently and silently repeated his personal oath to return with a cure. He must not allow himself to forget the reason he was here.

Bottles filled, they moved on, and three hours later Shade was the first to spot in the distance the flat, low building that held the thirteen men of the south post.

'There's life ahead, Shel old mate, and they are well armed if the one I can see is the norm. Do you want me to rip his throat out or have you a more subtle approach?'

'I only know part of what you speak, but there will be no bloodletting. The men of Ontrades are our friends and we have some part to play in its story if the portents I have been given are true.'

'And you don't understand *me*. Ha. Speak English, mate.'

'They are our friends and will be treated as such until something makes me think to the contrary. In a couple of minutes we will be with them. I ask you to be quiet.'

'OK, Shel, no problemo. But if that bloody phone starts ringing you had better answer it.'

Five minutes later they arrived at the camp and Shel dismounted, bowed low to the young guard facing him and greeted him in the manner of the lands, 'By my elders. My name is Sheldrak and I am on my way to the city of Ontrades where I have business to undertake. Would it be possible to spend the night here before travelling on tomorrow? There is only me, my furze and the mangy lupine that seems to have become attached to me.'

Shade looked up at Shel and opened his mouth to tell him he didn't smell that hot himself, when the guard spoke.

'Let me ask the corp, but there should be no problem. Don't know about that evil-looking bugger though.'

Shade was already getting sick of this but Shel crouched down and, taking the animal's head in his hands and, looking into Shade's eyes, said, 'Never mind, old boy. Nobody loves you, but don't worry, Shel will make sure you're fine.'

Shade kept his cool and bit his lip, which if you are a lupine can be quite a dangerous undertaking.

A moment later the guard returned with his corp by his side. 'By my elders, young man, these are dangerous times to be travelling alone. You are more than welcome, but you must take care, for there are hordes of wandering Morgs out there and rumour has it that it will not be long before war once more hits our land. But let us not think of these things tonight. Come and eat with us. We do not have a lot, but our rations divided by fourteen instead of thirteen will not make much difference.'

Shel met the rest of the men and sat and ate with them, listening to their talk of impending battles and how they would be heroes. They asked him questions about himself that he managed to fend with accomplished ease. He never lied, he just never told the whole truth.

They shared their beer rations with him and after eating ham, fresh fruit, bread, potatoes and carrots, Shel soon became sleepy. For most of the meal Shade stayed at Shel's feet and kept his head down, but the corp was no fool and saw that the creature was remarkably intelligent, turning its head at certain points of the conversation. It almost seemed to be following what was being said.

As Shel began his second beer Shade stood up, looked at Shel and then looked at the outside door. Shel understood the code and let the lupine out into the night air, whispering to Shade as he did, 'Meet me at the top of that small hill over there in two hours. We need to see what Northstar has to tell. Look, it's a full moon.'

Shade howled at said moon and ran off into the night.

Approximately two hours later, Shel stood waiting at the top of the small grassy knoll 200 yards to the left of the wooden barrack room and sleeping quarters of the south post guards. The acid churned in his stomach as the thought of using the sword for the first time generated a nervousness in his body.

'Was I glad to get out of there,' said a voice from the darkness. 'If I had to put up with one more insult I would have pissed on somebody's bed.'

'I would recognise that charm anywhere,' said Shel. 'Quickly, get here where I can see you. I don't want anyone else to spot us or see what we are doing. Word will travel fast if it becomes known we have the Sword of Destiny with us. Sit still, Shade, and let us see if we are heading in the direction of the sword.'

Shel took the sword from the scabbard hidden beneath his cloak and lay it on the ground. Isthmus came to Shel and said, 'By my elders, Sheldrak, you have done well to keep the whole truth from the soldiers, but I fear what you do now will be seen for many a league. You have no choice, you must test the sword. Let us see if it truly is Northstar – but I have no reason to doubt.'

'By my elders,' Shel replied, 'is this all I must do, Isthmus, lay the sword down and sit and wait?'

'No, Sheldrak, you must lay the sword so that it points back to the start of your journey, which is almost due south, back to Jost. Then you must quote the ancient incantation.'

Shade stood watching Shel as he turned the sword around so that it pointed back towards himself, and then Shel began to repeat the words of Isthmus.

> Northstar, Northstar, this is whence I came.
> If you be true, then turn and lead the way.
> If you be false, then die and be no more.
> Northstar, Northstar, by Faith, where is Tremain?

They waited, but nothing happened. Shel looked at Shade and was about to start the spell again when the sword vibrated gently against the thick grass on which it lay. A light came out of the sword, shining brightly in all directions like the birth of a new star. It was a beautiful blue-white light that instantly delighted and also terrified. It had a power that vibrated through the earth. The sword hovered an inch, two inches, a foot above the grass. Shel and Shade stepped back into the receding darkness as cries came forth from the barracks.

There was little Shel could do about the Ontrades guards knowing, because the sword was now spinning two feet off the earth, faster and faster, turning and sending flashes of light cascading around the already bright night sky. The moon flickered on and off, reflecting off the sword like the largest children's spinning top, dancing in the light of a fire. The sword stopped, the blade pointing right at Shel's midriff and beyond that, back 180 miles to Jost.

It turned for one last time, ninety degrees towards the West, rotating further another ninety towards the North and Ontrades. Again it rotated slowly until it pointed to the East and the great river Landsplitter, and finally it turned another forty-five degrees until it pointed approximately south-east. It stopped, the wonderful lights went out and it fell with a heavy thud back to the earth.

The corp grabbed hold of Shel and, with his men standing around him, said, 'I think you had better start telling the truth or you won't be taking another step towards Ontrades.'

Within thirty minutes Shel was sat alone in a guarded unit of the barracks with naught but Isthmus for company. Shade, in true heroic fashion, had scooted off into the night the second the guards appeared, although Shel knew that if there were to be a fight then Shade could be relied upon. Under the circumstances the lupine had done the right thing. They were in enough trouble now without the 'talking wolf' routine to explain.

The corp walked in and threw the confiscated Northstar back to Shel.

'I don't know what magic has been used on that sword but two of my men have badly burnt hands from trying to pick it up. Keep it. I was concerned about you anyway, which is why a fast rider took word to the Elders earlier today and has just returned. It seems you are in demand, for tomorrow I must ride you the rest of the way to Ontrades and deliver you. Not just to anyone, but to one of the best Inners in the history of the city.

'Tomorrow you will be under the close watch of Hemm, son of Hemm. Sleep well this evening as you will need your wits about you if the Inners and Elders want you.'

Shel lay down on his cot and slept while outside a wolf howled long into the night. He thought about the sword laying on his hip and wondered why it had not pointed to Ontrades – because, like it or not, that seemed to be exactly where he was going.

Sheldrak and Hemm

Sheldrak was led into the city with Shade by his side and his furze, Randeed, walking behind him. While he wasn't exactly under lock and key, it certainly wasn't how he had envisaged his arrival in Ontrades. He had thought that he and his colleagues would creep in a side door, not strut in alongside five guards of the south post. Everyone who wanted, needed or was interested enough to bother was able to see who he was. He even heard whispers from the onlookers of 'strange goings-on' and 'magic swords'. Well, it had happened now and no talk could detract from the fact, so he might as well make the most of the situation and see if he could persuade the elders of the city that he meant no harm. At least Shade was quiet, always a bonus, and Isthmus was saying in Shel's head that this was what they wanted. Access to the most learned people in the city, the Elders, could only help them solve the puzzle over the direction the sword had pointed. Why were they here when Northstar had virtually pointed south? It was in direct conflict to where Greeg, the village sayer, had told them they must go.

He forgot his problems for a moment when he looked around his new surroundings. Ontrades was spectacular to any newcomer but, to someone whose jaw had dropped in wonder at the size of the neighbouring village barn dance, this was something beyond Shel's imagination. The huge gates they had just passed through reminded Shade of the ones in *Jurassic Park*, but to Shel they were bigger than any building he had ever seen.

Shade thought, if a bloody T rex comes around the corner

now that's it. Quest or no sodding quest, I'm back to the forest and making the most of Lupine Land.

Neither of them had any such concern, for all they had to worry about were the hundreds of people scurrying back and forth, obviously on their way to a very important meeting with someone far more significant than themselves. The backdrop was a large, wide path, thirty paces across, full of horses, furze, carts and wagons of grain and roots, women with children and hundreds of men in uniforms of differing sorts. The path swept off into the distance on a gentle incline with many subsidiary paths running away from it.

Everything from this point was uphill, and a mile into the distance was the shining white tower of the Citadel cradled in the cushioning bosom of the Bluetop Mountains. A man of some importance came towards them and bowing low but never taking his eyes of Sheldrak, he greeted them in the manner afforded to allies and not enemies.

Striking his breast three times and speaking in a clear and strong voice, Hemm, son of Hemm said, 'By my elders, Sheldrak, I am Hemm son of Hemm and it is my duty to take you to the Citadel. There you will wait in comfortable surroundings until it is deemed necessary by the Elders to consult with you. By my Faith, I hope this meets with your approval.'

Sheldrak, somewhat taken aback for the moment by the courtesy shown to him, forgot his place before he too blurted out, 'By my elders, Hemm. You have my apologies, I did not expect to be treated so kindly.'

'Why is that? Are the men of Ontrades spoken about with a bad tongue or do you have good reason for expecting poor manners and ill treatment?'

'No, of course not. Neither. I just assumed when I was marched by five guards into the city that I was under some form of arrest.'

Hemm looked blighted again. 'Have you been told you are under arrest? Have you done anything for which you think you should be arrested? Do you not still carry your sword under your tunic, which you think is hidden, but which every soldier within 100 square miles knows you are carrying?'

Shel could see this wasn't going very well, so he chose to start again.

'Hemm, son of Hemm. Forgive me, for it is the first time I have ever been in a city the size of Ontrades and while I am aware of the military history attached to it, I am not familiar with the manners and customs of your fine people. I have not been harmed in any way, and you are correct, I still carry my sword, hidden, but not for the reasons you think. I thank you for your kindness and believe that your enemy is also mine. Where I come from that makes us friends.' Shel actually sighed with relief after this little speech.

'Well said, young man, you have my forgiveness. As for friendship, that decision is ahead of us. Now, grab your things, we must go on foot from here to the Citadel and it may look close but your breath will be short when we arrive. Leave your animals and they will be looked after.'

Shade looked at Shel and, ensuring that no one but Shel could see, moved his head from side to side. Please don't speak, thought Shel.

Hemm had turned and started to move away, expecting Shel to follow, but turned when he realised that he was on his own.

Shel spoke. 'By my elders I can leave my trusty furze but not my lupine.' Shel took a chance and said, 'He's enchanted and I have sworn by my Faith not to leave him.' This may not have sounded true but as Shade was one of the Seven, chosen to help Sheldrak oppose Essdark, then it was almost true. Shel *had* sworn not to leave him, even if it was indirectly sworn.

Hemm walked back to them, his patience wearing as thin as the cloth on a child's favourite rag doll. He leant into Shel so that only he could hear. 'I am tired. Your arrival has given me double duties and I am missing my wife. Now get the mangy mutt and bloody follow me or you will have a nice fur cloak to accompany you on your future travels. Enchanted or not.'

This time Shel went running after Hemm, hiding his astonishment as Isthmus told him that Hemm was indeed one of the Seven.

Essdark had been into her mind. He knew he had her. She was a willing accomplice as long as he could continue to give her the means to fulfil her desires. Her little trips down into the Pass were increasing and she was becoming ever more unhinged, but that would serve him well at the moment when the deed had to be done. He just hoped she wouldn't lose her mind completely before then and kill the brat. He hoped he wouldn't have to use too much of his strength, as controlling women was sapping his energy and he hoped to 'walk' soon.

He decided to pay one of them a visit.

She was lying on the cot in the house with the door coloured by dead men's eyes. The dirty, naked man stood by her side and pushed the sleeve of her dress up, exposing a gnarled but muscled pale, white arm. It stood out in the murk of the room as the palm of a dark-skinned man stood out against the ebony of the rest of his body. The naked man took her arm and, rolling the needle in the brown powder in the bowl, jabbed it hard into the throbbing vein that stuck out on her engorged skin, forced up by the thick twine tied around the uppermost part of her forearm.

She screamed in both pain and anticipation as she experienced the rush up her arm and into the main bloodstream of her torso. Her legs had been tied to the bottom of the cot, as some of the 'pleasure seekers' had sometimes run out into the paths of the Pass and on occasion had even had to be 'removed' so as not to attract the guards.

Her body arched on the cot and a stream of spittle ran out of the corner of her downturned mouth. Essdark entered her mind at her weakest moment, as the contorted body fell back on to the cot. He was most powerful when her mind was elsewhere and he spoke gently, probing the darkest secrets of her warped subconscious. Her mind was being eroded by the digging of a being far greater in mental ability than she was but also by the thick, brown substance that now oozed through her bloodstream.

He told her what she had to do and of the pleasures she would receive when she did it. She would live for ever in eternal ecstasy and what she felt now was but a tenth of what he would give her.

'Do my bidding and the lands shall be yours. Take that bitch married to Hemm if you want. But only when you have completed the task I have set you.'

The naked man at the side of the cot untied the straps holding the haggard old woman to the dirty, stinking mattress she was lying on. He was amazed she could keep coming back here for more. She should have died months ago, but something was keeping her heart beating. She must be strong-willed to live through this, he thought, or else her death is being held back for some darker reason. While she slept he took his payment.

The four Elders held their own council with Emperor Daynor in his personal chambers. Present was Rawt,

Capatain of the Inners, Travil, responsible for law and order, Trenc the sayer and of course the warlord, Shint.

'So, my learned men of battle,' Emperor Daynor began, 'how close are the Morgs and are we ready for them?'

Shint stood up from the low stools that had been brought into the room and placed around the emperor's ornate satin-backed chair. He spoke.

'By my elders, sir, we are as ready as we will ever be. We have 9,000 men prepared in their quarters to be moved to the front of the city at the sound of your order. We have 3,000 other men, mostly on horseback but some also on furze, ponies and mules. We even have the giants in the city who are worth at least ten men each and, finally, Rawt has granted me the power of warlord, which means if the worst happens then the fine men and women of the Inners are ready to fight. Faith forbid it should come to that.'

'And, according to your outriders, when will the Morgs get here?'

'They have not pushed the pace, my lord, and if you were to force an answer then I think we should take our men out on to the flatland two days from today and be ready to fight on the third. Ontrades must not fall to these foul Morgs, especially if the Grey One wants to take up residence in the Citadel.

'Gentlemen, you all know as well as I do that it would be better to take our own lives and the lives of our women and children before we hand them over to him,' explained the emperor.

Shint addressed him. 'Unless, my lord, they have some power of which I am not aware, we will win. The men and women of this city are the finest fighters in all of the lands and we may lose many brave soldiers, but we will retain control.'

Daynor turned to the sayer, Trenc, and asked him if had any counsel to give. Trenc replied, 'By my elders, my teachings tell me that the young man who has come into our city has a power and a part to play that we must be aware of. As I have already indicated to you, he could be the Chosen One and rumours are rife that he has the Sword of Destiny with him. One thing does confuse me. There will eventually be seven, but I thought that he was one of three. Reports back from Hemm, whom Rawt has wisely chosen to stay with the stranger, are that the only thing with him is a very large wolf or lupine.

'I may be wrong, but I know not why. My counsel is that we summon him to take his evening meal with us while we learn more about him. I think also that we should ask Hemm along to take a stay of duty on the door.'

Rawt butted in. 'Trenc, you know many things but Hemm has already worked a double duty. To ask him to complete a third is foolhardy. As Shint has already spoken, we need all the Inners to be ready for battle should they be required.'

'I am sorry, I forget my place. What if we invited Hemm and his wife also for the evening meal? Then they would not be on duty and it may also make our visitor, who is named Sheldrak, relax and loosen his tongue.'

Daynor then brought the meeting to an end. 'So be it, dinner in the Citadel dining room at eight bells.' And with that they all took their leave.

Sheldrak had indeed been given quarters that were as lordly as anything he had stayed in during his short life. He had been allocated a two-room suite in the Citadel, which was plain but suitably accommodating. The main chamber was large with simple pale drapes over the walls and one large window and balcony overlooking the city. The cot was spacious and could be used by two if necessary. Table, chair and writing equipment had been provided should he need them. Four large candles spread evenly around him gave more than enough milky light, which was greedily lapped up by the shadows of nightfall.

The second chamber was a primitive bathing room with a hand-drawn cold-water shower, a large, rough, shaggy drying towel and a set of fine silken clothes he had to change into for the dinner he was to attend with the Elders at eight bells.

Shade, curled up miserably on the one rug in the main room, complained, 'Am I invited to this posh dinner you're going to or do I have to stay here on my own? It's not much fun being a bloody lupine but even less when you are treated like a bride's first husband at her second wedding.'

'You have a complicated way of expressing yourself, my friend, which I cannot admit to always understanding but I do owe you my thanks for keeping quiet as I didn't think you would be able to do it.'

'Come on, Shel mate, take me out. I'm going mad in here. That bloody phone keeps ringing and if I don't get it, who will? Let me out. I fancy a nice rabbit pizza or a rat soufflé or something equally as filling.'

Shel looked at the unfortunate creature and said, 'Do not worry. I promise you will attend but only if you keep quiet. Isthmus tells me you have an important role to play but one which—'

Shade butted in, 'Who is Issy Arse? Is that the bloke you talk to sometimes when I'm not around?'

Shel, realising his mistake, was thankful for the rap on the door and only replied, 'Shhh, no more speech,' before opening the outer door to find Hemm, son of Hemm, alongside a woman of such strength and beauty than Shel stared, reddened and then, helped by a low howl from Shade, remembered his place. Bowing so low his baggy silk tunic nearly touched the floor, he said, 'By my elders. I am Sheldrak, son of Whinst, from the far southern village of Jost. My lady.'

Hemm, smiling only to himself and not allowing anyone else to see, growled, 'By my elders, Sheldrak, meet my wife, Marggitte, loyal member of the Inners.'

Marggitte, sensing Sheldrak's discomfort, linked her arm through his and said, 'You are an honoured guest to take dinner with the Elders on your first evening ever in the city. You must be a man of great power or, if not so, great expectation. Come, take my arm and the two best men in the Citadel will accompany me to dinner. You can tell me why you are here and perhaps shed some light on why Hemm and I are on special duties.'

The three walked away from Shel's quarters and away towards the dining room three floors above, with Shade strutting haughtily behind.

Joice stood over the sleeping form of Princess Arrara. The nanny looked dishevelled, even more so than usual, and the shiny dagger held in her thin fingers sparkled hungrily with the moonlight from the open window.

'Sleep well, Princess, for soon your sleep will last for ever. Your blood will taste sweet and then I shall have all.'

The child murmured in her dreams and turned away from the female scarecrow at the side of her bed.

Joice sat on the edge of the cot and, holding the child's hair in her hands, cut small clumps from the girl's head. As she cut, she hissed like a kettle coming to the boil. Cut, hiss, cut, hiss.

'I do hope I can do it, child,' she whispered. 'I would hate to waste all that pleasure after waiting so long. My reward will be great but my punishment will be greater if I don't.'

The sleeping child started to stir and the once-caring nanny, who was now totally insane with drugs and an even darker presence, faded back into the shadows against the wall and vanished.

Essdark walked. Isintress walked. Juunes walked. Millghrew walked. He was known by all these names and many more and now the Grey One walked the earth once more. He had been getting stronger with first the brat and now the women, and he had reached the point whereby he could take human form again. The time was right for him. Battles would be fought and he would become the dark sentinel of the lands. All that stood in his way was the Seven, but he would stop them.

If the Morgs could take Ontrades it would be a great battle won. If he could kill Sheldrak and get the sword, the war would not be far behind.

The Morgs were two days and nights away from the plain where the greatest battle in living history was to be fought and the tent of the warlord, Krarg, was set at the rear of his 20,000 warriors. When the battle was fought he would be right at the forefront, leading the charge. He wasn't one of these elders who sat at the back and shuffled pieces around a board. He led, and he led from the front.

Krarg was a seven-foot Morg, mostly covered in long coarse hair with a thick mane, like that of a horse, running from the nape of his wide-set neck down his broad back. His prominent forehead and flattened facial features were common to all but the luckiest Morg. Thick, slightly splayed legs gave the Morg race the stance of a gorilla, apart from the large flat feet with three toes also covered in hair.

They were renowned for their stupidity, their hatred of all but their own kind and the ferocity of their killing. One Morg would willingly run headlong into 100 men – bravery or stupidity? One would like to have said they were brave fighters, but there was nothing brave about slaughtering children.

The one old man who dressed in grey was neither brave

nor stupid, just evil as he walked into Krarg's tent. Krarg couldn't imagine any Morg who would have the audacity to walk directly into his tent on the eve of a major battle, and yet here was a mere man.

'Krarg, I believe I'm just the person who can help you win your petty fight,' spoke Essdark. 'In return there is a little something you can do for me.'

Food and War

Shel walked into the dining hall on the seventh floor of the Citadel on the arm of the most striking woman he had ever seen. Even though he was the sort of young man who had taken the company of girls before, none compared to Marggitte. The difference was that Marggitte wasn't a girl. He had courted many of the girls in his village but, as he believed in Strepsay, had never mated with them. According to the Faith he had to love them first and so he was saving himself for that time.

Hemm walked with them, but two strides to the rear. He was starting to like Sheldrak more and more, and Shel's obvious admiration for his wife was nothing more than a compliment. Hemm and Marggitte had only love for each other. Until death, they had promised, and that was how it would be. Alongside Hemm trotted Shade, bells buzzing angrily in his head like bluebottles around a rotting piece of offal. Shade would not be able to keep his silence much longer.

Inside Shel's head, Isthmus whispered words of encouragement and told Sheldrak that as long as he listened to his advice then everything would be fine. Isthmus had eaten banquets with elders on many occasions, but then he had been alive and not between the living and the dead.

The five moved into the room for the only time in their lives that they would all eat together. Isthmus might not eat but he would find his energy from some other part of the universe.

Emperor Daynor and his queen sat at the head of the longest table that Shel had ever seen. It could easily have sat fifty but tonight the royals would be joined by the twelve Elders, the two members of the Inners, Hemm and his wife, and of course the guest of honour, Sheldrak, son of Whinst. Shade looked disconcertedly at the bowl lain at the foot of the table which he assumed would be for him.

The other guests had their seats and Shel took his place with Elder Trenc the sayer to his left and Hemm (he would have preferred Marggitte) to his right. Trenc was sat at the top left of the table, to the immediate right of the emperor's wife, and sat facing Shel was Shint, the warlord.

In the centre of the table was a full roast pig surrounded by sweet-smelling cooked apples. Each silver platter had already been laid in front of each of them, full of as many different vegetables as Shel, or Shade for that matter, had ever imagined: carrots, sweetroot, beets, turnips, potatoes both small and large, artichoke, asparagus, beans broad and green, cauliflower, cabbage and tiny cabbage, courgette, marrow and mushroom. There were others for which Shel had no name, and Shade would tell Shel later that in his world, 'Nobody likes Brussels sprouts apart from at Christmas, because they make you fart.'

Every one had his or her own pitcher of rich red wine made from the finest vines in the lower regions of the Bluetop Mountains, and the final touch came in the form of flagons of different kinds of broth for pouring as sauces over the pork and roots. This, thought Shel, could keep the village of Jost for the whole of the winter, or Divad for one night. The joke almost made him wince as he remembered the condition his friend had been in when he had left Jost. The past fourteen days had seemed a lifetime – but whose lifetime?

'By my elders,' the voice of Emperor Daynor boomed around the circular walls of the Citadel, 'let us welcome our guest, and perhaps our saviour if Trenc is proven correct, Sheldrak, son of Whinst.'

Shel's jaw fell open like a pocket to a thief as each member of the feast in turn stood, struck his or her breast and, bowing low, paid homage to Shel as though one of the great kings had come back to walk the lands.

Sheldrak, young though he was, knew through his learnings that he was expected to speak. He heard Shade beneath the table whisper, 'Don't balls this up or you might end up like the pig.'

Shel coughed. The room went silent. He picked up his pitcher of wine and took a large mouthful and gulped it down like a bullfrog with a fly.

'I know not if I am here to save anyone, my lords and ladies, but I do know that I am here in friendship. I have been told things by a sayer that to this time has been proven true. I know that soon we go into battle and if my part is to fight alongside the good men and women of Ontrades then I am proud and honoured to do so.'

Nods of approval went around the table and Hemm acknowledged the honourable words. Shel took another gulp of the dry wine and continued.

'But I am yet young and learning my Faiths of Strepsay. I also have a personal quest to save my best friend, left lying with no sign of life apart from the occasional rise and fall of his chest. I hope that I express the Faith of Honour because that is what I now feel.'

Shel paused as a single tear fell from his dark brown eye and trickled down his face like the smallest river in the world. He cleared his throat and whispered, 'I think I have to fight the Grey One.' The gasps sneaked into the room like intruders into a darkened cottage in the depths of night.

In Shel's head, Isthmus spoke. 'Use his name. Show them you have respect for evil but are brave enough to fight it.'

'I will face Essdark for you and for all the lands and by my Faith I hope I am strong enough for the sake of us all.'

He bowed his head and sat. Everyone in the room had slowed their breathing so that all that could be heard was the thumping of hearts in the chests of the brave.

Shade howled and the silence broke like a smashed mirror, and even the bravest felt the breeze blowing across the napes of their necks.

Trenc spoke on behalf of the people of Ontrades. 'Your words are both comforting and terrifying. I know you speak the truth and I sense that you are indeed the Chosen One. For tonight let us try to forget what evil lies outside these doors, for it could be a long time before we again have the chance to eat in such pleasant surroundings.'

The emperor clapped his hands and the main doors opened for four minstrels and singers to enter. The room became immediately lightened as the singing voices and then conversation and laughter picked up and circulated the room.

Shade whispered under the table, 'Not the Spice Girls, but better than nothing. Get that phone, Shel.'

The meal went on for several hours and Shel became increasingly relaxed as the night wore on. He noticed that Hemm never took any wine and presumed that he was still on duty, minding him. He learnt from the Elders sat at his end of the table how close the Morgs were to the city. He had heard of Morgs as a child when they occurred in stories but he never expected to be attacked by several thousand of them.

Marggitte caught his eye and said, 'So, Sheldrak, how are you enjoying your first meal at the Citadel?'

'Well, I must admit that to start with it was a little daunting, but now that first words have been exchanged nobody seems to be paying me much notice. Do you know what will happen to me when the battle commences? Am I expected to fight? I will if that is the case.'

'I know not, but come, let us move to the other end of

the table and I will speak to Rawt, the Elder who is in charge of the Inners, he may know.'

The diners had become less formal and, apart from the emperor and his wife, were moving around the table and changing seats, as they needed to speak to each other. Only Hemm never moved until such time that Sheldrak did and then he followed his wife and Shel over to his leader, Rawt.

'Marggitte, it is always a pleasure,' said Rawt by way of greeting. He was in conversation with Gedar, one of the younger members of the Elders, who took his leave to allow Rawt, Shel, Margg and Hemm to form a close-knit quartet.

'So, Sheldrak,' said Rawt, 'we need to look after you if you are to fulfil the sayings of Trenc.'

Shel replied, 'By my elders, Rawt, I do not think I am supposed to get special treatment. If you fight then so do I.'

'Has nobody told you yet, Sheldrak, son of Whinst? You will not be fighting any battles. When the three bells of the Citadel ring out the chimes of war you will be confined to your quarters with the very best Inner in the city, Hemm, to look after you. His wife, Marggitte, will guard the emperor and his family. You are too important to be lost in a frenzied fight against the Morgs. These uprisings occur every ten years or so and we have fought before and will fight again, with or without young Master Sheldrak.'

Isthmus spoke to Shel inside his head. 'Sheldrak, do not worry. You are not meant to fight but to win over Hemm. He must leave the Inners somehow to join us in our quest to face Essdark.'

'Rawt, has anyone ever left the Inners after becoming one?'

All three of the Inners smiled and this time it was Hemm who spoke.

'The only way anyone has ever left is through moving upwards into the Elders. There are a few old stories which cannot be proven, saying that hundreds of years ago some

Inners left their posts to save an Elder and had to take themselves away, but that is only a rumour.'

Marggitte said, 'You must understand, Sheldrak, that we live only for honour. It comes before all and we would rather die than not do our duty. We would never leave our post, ever.'

Trenc walked over to the four of them and said, 'Let me take your hand, Sheldrak. Let me read you.' Before he had chance to pull away, Trenc had grabbed Shel's arm and looked deep into his eyes. He left go as quickly as if he had thrust his arm into the embers of a fire.

'My Faith, you are possessed. You have a presence within you.' He then turned to Hemm and said, 'And he means to take you next.'

Needing to reply quickly, Shel said, 'I am not possessed, Trenc, but you are right about Hemm. He is one of the Seven and if the Grey One is to be defeated then Hemm must leave Ontrades with me.'

Hemm took one step backwards from Sheldrak, the only backward step he had ever taken in his life, and said one word. 'Never!'

Krarg sat drinking buckets of ale among his comrades in arms, preparing for the fight ahead. Nothing better than to charge into war steaming drunk, he thought. His mind was full of stranger thoughts this evening since the grey-cowled one had visited him. He had been given a weapon of great strength, but a weapon that frightened him also. He did not like to use sorcery and the green bottle covered in strange runes that was strapped to his thigh made him very uncomfortable.

All he wanted was to kill those bastard sons of bastards in the Citadel. For centuries they had ruled the pass through the mountains and grown rich, while his people had fought and scrapped for a living on the banks of the Landsplitter.

The port of Seathon controlled the river from the north, the Ontradeans controlled the pass and the giants of Arbrain had the South and the plateaus. His people had jak all, nothing. The Grey One had promised victory and the price was that he had to use dark magic to get it. Magic worried him because he couldn't control it, at least not with fear.

One other thing the grey one had said had unsettled him even more. He had to find a boy, 'Spawn', he had said, by the name of Sheldrak. He would be easy to find for he carried the Sword of Destiny. The Sword of bloody Destiny was a myth. Who was he trying to fool? But when he looked into those grey eyes he knew it was no tomfoolery.

Krarg had never been scared in his life. The only way to the top of the Morg community was through fighting and never feeling fear. When he looked into those grey eyes he knew more fear than he thought possible.

He drank his ale and weaved his way back to his tent.

Essdark kissed the old woman gently on the lips. 'Tomorrow,' he said, 'when you hear the three bells, you may kill her. Make it slow if you can, and don't forget you must get him to witness the child's death. He must realise I don't intend to make this easy for him. Princess Arrara must die and the Seven will be split before they have even been joined.'

Essdark faded away and was back in his cave. It would be a long time before he had the energy to 'walk' again. The Spawn's mind was incredibly strong and he couldn't get close to him. He had to find him before the Spawn realised his own strength and harnessed it against the Grey. Not to worry, he had plenty of others who were prepared to do his bidding.

Honour or Love?

Sheldrak was forbidden to leave his own quarters. How ironic was that? He had thought his biggest issue would be to convince the people of Ontrades of his quest, but they knew more than he did and had decided he was too important to leave to the mercy and chance of combat. Isthmus had advised him to keep his peace and to wait patiently.

How many sixteen-year-olds wished they had the wisdom of experience to call upon when needed? According to Isthmus, he was here because it was Faith.

Shade was now allowed to come and go as he pleased and was well known around the Citadel and among the guards. This at least meant Shel knew what was happening outside the walls of his comfortable prison.

Hemm was the Inner who guarded Shel most of the time, but others occasionally took over. Shel preferred Hemm as at least he would enter the room and talk to him, but the others never said any more than the greeting, 'By my elders.'

The turmoil that Hemm was in never showed for a second. His wife knew, of course, but no one else. Hemm had gone as far as he could with his poor upbringing but was not from the 'right' family to become an Elder. He lived for his honour but had always thought that there must be something else for him and now along had come a sixteen-year-old boy-man from the South who purported to be the Chosen One.

He had heard these terms used before but never took too much notice. He dealt with the practical of the here and now, not with the world of dreams and sayers. Yet there was something about him, for such a young man, that made him stand out from the rest. If Hemm knew what that was and believed he had a role in the greater story then he could address the issue of leaving the Inners. The Elders believed in Trenc's saying abilities and were even now discussing whether the first Inner ever would be allowed to leave.

If Hemm got offered the chance, could he leave his wife? His honour was going to be tested to the full, but in the meantime he had to continue to prove his worth. He had to keep Shel in his room during the battle and not forget that the strength of the Inners lay in their ability to attend to the smallest and most mundane of tasks with the utmost honour and integrity.

Marggitte was now attending to another of the mundane tasks, but it was one the Elders had specifically requested that she did. It was her duty to guard the royal family, along with two other Inners, and her role was to keep Princess Arrara under lock and key. Not even that nasty nanny would be allowed in today, which was a good thing. She had been getting stranger and stranger by the hour and, today of all days, had not reported to the Citadel.

Of all days, because for the past twenty-four hours the men and women of the military had been positioning themselves on the flatlands to the east of the city in readiness for the Morgs, who themselves had set up camp less than a mile from the closest Ontradean soldier. Twenty thousand Morgs versus 12,000 men, women, giants and horsemen representing the emperor and his city.

The bright red flag of the Ontradeans blew towards the Morgs, whose blue flag flapped in their own faces. The battles were contested under simple rules of engagement. Firstly, both armies would take up their positions on the chosen field. Secondly, the defendants, in this case the Ontradeans, would signal the start of battle by the ringing of bells. Today these would be the bells housed at the top of the Citadel.

Thirdly, all hell broke loose until one side decided to surrender. This could mean the capture of the opposing warlord or the capture and slaughter of every child of the opposing army. It really did depend upon what 'lit your candle'.

The emperor would only fight a fair battle but the Morgs, in the past, had been known to commit appalling atrocities. Hence the heavy guard at the Citadel and the Inners not being allowed in the midst of the battle.

Marggitte was stood outside the Princess Arrara's room, on a mundane watch but one that would turn out to be so important. The emperor had sent word and the bells at the top of the tower were about to ring and change the path of Marggitte's life for ever.

Shade turned to speak to Shel and said, 'Look, Shel, I'm not here as a lupine for nothing. I sense something is wrong. These bloody phones will not stop ringing in my head. I need to get out. The battle is about to start, but the danger is much closer. I smell something bad and it isn't coming from me.' The animal then bowed its head and covered its muzzle with its front paws.

Shel rested his hands on Shade's head. 'What is wrong, Shade?'

Shade slowly uncovered his eyes and said, 'I wish I knew. These bells. Please answer the phone for me, Shel. If these carry on I think I will jump from one of the windows. The sodding bells won't stop ringing today. Answer the phone, mate. Please?'

The door opened and Hemm stood silhouetted in the doorframe. Shade took the opportunity and ran out through the door, howling as he went.

Hemm said, 'What is wrong with your lupine? "Shade", you call him. Is the fear in the city getting to him? They say that animals can sense fear better than a man can. The bells will be sounding the start of the battle soon and you and I are trapped here, waiting for any news. Can we talk? I need to know why you think I am one of the Seven.'

Shel then told Hemm the full story, starting with Divad and the Great Race, through to where he was today. He omitted one part of the story, Isthmus, but he even told Hemm that Shade could talk and had come from another world where bells rang all the time.

In the meantime Shade was running down and up the hills of the city, as mad as a man who has been hit by a bus and woken up in a strange land in the body of a large yellow wolf.

'Got to stop these phones, bells, noises,' Shade panted to himself as he reached the city's outer wall. He hurtled around the perimeter looking for a way out until he saw a small archway made out of lighter-coloured stone and ran through to find a circular flight of stairs in front of him. Pausing only momentarily, he ran up and around for a minute until he found himself on the battlements. He stopped and took in the spectacle ahead of him.

About a mile away he could see the last line of defenders of the city awaiting the notification that the battle was about to commence. Further away, too far for him to judge, was the bold red of the lead battalion's flag and, even further, his keen yellow eyes could just pick out the blue of Krarg's standard-bearer. He could see thousands upon thousands of men and women, prepared to give their lives for the city and the good of all. Also, thousands of Morgs ready to die. But for what?

Shade cried out loud, which became a long, hair-raising howl. The bells in his head were getting louder and louder and he swore in English, but there was no one to hear him. Most of the guards were closer to the Citadel, with a small troop on the main gate. Those bastard phones would not stop ringing. Please someone, help me. Shade climbed on to the corner battlement and was now at the highest point of the wall and could be seen from the Citadel windows and by the men out in the field.

It was then that the Citadel bells rang out three times. They chimed in unison and grew in a crescendo over about a minute before they ceased and a deathly silence rushed across the battlefield like water from a floodgate. No one moved. It was as if now that the time to fight had come, everyone had decided that there must be a better way to resolve their differences. Time stood still until at first a low, plaintive cry and then a howl of derision echoed around the fields as if the great kings themselves were speaking.

'Someone please answer the bloody phones!' screamed the lone wolf on top of the battlements and the two armies, as though released from their tethers, charged at each other across the worn green grass of the plains. Never in the history of the lands had a battle started with such a strange war cry and nor would it again.

The bells were heard not only by Shade in his madness but by Hemm and Shel, talking in Shel's rooms. It made them both sit up and take notice but, as high up as he was, Shel could not see the battlefield. Hemm took his leave and went to stand outside the room, on his post. His orders had been simple: he could enter the room if Shel wanted anything but could not move away from the doorway or let Shel leave the room. He decided that he would be better outside, in readiness for the worst.

He wished he were closer to the fighting. After years of training to be the best, Faith had placed him furthest away from combat. Peculiar, really – let the poor souls who could not fight as well as he could go to the front to die first.

The bells had caused Hemm to think about his role in the Inner Guard and were the catalyst to return him to his post in the doorway, but for Joice the bells were the final trigger to send her into the oblivion of absolute madness. The bells woke her from an uneasy sleep in the small room she had taken in the slums of the Pass. She wished to be close to her 'pleasure' and the trips between the Citadel and her home and back to the Pass were taking their toll on her weakening body.

She rose, and it was clear to any observer that there had been more water falling from the sky in the desert's summer months than had fallen on her skin in the past few weeks. Her lank, sparse hair fell around her face and shoulders and in the dark it looked as if she had a carnival head on a small, withered body.

She had slept in her clothes for several nights now and smelt like old cabbage water covered up by sweet talcum powder. But it was the eyes that were the most startling thing about her. The whites of her eyes were deep red, as numerous blood vessels had burst with the demands of the substances she was introducing into her body, and the pupils were completely black.

She took a knife from the top of the black vegetable box doubling as a cot-side table and pulled upright. One last effort, she thought. Walking to the door, she took from a small hole in the wall two hidden bottles, one clear with a small quantity of clear liquid in it and the other dark green with a small yellow label on it but no indication as to what it contained. She took the knife and dipped it into the clear liquid then, putting the green bottle in one of her numerous pockets, she re-hid the clear bottle.

She had not been asked to do this, but he had said 'slowly, if possible'. In the deep recesses of her mind a voice, that of the nanny as a young woman asked, 'Do you really believe you can go through with this? Your husband beat you and probably got what he deserved, but since when have you been a child murderer?'

Joice physically shook her head, like a cow in the summer shaking the flies off, as though she could dispel these questions from her younger self with a flick of the head. Mentally returning to her plan, she told herself the green bottle was also her insurance if she got caught. She really had gone mad if she thought she could ever bargain her way out of this.

The overcast sun was enough to make her duck and squint as she hobbled her way slowly up the hill to the Citadel. She knew that she wouldn't be allowed inside in this condition, but he had shown her secrets. The way she passed, only she knew, and then her pleasure would be eternal. She wound her way through the Pass and then east towards the whitewashed wall of the tower.

Before she got there she entered a stinking inn called the Duck and Bedago. No one was at home, as she had been told they would not be, and entering the cellar, she walked to the last large barrel. Moving around to the back in the corner, under a wall of wine bottles, she pulled the last bottle on the third shelf.

The rack clicked away from the wall and, squeezing through into the darkness beyond, she pulled the rack back behind her with another click. To her left, in the wall where she had left it, hung a lantern. She lit it and without a moment's consideration set off down the earthen tunnel ahead of her. Soon she would come upon a set of stairs that she had already used many times to move around the Citadel unseen, but today she was going straight to the room of Princess Arrara.

Krarg lined his troops up in tight formation. There was nothing subtle about the way he intended to win. At the front of the hordes he had his riders. Morgs, seven feet high from toe to mane, sat on all-black stallions especially bred to carry them into battle. They had rough sacks thrown over their backs for saddles and the Morgs, over the years, had developed the skills to control the creatures with naught but a leather harness that pulled on the sensitive tissue at the corner of the animals' snouts.

Each Morg was well covered in wrought-iron armour that, on a normal man, would have rendered him immobile, and each was topped with a full helmet with a slit for vision. Each helmet had a blue plume on the top. The Morgs were fully eleven feet up in the air, and to the opposing army a frightful sight.

Two thousand Morgs sat on stallions followed by 18,000 foot warriors, again all dressed in some form of armour. They walked behind the riders forming a wedge that spanned out into a giant V shape. Krarg felt that he had no need for subtlety. He had bigger fighters, 8,000 more than the Ontradeans, and was going to walk straight up to them and bludgeon them into submission with sword, lance and club.

He could afford to lose one for one and have thousands of Morgs left to enter the city; and if that's what it took, then what were a few Morgs for the capture of the trade centre of the North? For the first time ever, history beckoned the Morg nation.

His last resort was the bottle strapped to his thigh, a 'gift' from the Grey One. He hoped he didn't have to use it.

Shint, the Elder warlord, had decided that he indeed needed subtlety and if, as usual, the Morgs were going to charge and hack then he would prepare accordingly. He was not going to lead by example from the front but was at the back of the troops using his skills as a tactician. The way of the Morgs was not the way of Ontrades.

Shint was old and had spent his years in the thick of battle. By command from his emperor he was not allowed any closer to the combat than he was. He had chosen as many divisions of giants as lived in the city and put them right to the forefront of the battle. A great warrior led them, a giant by the name of Gregorn who was even admired by the Inners for his fighting skills. He was one of the few who could probably give Hemm a fair fight. Shint put his biggest up front with a view to matching the Morgs on horseback, at least in size, if not number.

His next phase of attack comprised 1,000 archers in position behind his horsemen, plus a further 500 archers riding every kind of steed he could muster. When the bells sounded these would charge off around the flanks of the Morgs and try to trap them by shooting across. The third stage of his plan would follow, if needed.

The bells in the Citadel sounded and echoed off the men waiting in their armour. The red plumage and colours of Ontrades flickered among the green grass like the fruit of a cut melon showing against the dark husk of its skin. No one moved. The Morgs stood their ground also, as the bells slowly faded. The long howl of a wolf, coupled with a strange cry of words that no one understood, unleashed the straining men and Morgs like dogs on a hunt released from their leashes.

War fell upon the plains of Ontrades like rain on a still pond and, as the two armies met and fought, the ripples moved further and further away from the centre as battle commenced.

The mighty horses met full on in the middle, lances crashing off body armour and foes spilling to the ground where their heads were removed with the sweep of a longsword before they had chance to regain their feet. The horses of the archers from Ontrades sprinted around the outskirts of the skirmishes, each one carrying three men until they had got behind the Morgs and dismounted.

Krarg was at the forefront, his huge frame hewing into the armour. In some cases, such was his strength that the metal split under the crash of sword. He wasn't on a horse – he liked to see the eyes of the men before he killed them and although he lacked in skill, he made up for it in strength. He planted his feet with his warriors around him and looked as unmovable as a 100-year-old oak planted in a forest of men.

Man after man fell by his sword and giants were proving no match either. Krarg thought he could win this on his own, such was the power surging through his limbs.

From a distance, through his eyeglasses, Shint could see that Krarg and the Morgs had taken hold of this battle roughly by the throat, and he needed to prise those fingers away.

Shint, with a nod to his corp by his side, gave the command and the stout man took a horn to his lips and gave three long blasts. Every single member of the Ontradean army immediately dropped back, disengaging himself from his individual fight. The field was awash with blood, red from the men and giants and a thick, black ink-like substance from the Morgs.

The men retreated further and then dropped to their knees, and the first wave of arrows hit the Morgs not in the chest or head but in the legs, which were unprotected. Now, some of them were so big that the arrows bounced off, but most of the Morgs to the front of the fighting took arrows in their legs and they started to fall like young trees. Morgs to the rear started to shout in their guttural voices as the archers deployed by Shint also released their arrows. The Morgs were falling and had difficulty moving forwards or back as hundreds of them dropped.

Krarg could see that the upper hand he had a moment ago was gone, and he decided to do something about it the only way he knew how. He jumped on to one of the riderless horses and charged at the archers, who fell back to let him through. But Krarg knew what he was doing and headed straight to the rear of the Ontradeans. If the Morgs were to win, then he had to kill the brains of the opposition. He was 500 yards from Shint, riding on the wing, straight at the Elder, and scattering all who got in his way. Shint looked back at Krarg as he drew closer and closer and realised he didn't have long to live.

But then Gregorn the giant walked straight in front of the charging horse.

She didn't run up the stairs, although her heart was beating fast in her thin, frail chest. Her drab clothes and painfully gaunt physique made her resemble a large sparrow flapping up the poorly lit staircase, and her heart hammered like that of a trapped bird beating in the hands of a young child. It was a very misleading look as the excitement and the thrill of the chase was what made her breathing quicken. She was a lot stronger than her appearance gave her any right to be.

She had made her way through corridors and past numerous doors and stairways on her way to the princess's sleeping room and play area, and now she stood on the other side of the door with her eye pressed to the tiny hole in the wall to see if the princess was alone. She was.

Joice flicked the small handle shaped like a tiny sword on the bottom of the door and slickly entered the room, gently clicking the door back into place behind her. From inside the room, the entrance was just a piece of wall panelling to the left of the princess's cot.

Arrara looked up from her playthings, still dressed in her sleeping garments even though it was now mid-morning. Surprised, she said, 'Nanny?'

'Don't be so surprised, my dear, I've been visiting you like this for years. It used to be a genuine visit of devotion. Sometimes to sit and watch you sleep was the only pleasure I had. But now I have other things to please me. You, my dear, are going to help me keep them.'

She moved with the speed of a striking snake and approached the girl, switching her around so that she could not see her face. She pulled her blade. Without a moment's thought she ran the blade across the young girl's palm so that she screamed in pain. Blood fell from the wound, pattering on to the stone floor like spilled red wine.

Within a second of the scream Marggitte was in the bed-chamber, her sword raised, head scanning the room like a predator smelling out its prey.

Joice backed away from Marggitte to the side of the bed with the secret door. The fingers of one hand were digging into the collarbone on one side of Arrara while the other held the blade at the child's throat, and she taunted Marggitte: 'Not so high and mighty now, are we? It's not much fun feeling helpless, is it? You have treated me like jak over the years and now it's your turn. But it's going to be worse than you think, because I want your husband here. He must see this.'

Margg's mind was spinning. Years of training had pre-pared her for this moment, but what could she do without the child suffering?

'Shout for your louse of a man,' Joice cackled, her voice rising an octave or two. The power was becoming a stimu-lant and her eyes started to glaze over.

Arrara was going the other way. The child's sensory system was switching off to take her away from this terror, and she slumped gently, almost dropping her neck on to the sharp blade. Blood dripped steadily from her gashed hand.

'Shout for him!' Joice screamed. Arrara twitched but nothing more. Marggitte could not leave her post. Honour was everything. Death or honour, that was it. No grey area with the Inners. But it was the same for Hemm. She also knew that he would not leave his post guarding Sheldrak. There was nothing in these lands that meant more to

Hemm than his honour. Marggitte, playing for time, shouted, but not so that Hemm would hear.

'Louder than that!' yelled Joice and she tightened the knife on the throat of Arrara, easing only when a thin red line appeared, which became thicker as the blood welled. The child's throat was not yet cut but another half an inch and her windpipe would be sliced in two.

Marggitte screamed with every ounce of effort in her body and one floor down in the Citadel, Hemm and Shel heard it at the same time. But only Hemm knew it was his wife.

Shel had been pacing the floor. He didn't belong here. Great deeds were happening outside of his chambers. Wars were being fought and men and women he had met during the past few days were fighting for him and the city. He was stuck in here like an old maid. So much for this wonderful Seven that was going to take on Essdark. He was here with a spirit babbling in his head being guarded by another of the Seven while the fourth, a crazy talking lupine, was running around the city screaming at people to answer something called a phone. As for the other three, Faith knew who they were.

He then heard a faint shout that came from somewhere above him. He walked towards the door of his chambers but before he had chance to place his hand on the wooden latch the shout was followed by a terrifying scream. He snatched the door open to stare directly into the eyes of Hemm.

'Did you hear that?' said Shel.

'Of course I did, but we do not move.'

'For Faith's sake, man, you can't ignore that scream. It sounded like someone was dying.'

'I hope not. It was Marggitte.'

Shel tried to push past Hemm, but was shoved roughly back into his room.

Shel implored Hemm, 'Please, we must go. What means more to you, your wife or your honour?'

'Without honour we have nothing. Love only comes through honour.'

'Hemm, you are wrong. I love my mother and father and that did not come through honour. Some love is unconditional.'

The scream was repeated and this time a voice shouted, 'Hemm, please come or she will kill us both!'

Hemm turned to look in the direction of the screams and for the one and only time in his entire life took his mind off his duty. Shel ran past Hemm and bounded up the stairs. Hemm had no option but to follow, knowing full well that he had just taken his own life.

The giant Gregorn moved his massive frame so that he was in a direct line between the charging beast and the Elder, Shint. The animal never took his eyes off Gregorn but with the huge form of Krarg working the beast's head, arms pumping, there was never any doubt that the stallion would not be stopping. Fifty yards, forty, ten, Gregorn never moved. It was the biggest game of chicken that could be imagined. At the last second, Gregorn jumped to his right. At the same time he swung his solid forearm, holding his lance back to his left, catching Krarg in the middle of his midriff and sending him sprawling from his horse.

The force of hitting Krarg broke his lance in two and he pulled his sword from its sheath. Krarg, though winded, knew he couldn't lie on the ground in the middle of a battlefield and expect to last very long, and was back on his feet in a moment. Krarg and Gregorn circled each other as all around them the fighting continued. Shint was only twenty yards away and had now managed to surround himself with men.

Krarg's plan had backfired. He was virtually on his own

in deepest enemy territory; Shint still lived, and he now had to battle this giant, whom he knew as Gregorn, one of the greatest warriors ever to come out of Arbrain. He wasn't sure what it would do, but he had no choice but to use the bottle given to him by the Grey One.

He tore the bottle from its strapping on his thigh and threw it to ground, breaking it into a thousand pieces. At first nothing happened, but then the ground started to tremble and crumble. Fights stopped as Morgs and men were thrown to the floor. A split appeared where the bottle had hit and then the earth rent apart like a paper bag, letting loose the spirits of all Morgs that had been killed in battles on these plains.

Krarg stole his chance and ran the remaining few yards to Shint. Men around were screaming and crying as hundreds upon hundreds of grey shapes swept in and around. They flew up into the sky, swooping and screaming down upon the men of Ontrades, and the noise was both deafening and inhuman.

The men and women of the city were dropping their weapons in terror and then the final blow came as Krarg savagely swept the head of Shint clean off his shoulders with one blow. Gregorn climbed back to his feet, looked around him and realised the battle was all but lost unless someone could kill Krarg. He moved towards the leader of the Morgs, knowing the spirits could do little to harm him physically as long as he could keep his mind together.

Something struck him from behind and he hit the dirt. The last thing he saw was the filthy, three-toed feet of Krarg before his eyes closed.

Shade was running around the battlements. 'Answer the phones.' Why was he here? Ring, ring. Why was he a lupine? Shel was his friend, he knew that. Didn't think much of Hemm, although his missus was a bit of all right.

Looked a bit like that woman from the stage show *Chicago*. That would do him no good, thinking about his old life. What did he have to do in this battle? Must be something. He could kill, fight, bite. Killed that wolf for Shel, didn't I? Ring, ring.

He charged back down the stairs from the battlements and continued running around the base of the city wall until he arrived back at the main gates he had come through days earlier. He ran up to the two guards on duty and howled at them to step aside and let him through.

'Bugger off, you stupid mutt. Times are dark and we don't need you barking at us.'

Shade thought for a moment and then frightened the two young guards to within a beat of heart failure by saying, 'I say, old chaps, would you mind awfully stepping to one side and letting me join the battle – or would you rather I bit your gonads off?'

The one who hadn't fallen over stepped gingerly over to the door and let Shade sprint off towards the fighting.

'Don't know what I'm going to do when I get there, but it's got to be better than sitting and waiting for it to come to me. And perhaps someone will have answered that bloody phone by the time I get back.'

Shel, with Hemm just behind, ran into Arrara's chamber, unaware of what to expect.

Marggitte screamed when she saw her husband. 'No Hemm, no, no!' She fell, wailing, to the stone floor, but Hemm never let anything distract him from the old witch holding the slumped figure of the princess.

A voice in Shel's head said, 'Leave this to me.'

Joice announced her intentions. 'Well now, what does it feel like to be flies drawn into a web? Essdark was right, you are so stupid with your bloody honour that you have become bit players in his stage play. The next part you have to enjoy is the slow, grim death of this little sweetie here. Any of you move and I will cut her another mouth to breathe through.'

She backed herself closer to the door that only she knew of and Hemm and Shel moved closer towards her. Arrara was now unconscious, being dragged by her neck. Shel spoke, but as he did a figure appeared directly in front of the old woman, causing her to scream, drop Arrara and back straight to the wall. Isthmus had appeared and the shock for all apart from Shel was indeed great. Shel leapt forward and snatched the young child as Joice's back hit the panel behind her.

Hemm spoke, but his voice no longer held the command that Shel had been used to hearing. Was it the appearance of Isthmus or the shock of having broken the code of the Inners? Marggitte was inconsolable.

'You have lost, old woman. Give yourself up and put yourself at the mercy of the emperor.'

'Lost, lost. Even now you cannot think for yourselves. The child is dead. She has an hour to die the most painful of deaths. The dagger had a peculiar version of dragon breath on it and only I have the serum to save her. Lost, ha! We will see who is lost.'

She clicked the catch behind her without turning and stepped backwards through the door, clicking it locked.

Shel ran to the wall, turned to Hemm and said, 'Help me, there must be a handle or switch somewhere.'

Hemm and his wife both sat and cradled the figure of Princess Arrara, whose breath was quickening. Her skin was already turning hot.

Shel continued to look where the nanny's hand had seemed to be when the wall turned on itself. Running his fingers under the decoration running down the centre of the wall, he found a small clasp that he pushed, and the wall clicked and moved back on its hinges. More people were running into the chamber to see what the screaming was about and Shel turned to Isthmus and said, 'I have to try to catch her. Come, please help me.'

To his surprise Isthmus answered, 'I'm sorry, Shel, you must find the old woman called Joice alone. It is your Faith. I must race and find Shade. If we are to have any chance of keeping the Morgs out of the city then I need to be with him.' With that he faded from view.

Shel turned to Hemm. 'I'm going after her. Get the princess to Nalla, the healer in the Elders. We have an hour to find that witch and the serum.'

He stepped through the doors into the comforting dark. He would never see Hemm alive again.

The men and women were valiantly fighting the Morgs with every last piece of their existence but they were slowly falling. They were the better fighters but were outnumbered and, apart from the giants, outsized by their opponents. Add to this the sheer panic invoked in many of them by the spirits and ghosts of fights long since fought and the battle was being dragged away from them. With it went the freedom and wealth of the city of Ontrades.

Krarg knew that with the slaying of Elder Shint he had taken control of the battlefield. He snatched up the head of his vanquished opponent and, ignoring the screams from all around him, stuck the head on the end of a lance and walked back towards his own men. The spirits screeched in unison at the sight of the Morgs' leader with the head of Shint paraded like a banner at a county fayre rather than with the dignity of one who had been a great warrior lost in his final battle.

In his haste, Krarg had walked over the fallen body of Gregorn, who had been clubbed at the base of his skull and who now wore a deep red cloak down his back made from his own blood. The blow had not been a deadly one and

Gregorn wearily pulled himself to his feet. As was the way of giants, he did not wait to be politely asked to continue in the battle but instead shouted at the retreating back of Krarg, 'You big, useless, hairy pile of jak. It'll take more than a cheap shot from a Morg to lay low a giant, especially Gregorn, best warrior ever to leave Arbrain.'

Krarg dropped the staff and the head and faced the direction whence the insult had been flung. His massive sword glistened dully with a slick redness before he charged at Gregorn, swinging it above his wild hair. Gregorn, though badly concussed, knew it would take a more skilled approach than that to beat him and easily parried the first swing aimed somewhere in the direction of his head.

The clang of metal as the two seven-foot-plus creatures swapped blows was three times louder than any other of the individual fights that continued to rage. Krarg made up in strength and fervour what he lacked in finesse while Gregorn, staggering with the impact of every clash, used his superior skill to keep himself alive. Gregorn's wound was slowing him down and he was almost drained of energy.

Krarg increased the pressure, realising that he could wear Gregorn down. He threw a shot to the head, blocked, and quickly followed with his other arm, holding a club, into Gregorn's middle. The dull thud into the body must have broken ribs. The sword flashed again, blood from previous kills arcing off and splashing all those within ten yards. Once again Gregorn parried, but he knew he was slowing and any second one of these shots was going to get through. His armour might not hold out against a Morg.

Gregorn decided to attack. Waiting for the swing of the club, instead of stepping backwards and away he caught Krarg unawares, stepping forward so that the club went around the back of his body and the impact was minimal. His face was close to the flat-nosed, ugly features of Krarg and he took his chance, slamming the flat edge of the sword into Krarg's face and getting soaked with the spray of black issue that came forth from the nose and mouth of the Morg.

Roaring in pain and defiance, Krarg dropped his club and grabbed hold of the collar of the tunic on Gregorn's back and pulled with all his might, creating a little more space between the two of them. Using one of his large, sharp-nailed thumbs he dug into the hole that was already dripping blood at the base of the giant's neck.

The pain shot down the spine of the giant, numbing his hand, and he dropped his sword without realising it while at the same time going down on one knee. He was helpless and about to die. Krarg pulled a short blade dagger and stuck it through the breastplate and into the ribs of the felled giant. Gregorn still looked into the Morg's eyes and said, 'You may think you've won, but as long as there is a man or giant alive in this land they will hunt you down to avenge today's carnage.'

Krarg laughed and said, 'For once, big fool, I agree with you. I do think I have won and to prove it I will kill you.' He lifted his sword to end the giant's life, but before he could apply the final blow a voice drawled from behind him, 'The hell you will.'

Marggitte had managed to get Arrara to her bed and guards from the Inners had been posted by Rawt to the room where she now twitched and moaned on her cot. The emperor and his wife had made their way to the chamber and there was now quite a crowd around the young girl, including the healer, Nalla.

Hemm positioned himself away from them all, head bowed, unspeaking. Eventually Rawt, the Capatain of the Inners, stepped away from the cot and moved to where Hemm stood.

'Hemm, son of Hemm. You left your post and you have allowed Sheldrak, son of Whinst, to leave his quarters, and we now do not know his whereabouts. There is no circumstance that exists which allows an Inner to take leave of his duties. Since time started you are the first to do this and you must pay the price. Do you have anything to say for yourself?'

Hemm could not even speak. Everything that he lived for, everything that he and his wife had built, his reputation, that of his family, the standing he had reached in the community of Ontrades had been taken as surely as a killer will take the life of his prey.

Hemm stood and muttered a couple of words. 'By my elders, I will abide.' He left and went to his quarters.

Marggitte, realising her husband had left, took her leave with the permission of Rawt and ran with all her speed to her and Hemm's room. She entered as Hemm was removing his uniform of the Inners and he stood naked by the end of their marital cot.

'Hemm, please Faith, tell me you will not do this?'

'My darling wife, it is the only way I can restore any honour to you, my name and the name of my father. I have for many years strived for the position we both now hold. I came from nothing, a large family who were lucky in that they had one son who could fight. I can fight no more.

'Marggitte, I love you always and hope we will meet on the other side, when we will renew our love. My love for you was stronger than my honour. I release you from our marital vows.'

Hemm took his ceremonial knife and slammed it into his own chest and straight through his heart.

He fell to his knees as Marggitte pulled out fistfuls of her own hair while stifling a scream with the back of her hand. Hemm fell forward as the blood gushed from the wound and a single tear fell from his eye.

Wisdom or Sacrifice?

Shel knew the old hag had only a couple of minutes on him, but the sound of her footsteps pattering in the dark below seemed to come from a great distance. He was also running in the semi darkness, and the rough-cut steps offered no firm purchase for him, with irregular drops and sudden twists and turns. He stopped for a second when he noticed that he could no longer hear the fall of any feet but his own.

By stopping he was in absolute silence. The noise from the usual day-to-day running of the Citadel would under normal circumstances have filtered through, but the Citadel was almost empty today, with all hands and eyes turned to the bloody plains where the roar of battle attracted all attention.

Joice had stopped to see if her hearing was correct and she shouted up from the darkness below, 'Don't think I don't know you are here and also don't think you can catch me. The bitch only has an hour and you are wasting it.' Her unreal laughter echoed off the stone walls.

Shel started again. Good Faith, if he could beat Arkel in the Great Race he could catch an old woman. It sounded logical to him and for the first time he missed Isthmus. What would he advise, to run flat out or try to pace himself? He had no time to ponder and went for the flat-out approach. Some lessons needed learning more than once.

He continued down, turning first in tight circles and then wider ones. Whoever had made this staircase was no stonemason. His eyes had adapted to the poor light and he no longer had to hold on to both sides of the walls but could lean with his inside arm and hand as he spiralled downwards, anticlockwise. This increased his speed but with the acoustics in this part of the Citadel carrying every little noise much further than normal, he had no idea if he was catching Joice.

Five minutes passed before he came to an earthen floor and, sprinting around a blind corner he ran straight into a solid stone wall, managing to raise his hands at the last second to soften the impact.

'Umph. Jak. Where did she go?'

Looking back the way he came, he could see no way out. There had to be one – she couldn't have vanished. He had to walk back slowly as he had no way of saving Arrara until he found Joice's way out. Two flights back he saw what he had missed in his rush the first time: a low earthen tunnel led down a rough slope. At the bottom he could feel a doorway in the wall but could not find a way through.

He felt all around the door, hoping he would find a handle or latch, but to no avail. His chest constricted as the first signs of panic set in. He did not have very long before the poison took its fevered grip and delivered the child into the hands of the dragon. That's how dragon breath worked, overheating the body until the heart burst.

He cried out in frustration and took the Sword of Destiny from its sheath and banged away on the door with all his might.

He spoke aloud to himself. 'Don't panic, Shel. Use your head, not your strength. The hag was weak. There must be a switch somewhere.'

He turned and walked back very slowly up the tunnel, feeling all down one side of it, and then down the other on his way back. Still nothing. In his head he heard the girl cry out as his mind played tricks on him. He stubbed his toe on a sharp piece of rock and fell to the ground, almost weeping with frustration.

'For the love of Faith, help me,' he cried out, sprawled

on the floor, getting back to his feet and then realising that his toe had not hit a chunk of rock but a slab of brick set into the earth floor. He stamped down hard on it and the thick wooden door clicked open into the barrel room of what looked like an old inn.

He ran through past some barrels up the stairway out of the cellar and into the back yard of a run-down tavern. There was no sign of Joice and the bright sun hit his eyes hard, sending shards of multicoloured points of light into his head. He had an idea where he was as this path in front of him led down to the Pass. Where else would an old murderer be held up?

He went sprinting down the steep hill, not knowing which way to turn or look. There were not many people about, only the old, infirm and cowardly, those who could not or would not fight. He was in the depths of despair. He had lost Joice, who held with her the only chance of survival for the princess, and it was his fault. He had brought this madness to the city of Ontrades, no one else. He screamed out loud and madness took his eye.

He asked all he met if they had seen a crazy old woman running down here moments earlier but information was not freely given in this part of the city. People only helped themselves, and normally helped themselves to someone else's possessions.

He heard an evil laugh from somewhere above.

'I have a deal to strike with you, but you have only two minutes to make your mind up. After that you will not have enough time to get this serum back to your precious princess.

'It's very simple. Your sword for the serum, or Arrara dies.'

Shade was running directly towards the battle, not knowing what action he would take on arrival. Never fought in my life, he thought, not until I became a wolf. Sorry, bloody lupine. Got pissed in All Bar One once and thought I'd shut that big daft lad up who had been singing all night. What a mess he made of me. Never mind, here goes.

'Wait,' a voice in his head said.

'What the bloody hell?'

'My name is Isthmus. I am a spirit who has been with Sheldrak from the beginning and I am here to help you. If you let me take over your body I can help you fight. I think we will have to help fight the Morg's leader. It's normally the only way to stop a Morg army.'

'Whoaaaa. Time out, Isbus, or whatever your name is. I'm a bloke, then a wolf, and then my body is being taken over. No bloody chance. Sod off. I've only just got used to being a lupine without being a spirit as well. How the hell do I know you have been with Sheldrak?'

Isthmus thought before replying in Shade's head, 'Because you were going for a sandwich... Got hit by a bus... And no one will answer the bloody phones. I think that's correct.'

Shade was obviously impressed. 'Welcome to wolfkind, oh spirited one. Now, let's get this Morg.'

Shade continued to run towards the battle, seeing the fight between Gregorn and Krarg and arriving as Krarg raised his sword to kill the fallen giant.

Speaking to Isthmus in his head he said, 'I'll give him my best John Wayne.' And speaking aloud, 'The hell you will.'

Krarg turned from his prey to find himself face to face with a talking wolf.

Krarg, turning, kept the pressure on the base of the neck of Gregorn, who had the look of a freshly caught fish landed on the shore. He looked over the top of Shade, trying to find the owner of the voice when Shade said, 'You, I'm talking to. Let go of the giant, you stinking great hairball. You look like some leftover from a *Star Wars* movie.'

The insults were lost on Krarg, but all the same he recognised them as such and, hitting Gregorn hard in the face with the handle of his sword, he spat the words, 'I'll see to you in a moment.' Facing Shade again, 'In all my days I have heard of different enchantments but never a talking lupine. You will make a fine pet.'

'I'm no one's pet, hairball, and when I've ripped your throat out you won't be able to take a pussy cat as a pet.'

Isthmus spoke to Shade in his head. 'Look ferocious, bare your teeth and raise your hackles.'

Shade did as required and threw in a long, cool howl for good measure.

Krarg raised his sword once more as his new foe prepared to attack. 'It will be sad to kill you, I could have made a lot of trade from a talking lupine.'

Shade was much bigger than the average wolf, as big as a Great Dane, he thought, and his size was going to be an asset now in this battle with the Morg. Isthmus told Shade that Krarg was the leader, from the markings on his armour, and they both knew that taking this Morg out was the only chance they had. The ghosts of the dead Morgs were still screaming around the heads of the Ontradean army and many men were lost as concentration deserted them and the Morgs took advantage to kill and maim.

Shade circled Krarg, waiting for his moment. There was no way he was going to run straight in at him. He had seen how Shel had dealt with the smaller wolves in the forest. He feinted in; Krarg swung his sword, hitting naught but the fresh air where Shade had been a second earlier. Taking his opportunity, Shade waited for the swing of the sword to complete its heavy arc and then nipped in, taking a nice large bite of the Morg's uncovered leg. A black substance, which was the equivalent of blood to the Morgs, gushed into Shade's mouth, but he didn't hang around and was out again quickly before Krarg had chance to lay a hand on him.

The combination of man, lupine and spirit was looking as though it could compete.

Isthmus guided Shade, telling him to keep away as Krarg, enraged by the pain in his leg, ran at him. The lupine was too deft, skipping easily out of the way and getting a nice chunk from the thick thigh of Krarg as he flew by.

'You taste like horseshit!' shouted Shade. 'Which around here is translated as bedago jak!'

The Morg had now lost all semblance of control and was swinging wildly at Shade in all directions, but to no avail. Isthmus was in control and he would not let Shade get close enough to be scratched. Krarg raged like this for a few moments while Shade continually kept out of reach unless he could get a nip or bite to keep the 'blood' flowing. Krarg stopped, putting his hands on his knees and taking in great gulps of air, his head lowered so all that could be seen was a mass of unruly hair.

Isthmus spoke quietly to the man in the wolf and Shade took a few steps back, never losing eye contact with the Morg. Isthmus concentrated all his energy into the lupine and Shade left the ground he stood upon. A couple of inches at first, then a foot, until from five yards away the wolf-like creature hovered in the heat of the battle with a stillness that stopped many individual fights as combatants turned to look.

Krarg raised his head to see the devil beast at his eye level and his gasp could be heard by many of his surrounding troops. For the only time in his life his eyes betrayed the fear that gripped his soul. The howl from Shade was as debilitating to Krarg as if someone had run a spear through his heart.

From the hovering position he was in, Shade shot forward like a large, hairy missile, hitting the motionless Morg square on his neck and ripping his throat clean out. The spurt of Morg blood plumed into the air like the world's darkest fountain and was seen all over the field. The Morg leader fell like a toppled monument and the ground shook for miles around.

Isthmus had one final act to fulfil and, leaving the spent body of Shade, he moved invisibly into the centre of the remaining battle. All around him Morgs lay on the ground, their legs enriched with the arrows of the Ontradean archers. The infantrymen of the city had then removed their heads. Men, women and giants also lay wounded or dead in their hundreds and thousands. If Isthmus could stop this, he would – enough blood had been spilled for one day.

He had no energy left to become visible but, taking his presence as close as he could to the old burial grounds of the men and women of Ontrades, he began to chant. He was heard and not seen until, from the ground, the dead of Ontrades walked again. Men and women who had fought in wars of times long gone rose for one last battle. Thousands pulled themselves from their graves to face down the bad spirits of the Morgs and to lift the hearts of the Ontradean army.

No war or fight could be seen by the living, but gradually the Morg spirits were dragged, screaming in a way that burst the ears of many, dragged back into the earth whence they came. It was a day when good had the ascendancy over evil.

The defeat of Krarg meant so much more than one death as the whole Morg army, seeing their leader beaten with such sorcery, turned and retreated. With the removal of the screaming banshees back to the earth, the battle was over and though there had been many casualties, the Morgs would not be challenging Ontrades again for many, many years.

The battle was over but it merely marked the start of the latest war against Essdark and his powers of evil.

No time for counselling or speaking to Isthmus – he had to decide now, on his own. Could he let a child die? One he had not known for very long? But it could mean the end of his quest. How could he face Essdark without the Sword of Destiny, without Northstar? In fact, how would he ever even find Essdark without the sword? It was now he needed his wisdom more than any of his other Faiths of Strepsay, and he had little time with which to make his choice.

'Come on, you dirty Spawn, child or sword? What is it?'

Shel knew deep down in his heart the choice he had to make. He had to sacrifice the sword for the child. He had already forced Hemm into betraying his honour and Faith knows what that would mean.

'You have me, woman. Where do you want me to put the sword?'

All this time Shel had stood in the midst of five broken-down houses with two floors each. He was shouting up to them, trying to ascertain which one the hag's voice was coming from. The cackle came again from above like some evil joke of a voice from the heavens.

'The bottle I have in my hand is easily broken. If it breaks, the child dies. You will come to the house to your left with the blue door and in it you will see a hatch. Wait there for me. I promise you that if you don't do exactly as I say the child will die.'

'Just hurry, woman, I still have to get back.'

Shel walked over to the door and waited. After what seemed like an eternity, but must have only been a couple of minutes, the hatch pulled back.

'Put your arm through and have the sword in it.'

Shel did as he was told.

'Drop the sword.'

'How do I know I will get the serum?'

'Oh, you will get the serum, you stupid bugger. You have no chance of getting back to the top of the Citadel.'

Shel dropped the sword. 'Come on, give the bottle.'

'Wait, I have to check the sword.' Joice picked up Northstar and it immediately burned into the sparse covering of flesh on her hand.

'Jak', she screamed, 'how do I pick this up?'

'I have no idea, use cloth or something – just give me the bottle.'

He felt something thrust into his hand and without wasting another second, turned and ran back up to the Citadel.

Shel had lost track of exactly how long it had been since the knife had cut the Princess Arrara for the first time but he knew that he would have to run at his fastest to have any chance whatsoever of saving her life.

His thoughts went back to over a month ago when he had taken on Arkel in the Great Race. He pumped his arms and legs hard, driving himself back up the unforgiving slopes of the Bluetop Mountains and back towards the Citadel. His heart leapt in his chest like a young hare trapped in a sack, for he had only ten minutes earlier been running in the other direction.

He was drained emotionally and the trip back to the Citadel nearly finished him off totally. The tunnel at the base of the Citadel was guarded by two of the Inners and they had received orders to let no one in, whoever they might be, until they got permission from Rawt, their capatain. Shel wept in despair as he tried to get past the two Inners. He tried reason, then shouted for all he was worth in the hope that someone with the authority would hear him and finally he attempted to fight his way past but nearly lost his head, literally.

The hour was gone and many other minutes with it, making the bottle in the pocket of his tunic as much use as a woman to an elder. He decided to take the secret passage through the old inn. Once again he ran back and down to the inn, through the startled bar which now had a couple of regulars, and down into the cellar.

He found the catch at the back of the last barrel and ran every step of the stairs before falling exhausted through the hidden door into the princess's room. He gasped, 'Quickly, I have the serum. It may not be too late.'

The emperor and Rawt walked over to Shel, who was sprawled on the floor with one arm raised in the air, waving the green bottle like a flag of surrender. Rawt pulled him upright and, taking the bottle from Shel's sweaty outstretched hand, said,

'Do not worry yourself Sheldrak. The old woman was tricking us. She could never have killed the child she had raised from a baby. It wasn't dragon breath at all, merely a sleep-inducing drug that raised the child's temperature to give the impression that it was dragon breath. Come, take a look. She sleeps peacefully now that Nalla has given her medication to counter it, but she will be in a condition of shock for quite a while.'

That was the final straw for Shel. He slumped in the arms of the strong Elder, knowing he also had been tricked after he had made the ultimate sacrifice, that of the Sword of Destiny, for nothing more than a bottle of coloured water.

On the other side of the room he espied Marggitte and crossed, half staggering, to speak to her. Her head was bowed.

'Marggitte, I have lost the sword.'

Marggitte replied, 'And I have lost my husband Hemm, son of Hemm.'

'What do you mean, you have lost Hemm?'

'The penalty for an Inner for leaving his post or ignoring an order is death by his own hand. Hemm has already taken his last command.'

With tears streaming down her handsome face she hit

her breast three times. 'By my elders,' she invoked, and with a nod towards Rawt she walked from the room.

The leader of the quest was alive but without the sword. The princess lived and the battle against the Morgs had been won, with Shade the new hero of the city. Isthmus was resting but would be back to guide Shel. Unbelievably Hemm, one of the Seven, was dead. How would Shel find the fifth, sixth and seventh without Northstar to direct him?

It was all too much for Shel to comprehend. He fell to the floor in a daze and closed his eyes in the hope that, when he opened them again, he would find himself back in his bed in Jost, getting up for his lessons.

Onwards

Gregorn and Shade walked through the marketplace in the Pass. They were inseparable after Shade had saved the giant's life. That had been more than two weeks ago and life in the city had taken on a semblance of normality again after the bloodiness of the battle and the shock of the deaths of some key personnel in the city hierarchy.

If it were possible for a four-legged creature to puff its chest out and walk with a swagger, then this was the very gait that Shade had now adopted. As he told Greg at least once every ten minutes, saving his life was, 'Nothing, mate. Just doing my job.'

Shel had remained in the Citadel for most of the two weeks, looking worried, spending time with the Inners and Elders, studying maps and charts of the known lands and listening to advice from all who were prepared to give it. In the Citadel, this was just about anyone with a mouth and tongue. Isthmus had come back to Shel and snuggled comfortably into that little gap between uncertainty and the rashness of youth in the back of Shel's rapidly expanding mind.

The Elders had decided without any doubt that Shel was indeed the 'one' and his deeds in saving the life of the young princess were already the topic of six or seven different songs. Depending on the imagination of the musician, the story ranged from a battle against ten Morgs to a battle of minds against the Grey One himself.

Shade and Gregorn had gone to the market to find a present for Shel to 'put a smile on that miserable mug', as Shade delicately assessed the situation. Gregorn put up with the chattering of his new-found friend with no annoyance at all and Shade took advantage of the opportunity with both paws. He hadn't been allowed to speak for two weeks – and was he making up for lost ear space!

'So, Greggy boy, what do we get old misery guts? Face like a wet weekend since he lost that bloody sword. I know it's important but, as we've all told him, he did it to save a life. Can't argue with that. Arrara one, Joice nil. But this bloody quest he's dragging us all on is bothering him big time. Nobody's seen the old witch since she got the sword. Everyone says she can't get out the city without being seen, but she got into the kid's bedroom easily enough. What do you think, oh tall one? Eh, eh, what do say?'

Gregorn took his chance to reply. 'Well I beli—'

'Forget it, Greg, we'll never work old Shel out. He's deeper than a taxman's pocket, that one. Look at that there, that's a brill prezzy. Come on, get your cash out, I'm all out of readies.'

Gregorn smiled. Perhaps if Krarg had taken that last swing it would have been swifter and less painful than being talked to death over 1,000 years, because that was how long he was prepared stay with this strange creature. One thing you could count on in this life was the loyalty of a giant, and if Shade were loyal to the strange young man called Shel-drak then Gregorn would be loyal to Shade. Even if he would have to buy earplugs.

'Come on then, Greg, let's buy it and take it back to Shel. You know what, mate, since I saved you I haven't heard one bloody phone.'

They walked over to the stall where Shade had spotted the present and, speaking to the proprietor, Shade said, 'Do you gift-wrap swords?'

In the Citadel library Shel walked among the high-stacked shelves. Many of the tomes in this dusty old place hadn't been opened in centuries and even if they were to have been, they were in languages old and no longer used. He knew that they must soon move on. He still had quarters here that were more than adequate for him, but his heart was still heavy in his chest. The loss of the sword had been terrible but the sacrifice had been made willingly and he knew his heart would never have let him choose otherwise.

The pain in his chest was not from this loss, but the wasted death of Hemm. He did not know whether he would have been able to convince Hemm to accompany him on their journey but he would rather Hemm had stayed in this dusty old library for the rest of his life rather than lose it. He had only spoken once to Marggitte since the funeral pyre had been lit but the pain had been too much for them both and they could not share more than formal conversation.

Shel had stayed too long in the city but was still hoping that the Emperor's men would be able to find Joice and return the sword to him. She had not been sighted since that day and Shel feared that she had already moved on. If that were the case, how long before Essdark had the sword for himself, and what did that mean?

Would Northstar be as powerful in the hands of evil as it had been in the hands of good? There was no point in worrying about that now. Isthmus had told Shel that he must call Shade and Gregorn to his room that evening, and Marggitte, if she were able. Shel had also asked Trenc the sayer to participate in the council. Decisions needed to be made and to be made quickly.

Shel sat by the open doors with the pale autumnal sun falling on his face. He closed his eyes for a moment and let the warmth seep into his body, taking the chill of his doubt away and replacing it with the confidence of youth. He had the decisiveness of one who knew that, at sixteen, he was already more of a man than many who had seen forty watery autumns pass by.

He afforded himself a smile: Divad, Arrara, Hemm, Shint, Shade, Isthmus, Gregorn, Marggitte, Rawt, Trenc and Emperor Daynor. A short while ago the only one of these he had known was Divad, and he must never forget that it was Divad who had driven him to be where he found himself today.

Feeling refreshed, he rose, ready to face the next challenge that this quest was about to throw at him.

The Elders had given Shel and his companions a small mess room on the second floor of the Citadel that was used by groups of the Inners to socialise. But tonight a table had been set for six, the food laden and then the room cleared. Two Inners of sound repute had been set at the outer door.

The table was a good oaken one, worn with the years of use and still resonant with the fine fighting songs that had been sung in its presence. Shel sat at the top end of it with Trenc facing him at the opposite end of the long side. To Shel's left sat a high chair for Shade, with Gregorn to his left. A place had been set for Isthmus, with no eating utensils, opposite Shade and to the left of Isthmus, facing Gregorn, was a place for Marggitte.

On the table was a large tureen of famous Ontradean stew, and bread and cheeses of many kinds. Each guest had his or her own jug of special Citadel ale, normally used only for birthdays or anniversaries, while Shade had his own drinking bowl filled with foaming beer.

Only four places were taken and Shel waited patiently for the appearance of both Isthmus and Marggitte. He knew Isthmus would only show when Margg did, but Shel was not certain that this would happen this evening. He knew she had received the written invitation but he had not received any affirmation back.

The fire blazed in the pitch-black open fireplace and the flickers of flame reflected weirdly off the odd-shaped shields decorating the walls. The many candles scattered haphazardly around the table emitted the radiance that would light the food and feed the light. Shel waited as long as he could without wanting to let the stew spoil and, just as he was about to give the word to commence, the door opened and the unmistakable physique of Marggitte rushed into the room as though she were trying to race some invisible rival to the last dinner place.

They all stood and Isthmus appeared. Shel addressed his friends.

'By my elders. I offer this meal to the memory of our many friends that have been lost in the recent fights against evil. By Faith, may their spirits rest easy.'

'By my elders,' everyone replied.

'Come on then, folks. Grub up. Greg, do an armless man a favour and pour me some of that lush-smelling stew.' Shade was good to be around now that he had stabilised a little, and always seemed capable of raising a smile or breaking awkward pauses. Not one person, giant, spirit or lupine, mentioned the fact that Marggitte wore a plain white mask with eyeholes and naught else but a gap to eat through. Two thick straps that fastened tightly at the back of her head held it on. She had also cut most of her hair off so that all that could be seen were small bobs of blonde sprigs sticking up on the top. She had obviously cut it herself with a sword or knife.

After the food had been shared and the ale had flowed, conversation picked up and inevitably talk turned to what Shel intended to do next. It was a question he wanted to address, but not on his own. One thing Shel had decided early in this quest was that it was to be a team effort. The less he had to undertake singly, and the wiser the counsel he could take, then hopefully the better the outcome would be.

He turned the question back to his fellow diners and asked them, 'Well, my friends, I do have some ideas of my own but I am also intrigued as to what you think my next move should be, as I have realised I don't always have any answer, let alone the right one.'

Shade blustered straight in. 'Well, we find the hag, get the sword back. Find the next three members of the good old secret seven. Go get Essdark, kick his butt. Find a way of making me human again, all go home and get pissed. Sorted. Who can argue with that?'

It was a couple of minutes before they all stopped laughing, after they had enticed from Shade the meanings of the words they didn't understand.

It was Trenc, the Elder and sayer, who picked up on a couple of points with Shade. 'Shade, you said "three more" but I see only three members here, which makes four more.'

'I am number four,' said Gregorn, smiling at Shade and then looking to Shel for acceptance. Before Shel could answer the eager giant, a quiet voice said, 'And I intend to be number five. If you will have me?'

The muffled voice was that of Marggitte.

'I thought of nothing else since the pyre of Hemm. I believe he would never have come with you, no matter what tale you could have given him about the "bigger story waiting to be told". But this was meant to be. I am the one who is meant to come with you for I now have nothing to stay here for. Hemm's love for me was greater than his honour for the doctrine of the Inners and therefore I intend to use his love and take it with me as my weapon against whatever is awaiting out there for us all.

'It is Faith.'

She paused and, though no tears could be seen through the mask, the slowly heaving shoulders expressed more grief than a million tears ever could. She composed herself and continued.

'I wear this mask in honour of the man who loved me. No man will ever look at me again and want me or see in me the attraction that Hemm did. This will be my death mask, for only then will I remove it in the company of others. These are my terms, Sheldrak. I leave the Inners as Rawt has granted, but my punishment is that I can never set foot in the city of Ontrades again. Will you have me?'

'By my elders, I cannot think of anything more right than that you join us. Gregorn, you also are one of the chosen. We are now five, but please remember all of you that my dream foretold that not all would return, and the travels I ask you to make will not be pleasant. No one could blame any one of you for not wishing to remain in my company.

'Danger and evil are in all directions and the steps that I ask you to take will be to face the biggest evil of all. The Grey One has walked recently and he grows stronger again as we sit and wait in this city. Shade is right. Let us "kick some butt".'

Shel received cheers and backslaps and howls from Shade for this little speech but it would be a long time before Marggitte would smile and even longer before that smile would take root and grow into a laugh without regret.

Isthmus brought them back to their senses. 'I agree with you, Sheldrak, we must move on, but, now that we do not have Northstar to guide us, where exactly would you have us move on to?'

Shel replied, 'I also have had these thoughts, Isthmus. Now that we no longer have a direction, where would we go? This is why I have asked Trenc to join us. Sayers have advised me well so far and with very limited options, I turn to them again.'

Shade butted in. 'Hold on a minute, Shelly. We have no reports of the old bag's movements. As far as we know she could be held up in the bowels of the Pass. If that's the case and we go trekking off, we are getting further and further from where the sword is, and I believe you need that to face Arsedark or whatever-his-face is?'

'Which is why, my furry friend, I seek counsel from Trenc, because not only do we need to get the sword back but we also need to find the last two members of our seven, as that also seems to be a condition of facing the Grey One. Trenc, will you hold my hand and give me a reading?'

Trenc, who had been silent until that point, content to listen to the thoughts of others, lifted his deep brown eyes and looked at Shel. Trenc was one of the younger members of the Elders' Council in Ontrades and his thick, tousled and unkempt brown hair and overly bushy eyebrows seemed out of keeping with the simple, plain cream habit that he wore. There was no mistaking the dignity with which he spoke.

'I can and will do as you request but remember, Shel-drak, I will not always be correct and things can change from what I see today and what I may see tomorrow. There is no science, only love and the Faiths of Strepsay.'

Shel moved to the other end of the table and pulled a chair to the side of Trenc. Trenc turned so that they were sitting face to face, and they grabbed each other's forearms. Trenc shut his eyes and a spark of blue electricity shot from the top of his head. His hair stood up on end, even more than it did already, and he jerked and swayed as though he were receiving strong electrical pulses from Shel's body.

This lasted for about twenty seconds and the others, including the hovering spirit, Isthmus, gathered around. Only Marggitte sat in her place, as she was already next to Trenc whose back was turned to her. She had seen Trenc do this before and wondered to herself how much of it was a parlour trick and how much was true.

Trenc let go of Shel and, after gathering his composure, said, 'I saw plenty but I will not share all as it seems contra-dictory. But I believe you must head east from Ontrades as a great river features in your future, Sheldrak, and that is where the Landsplitter flows. I also predict that your two future companions lie in that direction. As for the Sword of Destiny, that will try to work its way back to you, but ultimately will head in that direction also.'

Gregorn the giant said, 'Are we to go to Seathon, the biggest river port on the Landsplitter? It is not far from the reaches of the Morgs.'

'Don't worry about Morgs, Greg, me and Isthmus will sort them out for you,' bragged Shade.

'I do not worry for myself, but if we are to be successful then it is better not to walk directly up to your enemy and invite a shot. At least, that has been my experience.' Gregorn said this with humour and no malice.

Sheldrak finally spoke.

'Tomorrow morning at break of day we set off for Seathon. We are five, looking for two more, and at the same time we must find Joice and Northstar unless they are already separated, in which case I care not to cross Joice again.'

'One more word for you before you continue with your ale,' said Trenc. 'I think your choice of Seathon is a good one, for they are decent people who have no history of trouble or fighting. War is not for them but, I warn you, I saw great sadness ahead. Beware, for not all will be as it seems.'

Trenc stood. 'I will take my leave. Ensure you say your farewells early to the Elders and the emperor. They have treated you well considering that trouble only came to the city with your arrival. Your stay has been short but it will never be forgotten. By my elders.' And with a swish of his cloak he had gone.

Shade, as ever, put his finger, or paw, on the point.

'I think you could say we've overstayed our welcome. But tomorrow we move onwards, onwards to Seathon.'

Part Three
Seathon

Flatlands

The five companions made an odd ensemble as they trooped across the arid rocks and sands of the flatlands. At the front was Sheldrak, back on his faithful furze, Randeed. Riding behind was the formidable figure of Marggitte, who from a distance looked to have no face. Features blank and stark, she sat on a beautiful white stallion called Bold, a parting gift from the emperor and Arrara. Trotting dutifully behind was the shaggy, dirty yellow-coated Shade and bringing up the rear was the solid presence of Gregorn, so tall he needed no steed to keep up with the others.

Finally, known but not seen, was Isthmus, occasionally inside Shel, other times away to wherever he went to restore his strength. Most of the conversation during the day was between Shade and Gregorn. Shel was pensive and torn between anger at himself for losing the sword and the thought that the good people of Ontrades held him in some part responsible for the happenings of the past few weeks. Was he some sort of siren, pulling trouble to him and whoever accompanied him, as in the tales of old when pretty young women enticed sailors to their untimely deaths?

Strange saying. He had yet to meet a person who would have considered anyone's death to be timely.

Marggitte was quiet for other reasons. She was still in a state of shock, her mind divorced from all that went on around her, as her whole being came to terms with the grief that filled her body. She felt as though someone had opened her up, scooped out all of her insides and filled her with wood filings. Her thoughts were to keep going, keep moving and to be away from Ontrades – not to help her forget, for her love of Hemm was something of beauty and solace to her – but to help her live again. One day, not next week, not next year, but one day she would start to live again. Never love, just live.

By going with Shel and his friends she hoped to keep some purpose. She did not feel it now but, if she could find someone responsible for the death of her beloved Hemm, then revenge might be just the catalyst to ignite the spark of life that had previously blazed so strongly in her body.

The flatlands were appropriately named. Only a matter of miles east out of Ontrades, the grasses became sparse, gradually turning to rock before the desert took over the landscape. Every now and then the desert gave way to huge outcrops of sandstone, sometimes lasting for miles.

It was difficult for the animals to carry Shel and Marggitte over these outcrops, which looked like enormous stepping stones put down by gods so that they wouldn't burn their feet on the hot sand. This ensured that making any real headway was difficult and they only covered about thirty miles in the first three days out of Ontrades. Even Shade's relentless chatter died down to the occasional caustic comment.

Shel was down, worried about his own morale first and then that of his colleagues. The desert sun burned hotly during the day, even as back home in Jost the leaves were turning. Sweat poured off them by day, turning them chill with the cold of the desert night. On the morning of the fourth sunrise, exactly eight long weeks since Sheldrak had first climbed on Randeed outside his father's small farm, he woke with a headache. By lunchtime it had turned into a fever. The sun bore down on him but he shivered with the icy sweat dripping from his body.

Isthmus knew instinctively that all was not well inside Shel's head, as the boy's answers to his promptings were not making much sense. The others could see that Shel was suffering but he had been much quieter than usual after leaving Ontrades and they put it down to his obvious guilt over the loss of Hemm and Shint (and possibly Northstar). They knew he was getting worse when, in the afternoon after climbing a steep side of rock that continually crumbled beneath their feet, remounting his furze, Shel toppled to the ground in a dead faint.

Marggitte was first to him. Bodily picking him up with the ease of a mother lifting her infant, she took him to an overhang of rock to provide him with shade. Within minutes Gregorn had erected one of their tents and made up a low sleeping cot that they used at night.

They got some fluid into him but when he came around he was still incoherent and soon drifted away into a restless sleep again.

Isthmus appeared to them and took them a small distance away to discuss the state of health of their leader.

Isthmus spoke. 'I don't know how unwell he is but I do know it is affecting the clarity of his thinking, which is not a good sign. He needs a healer, but we are still 120 miles at least from Seathon. At the speed we have been going that is over a week away.'

Shade replied, 'Not only that. If we cannot travel at the same speed we've managed up to now, we'll be clean out of water and I'm already as dry as a witch's ti—'

Marggitte interrupted the coarse lupine. 'It's a simple solution. Bold is strong enough to carry both Shel and myself. I will ride on to Seathon and get him to a healer and will meet you there when you arrive.'

'But,' said Gregorn, 'how will we find you?'

'That is easy. It should take me no longer than two and a half days if I ride through the night. If you push on from here you will be with me in six, at the outside seven. It will also give you more water, as Shel and I will need less as we will be quicker to the river port.

'So, seven days from today I will find the biggest worship house in Seathon and meet you in the inn closest to it at eleven in the morning. If you are not there I will go back every day until you arrive. If you are not there after ten days then, my friends, I will head back out here and find you or die in the search.'

'Bloody hell, Maggie, biggest speech I've heard you make. And less of this "until I die" business. The five of us will be in this mess until the end. I can feel it in my bollocks.'

'I know not what your bollocks are and have no intention of finding out but, by my elders, I thank you for what I think are kind words.

'Isthmus, Gregorn, do you agree? For we must decide together in the absence of Shel's thoughts.'

'I agree,' said Isthmus, 'but I stay with Sheldrak. It is my reason for being here and I take up no space on Bold. Shade can have my share of the water.'

'My God. That's a first,' said Shade, 'a joke from the see-through one. But seriously, me and Greggy boy will be OK. It's only a week.'

Gregorn nodded his acceptance of Shade's words to Marggitte, who said, 'It is decided then. I will take food and water for three days for the two of us and leave the rest for you. I will leave Shel to wake naturally but if he doesn't change by nightfall then I will ride whatever.'

The coughing and spluttering that then burst forth from Shel broke up the impromptu meeting and Isthmus faded from sight. Marggitte went to him and, gently taking his head under her hand, raised him so that he could drink. This caused another coughing fit during which large wads of dark phlegm were dredged up off the young man's chest. He laid his head back down and in the shadow, the pale of his face stood out more than the white mask adorning the face of Marggitte. Unlike Sheldrak, she did not have heavy purple rings underlining her eyes.

'That's it,' she said, 'I wait no longer. His illness tightens by the minute and I refuse to wait another three hours until nightfall. I leave now.'

She quickly loaded Bold with packs, food, water and tents before scooping Shel up once more on to the stark whiteness of the stallion.

'By my elders,' she shouted as the horse charged off over the sands, 'we will meet in a week.' She was so very wrong.

Joice had not eaten for over five days. Yet wandering off into the flatlands had seemed like a good idea. She had taken water for one or two days but even she in her heightened state of madness had the sense to reduce her intake to make it last as long as possible. Add to this the withdrawal of 'pleasure' since leaving Ontrades, and her life expectancy had taken on that of a horsefly's in summer as it hovers around an old shire.

She slept fitfully on top of a rock about fifty miles away from where Shel slept fitfully underneath the tent that Gregorn had put up. Joice had managed to keep herself hidden in the various underworld locations she frequented in darker parts of the city. Essdark did not come to her as he had before and, with the reducing poison circulating her frail body as the only crutch to keep her upright, she wasn't sure if he came to her or if the ramblings were of her own demented mind.

Either she had decided to leave the city or someone had advised her, but she was not equipped to last out here for ten days. She had had enough food or drink for five days, so ten was stretching her battered old body to the limit. The Joice of two months ago could not be recognised. Her skin had turned leathery brown with the sun, apart from the red, open sores that gathered around her slit of a mouth like maggots around a rotting corpse. What teeth she had left had been falling out with the regularity of her meals and her whole painfully thin body was covered in the dark red dust of the crimson desert sand.

When she woke and lifted her tired bones to her feet she looked like the world's worst-dressed scarecrow, dragging itself off its pole and going after crows rather than waiting for them to come to her.

The voice in her head, whether her own or belonging to some darker force, indicated the direction she should walk. Picking up the end of the rags she had tied together to form a rope, she set off, dragging the bundle with her meagre belongings enclosed. Northstar resisted every step she took and it took all the will of Essdark to keep the frail old woman's body moving.

After all, she had failed him. The plan had been to kill both Hemm and the emperor's brat of a daughter and, even though she had managed to get her hands on the sword using her own initiative, her body would not last long enough to get the sword to the Grey One. Essdark wondered if the sword was better placed with the Spawn, as at least he was heading back to Tremain with it. Now that Essdark couldn't totally control the woman, he felt a little exposed. She was too far gone now to manipulate.

Weakened by the efforts thus far, Essdark would have to turn to his other followers. And as for the bitch with the sword, he would keep her alive as long as possible and try to get the sword into the hands of someone he could trust. Trust, pah, you couldn't even trust a Morg to win a hand-fight in these times. He pointed Joice in the right direction and turned his mind to other things.

Joice, with no clarity of thought, dragged her feet, body and the sword along the rock and stuttered down the other side, walking as though her legs belonged to a wooden puppet. This at least enabled her to stop herself going arse over tit down the sandy concourse. To be exact, she had lost so much weight that the saying was wasted on her. It was more like stopping herself going coccyx over sternum.

In the distance, a Sandman with an eyeglass spotted the old woman. He mounted his kamer (a humped beast with large flat feet especially suited for running on the sand, smaller than a camel but similar in shape apart from its rabbit-like ears). He turned and headed back to his camp with the news.

The Sandpeople were a small, squat race, not as small as dwarfs, but not as big as men. They were totally hairless with tiny eyes and ears. The rest of their facial features were delicate and almost angelic until they smiled, showing off their three rows of tiny but razor-sharp teeth. They were a nomadic race who entertained no one but their own and lived off anything they could find in the desert. As far as they were concerned this was their land, and if you wanted to enter it then fine, but don't blame the Sandpeople if you became dinner. What was left from dinner would be finished off next morning. As Shade put it, 'Like a little leftover cold pizza from the night before.'

They had been rumoured to eat their own kind if nothing else could be found, starting with the eldest and infirm and working through the community like a Chinese menu.

Rizzer, the scout who had seen Joice, knew one thing for sure. His leader, Qwant, couldn't use this old one as a first course, but her bones might be tough enough to chew on for an hour or so.

Poor Joice. She hadn't led a good life, but finishing up as a set of pre-dinner dips for an extended Sandpeople family get-together was not a nice way to depart for the other side.

Fifty miles away, Marggitte was getting on her stallion, Bold, and riding in a direct line to Seathon, a direct line that would take her straight into a marauding family of Sandpeople.

'Well, Greggy old mucker, it looks like it's me and thee again.'

'I take from the gibberish you talk that you mean it is you and I together again.'

'That's exactly what I said. Didn't like the look of Shel, though. I don't know what was coming out of his mouth but it looked like a twenty-a-day cough. Do you smoke in this land of yours?'

Gregorn replied, 'In the lands of my people some will smoke a pipe and in the mountains of Mina there is a weed which, when smoked, can give you the power of a sayer for a short while.'

If a wolf could look astonished then Shade gave a good impression of one.

'Weed? You mean "the weed"? Hash, dope, pot, the holy smoke? In this wonderful land of yours, do animals ever get the chance to try a little of this weed?'

'No. Now come. We have far to go and I am worried about our little friend. He may be the Chosen One but this morning he did not look as though he would last to Seathon. Let us march.'

'OK, Gregg, keep your armour on. My legs are not as long as yours.'

'No, but you have twice as many. And also, I have no intention of taking my armour off. It may be approaching winter but in this sun I would still burn.'

'What I meant was... Forget it. Let's go.'

The two friends marched onwards, also heading towards rows and rows of tiny, sharp teeth.

Kurn and Dee

Bold was as swift as he was strong and this present from the emperor was serving both Marggitte and Shel well. He ate up the ground, galloping over the thick sand. Sometimes he became a little timid when climbing over the steeper rock fragments but, by dismounting and leaving only Shel cradled in the saddle, Margg helped him overcome his fear by gently leading him by his soft leather bridle.

The sun beat down upon them for an hour. But as the afternoon moved on and turned to dusk, the chillier desert air started to show the breath of Bold, which plumed from his mouth like the steam from a locomotive's funnel. As the dark collected itself around them, Marggitte had to slow down a little. If the ground suddenly fell away into a dip that Bold could not see, then the chances of him breaking a leg or even throwing and rolling over the top of his riders was just too great a chance to take.

Shel was in another place altogether. He walked hand in hand across a beautiful meadow with a young woman who looked just as he remembered his mother from when he was very little. He then grew, and the woman he was with shrunk and he became a father figure and the child in his hand was Princess Arrara.

She turns and smiles at him and the teeth fall one by one from her mouth. Her face ages. Wrinkles appear, wrinkles which should have taken decades to form do so in seconds. The blonde hair falls from her head and what remains turns grey.

The not-so-beautiful face of Joice is grimacing up at him from the body of a young girl and the sight makes him raise his hand to stifle the scream caught in his throat like a bird in a fox's jaws. Then the fields turn to red in a flow from the edges of his vision and a familiar voice says, 'You are mine.'

Shel shouted out in his sleep and then his eyes stared up at the stars in the cloudless desert sky. Into his sight came the bobbing white mask that is now the visage of the once strikingly handsome Marggitte, and he realised from the motion of the horse that he was moving very fast.

'By my elders, am I glad to see you open your eyes again. You have not stirred for most of the night and dawn cannot be far away. How do you feel?'

Shel took a moment to answer. His throat felt as though the members of a small family of burrowing rodents were nesting in it and using his windpipe to rub off their summer coats. Marggitte reined Bold to a shuddering stop and lifted Shel down to the desert floor.

'I have bad dreams,' he croaked, 'and I still feel very sleepy. Hot and sleepy.' He closed his eyes once more and then shivered. Opening his eyes again, he said, 'I have pains deep down inside my chest and I don't think I could even stand up if I wanted. Where are we, Marggitte, and where are the others?'

'Do not worry about them, they are following on. Here, drink this. We will make Seathon in about thirty-six hours. Bold is making good distance and hardly feels our weight. Try some food.'

She tried to get him to take some dried fruit but most of it came straight back. He coughed long and hard and his young, muscular body racked with spasms as his lungs could not get enough good air into them. Marggitte panicked as Shell's face turned blue as he retched, trying to take in air.

Isthmus entered Shel's body and worked the diaphragm and ribcage, massaging the lungs until he started to breathe a little more normally. He then appeared to Marggitte.

'He needs a healer and quickly. For some reason he is much sicker than we imagined. He undoubtedly has picked up an illness but it seems that the guilt he has taken on himself for the events in Ontrades has turned an ordinary sickness into some black wretchedness. It lies heavy on his lungs, forcing the breath out of his body. You must get back on your steed and do not stop until you reach Seathon. I will go back into him and help his breathing.'

Picking Shel up, she remounted and soon they were galloping off into the East as the watery sun rose and beckoned them onward.

The sun climbed above them, throwing their shadow back, trailing like some dark spirit forever trying to catch its owner. The black shadow eventually caught them up and then undertook them before taking the lead as the miles thundered under the heavy, ironclad hooves of Bold.

During the afternoon they sped past a tribe of Sand-people. Marggitte knew of their reputation but was not about to slow up to find out if it were true. She was never frightened; her fear was all being channelled into the spasming body she carried in one large, muscular arm as she urged on the neck of Bold with the other. If she had known that the Nomadic tribe far enough away to her left had captured an old woman whom she knew only too well, and was contemplating eating her that night, then what would her decision have been? What if she had known that the leader of the tribe, Qwant, had bundled up in rags a certain sword by the name of Northstar?

Northstar was keeping Joice alive.

Marggitte paid them no heed and kept Bold galloping forward. As night approached for the second time, Margg had stopped only three times in more than twenty-four hours, and that had been to get some fluids into Shel.

Imagine if she got him to the healer, only to find he was

going to die from lack of water. She was now getting weary and she knew that she would have to stop, if only for a couple of hours. If she did not then she might topple from the horse with Shel in her arms, and that would be the end of both of them.

The night air was getting increasingly cold in accordance with the moving of the seasons. Marggitte quickly set up a tent for them to lie in and then held Sheldrak in her arms as she shut her eyes. Her training with the Inners had included powers of meditation and she moved off into a part of her mind where she could achieve rest while at the same time keeping her senses alert enough to register the presence of danger. Sheldrak's body was far hotter than it should have been and his heat was unsettling for Margg, but she set her internal body clock and two hours later opened her eyes, refreshed enough to ride on.

The sun rose on them for the second time and with the daylight came new hope. In the distance, reflecting the newborn rays of light, was the vast expanse of the river Landsplitter. Marggitte knew she had made better time than she had hoped and patted the neck of Bold gratefully. He whinnied in appreciation, as if knowing the importance of speed to the hot bundle lying in the arms of his new master.

Seathon was not a city such as Ontrades. It was smaller and spread itself thinly along the banks of the river. The houses were mostly wooden, made from the thick water reed that was to be found at every turn. The reeds were thick as a giant's forearm, easily available, and provided the necessary height to keep the houses high off the ground, to combat the numerous instances of flooding. Away from the piers and wharfs at the edge of the great river, the dwellings became more traditional in height, but were still made of the thick bamboo-like material.

The people of Seathon were peaceful and had never got involved in the trade disputes that Ontrades defended so forcefully. The atmosphere was far from the military one experienced in the 'city of rock' as the Seathoners called Ontrades. It was even known that Morgs would come to Seathon and, although they tended to drive a hard trade, would nevertheless do so with little violence.

There were many small wooden fishing boats dotted along the river, as one of the main trades of Seathon was the buying and selling of seafood. Other boats were used for pleasure trips. A small trade exchanged for an afternoon spent lounging on a boat while someone else did the work seemed a fair deal to the diplomatic people of Seathon. Many other vessels were for leisure only; canoes, kayaks, small, brightly coloured sailing dinghies and one or two very old antiques with rusted-up propellers utilised the rest of the docking berths.

After another hour of relentless riding, Marggitte arrived at the closest dwelling to her, and the furthest from the river. No guards were needed for entrance to this community, just normal sentries policing the port for trouble, as in any large township. Leaving Shel lying on Bold with Isthmus to ensure he didn't roll off the horse, she banged heavily on the door of the reed cottage. After what seemed to Margg the lifetime of a small woodland creature, a very old man came to the door. Observing the strange white mask of his visitor, he whimpered, 'By my elders, can I help you?'

Margg forgot all about her etiquette and said, 'I need a healer, a good one. There is a man on my horse who has a fever that is stealing his breath away. Who is this port's most skilful practitioner?'

The old man, whose seven strands of grey hair were whipping in several directions at once, giving him the look of someone who had some tricity in him, realised that the strangely masked woman meant him no harm. He said, 'Well, there is some debate about who is the best. There are two schools of thought depending on whether you want the traditional leech-in-a-bottle approach or this newfangled business with herbs and flowers and "healing through the mind", which personally I think that if Faith had intend—'

'For Faith's sake, sir, I have no time for the debate. Which is closest?'

'Oh, sorry, yes. Dee's boy Kurn is closest. Newfangled he is, and as strange as an Ontradean fisherman. Look for pier seventeen. Go directly east to the river then head north alongside until pier seventeen. Only one hut there, tallest in the port. Can't miss it. Now his mother, Dee, is a strange one, traveller she was, been all over, as far as Mina, some say. Well, this boy of hers...'

The old man was stood alone, muttering to himself, and felt the rush of wind as Bold swept by. Marggitte shouted from the back of Bold, 'By my elders, and thank you,' as she raced for the river and pier seventeen.

A middle-aged woman opened the door, her long black hair streaked in places with flashes of grey. Her face was care-worn but friendly, with deep laughter lines and dimples at the corners of her mouth. She was plain but her smile, coupled with the clearest of grey eyes, more than compensated for plain, and here was a woman who had had no problems in finding a partner.

She took in the tall, striking woman in front of her and if she was concerned at the sight of the white mask she never let it show. A mask in return for a mask. She looked down upon the bundle, which moaned and introduced itself as something alive, well, hopefully alive. Marggitte was nearing the end of her capacity after carrying Shel up the eight flights of stairs, some which had groaned disturbingly under their combined weight.

This time she remembered her manners. 'By my elders. I have ridden over 100 miles to get here. You must be Dee, mother of the healer, Kurn. Please say your son is in and able to see the sick man I carry in my arms. His name is Sheldrak, son of Whinst, and he is from the faraway village in the South, called Jost. My name is Marggitte and until recently I was a member of the Inner Guard from the city of Ontrades.

'Now, for Faith's sake, let me in and see if we can keep this boy alive.'

Dee, taken a little aback by the outburst from Marggitte, stood back and let her enter their abode, keeping her composure. Here is a woman not easily rattled, thought Marggitte as she took Shel across to a cot on the far side of the room and laid him down.

Dee said, 'I will go and get Kurn. He is collecting plants from the water's edge a little further down the river. Do not worry, I will not be long.'

Dee threw a shawl around her shoulders and ran down the stairs that Marggitte had just come up. True to her word she returned within ten minutes, entering the room behind a tall, gangly youth. Kurn was twenty years old but looked younger. He was painfully thin and his elbows jutted out at right angles from his body, giving him the look of a tall wading bird strutting into the marshes. Across his back he had a huge bag, stuffed to the top with greenery, leaves and tops of flowers. If Kurn had been able to see behind the mask, the mask that hid all emotion, he would have seen a frown cross the face of Marggitte, as she was about to entrust the life of her friend to someone who looked the same age as the patient.

The youthful Kurn read her mind. 'I know what you think but you need not worry. I have been lucky with my parents. I inherited my mother's grace and charm and my father's ability to read nature the way you can read the movements of a warrior in battle. I see from your armour that you are a great warrior, but my mother has already told me that you were a member of the Inners and so as well as your fighting ability you must have great wisdom. Let me see your friend and I will help.'

Marggitte stood to one side, away from her position as mother hen at the side of her nest and Kurn sat on the cot and then lay with his head on the chest of Sheldrak. Shel's chest eased in and out but the bellows pumping within wheezed as though they had sprung a leak.

'How long has his breathing been so difficult?'

'About three days, two for certainty, but I guess he hid it from us for the rest of the time. Can you help him?'

'You have brought him to me not a moment too soon. He has the blackness on his lungs. With rest and my help we can have him well again, though I think it will be many days before he runs for the last boat.

'Keep him warm and give him fluids, as much as he will take. I have to make something for him.'

Kurn went down the stairs revealed by the trapdoor, into the darkness below, and for ten minutes the noise of his industry filtered up into the sunlit room above. Shel continued to struggle with his illness. Kurn came back up, his thin body entering the room via the stairs, looking like a baby giraffe popping its head out of the tall grass. In his hands he carried a large, brown, shallow bowl in which lay a thick greeny-black paste.

'Take his tunic off, please, oh, and by the way, I'm Kurn. By my elders.'

Struggling to pull Shel's tunic over his head Marggitte replied, 'Sorry, excuse my manners. By my elders. I can't get—'

Dee stepped in before Marggitte finished her sentence and, smiling, held Shel upright while Marggitte tugged the tunic off. Kurn sat by Shel's side and applied the thick goo in deep swathes across the pale, exposed chest. Like a child with a colouring book, Kurn filled Shel in until no white could be seen.

'That's fine, but we need to help on the inside also. Mother, make some thin stew, not too many solids in it, and apply this herb. One spoon for every bowl we hope to get inside him. With any Faith, it should break the blackness into smaller chunks. In a couple of days we will give him something else which, unpleasantly, will cause him to bring those smaller chunks to the surface.

'Marggitte, will you be able to nurse our patient?'

'Yes, of course, but I have also left our other travelling companions in the desert. If they do not arrive then I have, by my honour…' She trembled as she spoke this word and mother and son exchanged a knowing look, '…promised to return to bring them to Seathon.'

Dee questioned, 'And you live by your honour even if you cannot look after your friend?'

Marggitte took a deep breath and replied, 'An Inner will live and die for her honour.'

Kurn, sensing the change in atmosphere his mother's tone of enquiry had brought to the room, moved the conversation on. 'Mother, it matters not, Menth will look after the patient when you and I are busy. She is always asking me to teach her the ways of healing, so she can start by looking after Sheldrak.'

'And Menth is?'

'Menth is my betrothed and the other love of my life, apart from nature and healing. Not forgetting Mother.'

No, thought Marggitte uncharitably, you wouldn't be allowed to forget Mother. She admonished herself straight away. By my Faith, I have only just walked into their home with a sick stranger and I am thinking badly of them. Under her mask she turned red in embarrassment.

Dee said, 'I hope you are right, Kurn. She is betrothed in your eyes but not yet in her own. Just Mother being protective I suppose.'

'Do not worry, Mother, Menth will do a wonderful job

if Marggitte needs to go and find her other friends.' He turned to Marggitte. 'But in the meantime, please sit and eat with us and tell something of your tale, including why you are here. We will understand if you cannot tell us all, for these are dangerous times with the Morgs declaring war once more.'

Marggitte said, 'I will tell you some of my tale and you must trust me to tell only that which will not put you into danger. I represent an example of the strange times we are in, for you must realise that this is the first occasion ever that an Inner has been allowed to leave Ontrades.'

Isthmus, listening to all this from within the improving Shel, thought, it seems we have found six, but I'm still not sure about seven.

Later that day Menth joined them for their evening meal and was introduced to Marggitte. Margg told them that they were a band of travellers looking for people to join them on a quest to find the lost sword of Strepsay, the Sword of Destiny, the sword known as Northstar. What she didn't tell them was that they had found the sword once already and had lost it to an old woman by the name of Joice – an old woman who was not looking forward to her next meal because she was the next meal.

Menth was a charming young woman, delightful to look at and equally delightful in manner. Marggitte noted the way Kurn never took his eyes off her throughout the meal, but also noted, the way only a woman can that, while Menth clearly thought a lot of Kurn, the adoration shown her wasn't exactly reciprocated.

Menth was a very confident young woman who knew how she looked but was not arrogant; in fact, she was a little humble. It was a trait of the Seathon people, who rarely left their birthplace and thus retained an air of innocence and humility.

The attractive young woman continually glanced at the white mask adorning Marggitte, obviously intrigued but too polite to comment. Finally Marggitte put her out of her misery.

'I know you all wish to know more about me and why I wear this protection.'

Dee answered, 'We would be speaking a falsehood if we said that we were not interested in your strange attire, but only speak if you feel comfortable enough with us. We are still strangers who have known each other a matter of hours.'

'I use the word "protection", but not as you think. It is simple. I have recently lost a loved one – my only reason, or so I thought, for living. The protection is for the rest of the world so that they do not see the grief that is written into every line of my face. It is a sadness that I must bear alone. You need not know any more.'

Menth, who had met Marggitte only an hour or two earlier, arose, went to Margg and placed her arms around her in a hug of friendship, saying, 'By my elders. Your inner beauty shines through your mask, destroying your grief minute by minute. One day I hope to be able to look upon you to see gladness in those sad eyes.'

Marggitte was totally taken aback. No one but Hemm had ever shown such concern for her. This woman was either very manipulative or caring beyond her young years. Marggitte, with tears in her eyes, was prepared to give her the benefit of the doubt.

Kurn broke the moment by saying, 'Come, we have finished our food, let us tend to the patient.'

He led Menth away by the hand, over to where Shel lay. His breathing was gentle now, and the healing of Kurn was working. Shel was not clear of the shadow yet, but the sun was moving back into his life with every passing hour. Marggitte watched the two lovers, comfortable with each other's company, as Menth learnt from Kurn how to apply the chest rub and how to feed and water an unconscious patient.

Dee turned to Marggitte and said, 'Let us step outside and leave them with some time and space.'

Once outside on the porch they could look from their vantage point over the whole of the community on one side. On the other, the quarter moon shone brightly out of the water of the Landsplitter, as well as above them from the starry cold night.

Dee shivered. 'I have seen you observe them. My son is totally head over heels in love, the only way a young man can be. They have known each other since the age of five, when they first went to lessons together. At the age of fifteen they made the promise of Strepsay to be as one for ever. Now, at the age of twenty, only one of them is still sure of their actions five years earlier. She would break his heart if she changed her mind now.'

A dark flying creature of the night passed in front of the moon, casting a shadow over part of Dee's face so she looked like a negative of Marggitte in her mask. She continued, 'But he is all I have since his father came and went. Came and went all inside one evening when I was only seventeen. Charmed me? Put me in a trance, more like. I remember nothing of the evening, and then, nine months later, Kurn. He is all I live for, you see. You understand from under that mask – you loved for only one person. My love is the same. No harm will come to Kurn.'

Marggitte replied. 'I have known them for a short while but I can understand your worry. But you know you cannot make her love him if she does not.' Dee looked aghast so Margg added, 'But I am sure that she does.' Marggitte remembered what Isthmus had said about six and seven and thought, I must ask Isthmus which of these three are our two companions, because I cannot see Dee letting go of her son without a struggle, especially if he cannot be with Menth. Come on, Shel, get out of this trance, we need your guidance. I may soon have to go and look for Gregorn and Shade, wherever they are.

Marggitte spoke once more to the troubled Dee. 'I must find a room for the night as I have slept for only two hours in the last seventy-two. Can you propose an inn?'

Dee snapped out of her self-concern. 'You will do no such thing. If I cannot find a room for the night for a weary friend then there is indeed trouble in the lands. Please, come, we have many spare rooms in this dwelling of ours. Kurn has turned our home into something of a shelter for the sick so we have many cots for you to choose from.'

Dee led the way back into the room where Shel lay and walked in on a passionate embrace between Kurn and Menth.

'Sorry,' said Dee, 'we are just passing through.' Dee gave Margg a reassuring look of approval as they went down the stairs into the depths of the lower rooms to find suitable sleeping quarters for the tired Inner.

Outside, tethered with the other livestock, Bold gave a small whinny of fear as another shadow passed over the sliver of moon.

Sandpeople

At the same time as Margg was sitting down for her evening meal with Dee, Kurn and Menth, Gregorn and Shade, leading Randeed, were setting up camp for the night.

'OK, buddy, you take the dried fruit and stale bread while I go and try to hustle us up a snake or two or even a tasty lizard. I'm that hungry, even old Randeed is looking appetising. Then again I'm a lupine, so he should do. In fact, Greggy, even you are looking a little burger-shaped, and with your size I'd say a king-sized Whoppa.'

'Shade, please go and find your meal. The more stressed and hungry you are, the greater the difficulty I have in making any sense of what you speak.'

'I'm going, don't lose your knickers.'

With no way of making any fire, Gregorn had been forced to eat dried products, eggs preciously carried in his own bag and raw vegetables. He was as lean, fit and strong as at any time in his life. Strength had never been a problem for him but giants do like their food, and his belly was being eaten away from the inside with hunger. As well as the continuous walking, he was eating far less than a giant his size needed, so the days to Seathon were counted down with relish.

Shade came back after hunting down his meal, blood sticking to the sides of his jowls. Gregorn had come to accept the man/wolf's ways. However, after having held reasonably civilised conversations with him all day, it was unworldly to watch him rip the head off a small animal, splashing blood as though it were gravy from a joint of well-cooked meat.

Gregorn lay on his back, looking up at the stars surrounding the quarter moon like ranchers about to round up a wild horse. Gregorn spoke in his deep, rumbling voice that echoed through his chest as he lay on his back.

'My people believe that when we die, a new star is raised in the heavens. The star remains up there for aeons, the time spent waiting proportionate to the integrity of the life you led when alive. Eventually the light will fade, dimming slowly over years until one night you will look up there and a star from the night before will be gone. The star represents the soul and will have passed on into a land where you will live for ever, never wanting for anything, reacquainted with your ancestors.

'Sometimes if you have wrongs to right and unfinished business you can come back to the lands. Some say you come back as a different creature but once you have put to rest the matter, you return. We call this place in the heavens Tremain. The same name as the lost city of Tremain in our world, taken by evil many years ago. Essdark is rumoured to reside there today. If Shel is successful we will all see this lost city and I can die in peace.'

Shade looked over at his gentle friend, for once ignoring the chance to make fun of him. Eventually he said, 'Perhaps that's what I am, an ex-giant come back to avenge the bloody bus driver who ran over my head.'

'No, Shade, you could never have been a giant. You are too reckless. Also, a giant is far more certain of himself than you are. Without food, you start to run around in circles trying to answer your "bloody phones".'

'So do you think this Tremain is the same place or a different one, or nothing to do with your heaven where you go when your star loses its twinkle? I just thought that was middle age myself, but I have plenty twinkle left in my star yet, I hope. Wouldn't mind meeting a lady lupine, actually.'

Gregorn continued. 'Thousands of years ago when the

lands had different shapes and the Landsplitter was but a stream and the Bluetop Mountains were small hills, my people, the giants, ruled all. The king of the giants, a vain male called Travest, thought that he was a god and wanted to build a land fit for his deity. Of course, he was quite mad. He ruled with fear and built the most beautiful castle the world had ever seen with hundreds of turrets, a moat of the most superb wine obtainable – jewels encrusted every wall, the finest paintings adorned every room and the library was the biggest and best across all the lands.

'He called it Tremain after the home of the gods. If it exists, because it is only Faith that keeps it alive in the minds of giants, then I will be the only giant to have seen it for centuries.'

'And if it doesn't?'

'Then at least I will have died fighting for good over evil. Better to have believed than to submit.'

'Bugger me, mate, this is getting a little too deep for me. But whatever happened to Travis?'

'Travest died. Stood on the highest turret in his castle, trying to reach up to the gods. He fell upon the jewelled walls he himself had instructed to be built. His last words were, "If I have upset the gods, so then my star will glow for ever. The star that remains in the sky the longest will be mine and the heavenly Tremain will never glitter under my gaze."

'He then threw himself from the turret, killing himself instantly. And if you look at that star there,' Gregorn pointed at the brightest and northernmost star in the sky, 'you will see his star is indeed the brightest in the night sky.'

'Nice story, mate, but I've got a better one. If you sit up and look directly in front of you, you will see a series of twinkling little stars, but if you look closer you will see they belong to some funny little things with Kojak haircuts. By the way, they also seem to have more than the average number of teeth. Get your sword, mate, I think you are going to need it.'

The Sandpeople had heard the deep baritone of Gregorn rolling around the desert air like a bass drum in a village hall and Qwant had gathered thirty males together to capture their next meal. They were dressed in thin, off-white robes that stretched from below their hairless chins down to their sandaled feet, tied in the middle with cord. Their dark, cherubic faces contrasted with the light, airy clothes designed to keep them cool during the day but warm them in the night air.

They circled themselves around the talking friends and awaited the signal from Qwant to attack. They carried no weapons; Sandpeople were born with them.

Shade repeated his warning to Gregorn, 'Don't want to worry you, mate, but there are quite a few sets of those beady eyes behind us as well as in front.'

Randeed, Shel's furze, whinnied away to their left. A dull thud followed, then a high-pitched screeching noise like a young puppy being dragged from its mother's milk.

'What in God's name was that?' questioned Shade.

'That is the unfortunate method of speech used by Sandpeople. Unfortunate for two reasons. One, we have to listen to the screeching and two, this means we are surrounded by them, and they are not noted for their generosity to strangers.'

'What do you mean, Greg? Tell me. Stop speaking in riddles.'

'From my knowledge they will try to kill us and eat us. If we are really unlucky they will catch us alive and we will die over a matter of days after being used as a live food store with, every day, a chunk or piece of us being chopped off.'

Shade grimaced. 'Enough said, we fight.'

The two of them stood, Gregorn with his sword raised, waiting, while Shade raised his hackles, drew back his black lips and growled deep in his throat. The sound was like an idling engine waiting for the accelerator to be pumped. Finally, Sandpeople edged close enough for Greg's night vision to spot their small bodies, which Shade's lupine sight had been watching for some time.

Gregorn spoke, 'I will turn my back to you, my good friend, and will defend it with my life.'

'Don't worry, Greg, these little Donald Pleasences won't get near to you.'

'By my elders,' they said in unison and the Sandpeople attacked, screaming in the manner of American Indians in a fifties B-movie.

Gregorn's sword flashed and a head rolled back quicker than the advancing Sandperson but three more hit Gregorn in unison, knocking him off balance. Shade had his own problems.

Much closer in height to his foes than Gregorn, Shade snapped his jaws, ripping dry skin as thick blood hit the sand. It congealed into a mud patch that no child would ever want to play in. As his teeth ripped so did those of the Sandpeople, one landing straight on Shade's back, trying to keep a hold on the fur while digging sharp teeth into the skin at the back of Shade's neck. His thick fur kept the teeth out and Shade rolled quickly, trying to dislodge the rider at the world's weirdest rodeo. No luck, the thing clung on.

Behind him, Greg brought the butt of his sword down heavily on to the head of the nearest Sandman. The head split, cracking like a child's Easter egg and in the light of the quarter moon the blood ran like chocolate down the broken skull. His scream pierced the air. Teeth bit into Greg's arm, then his leg, and he dropped his shield. Crying out, he shouted at Shade, 'I'm losing, you must run. Save yourself.'

Shade replied, 'Never. Together or not at all.'

Shade was still pitching and jumping to move the creature on his back but to no avail. Greg roared and renewed his efforts, using brute strength to throw the much smaller fighters off him. Metal cut into flesh again and more Sandmen died, screeching. Greg spun around, proving his mastery of the sword by taking one swing and cutting both hands clean off the thing on Shade's back. The hands clutched on to the fur like two extra limbs growing out of Shade's neck.

'Christ Almighty, Gregorn, that was close. You gave me a haircut with that swing.'

'Fight. Then on my shout we run in the direction you face, towards Seathon.'

Greg's foes had stepped away for a moment to regroup, chattering animatedly like children squabbling over the rules of the game. The rule they didn't like was the one where the bloody big giant swung his sword and chopped your head off. To quote millions over centuries in many different worlds, 'That's not fair.'

Shade continued to snap and snarl. As he took a bite, his enemy took a bite. His fur was matting with blood but for him the wounds were superficial because of the protection favoured him by his shaggy coat.

Greg took the lull in the fighting as his opportunity. 'Run, Shade, run with all you have left.'

They both charged at the remaining Sandpeople, scattering them with their greater size and unity, picking up speed until they were both sprinting away from the clotted, blood-soaked sand behind them.

They only saw the thin grey nets as they folded around their rushing bodies, their momentum perfect for the trap that had been set. Within seconds of becoming entangled they had both taken heavy blows to their heads. The last things they heard were the triumphant spiralling screeches of their captors as darkness took them.

Menth

Five days had passed since Marggitte had reached the home of her new-found friends in Seathon, but Sheldrak had yet to come out of his deep sleep, apart from on one or two occasions when he momentarily spoke in his dreams or shouted someone's name. Marggitte had been reduced to tears when she heard the name of her dead husband called out in the still of the night.

Marggitte chose to take the nightshift, while during the day it was Menth who continually applied the rub and kept a constant stream of water and medicinal draught flowing down the sandpaper that Shel's raw throat had become. Kurn was confident that Shel was past the worst but it was important that he continued to rest, to fight off any relapse that the fever may have in store, should Sheldrak decide he was over the finish line.

Menth sat by the cot with Shel's thin body lying on the covers. Marggitte was asleep in her new room; Dee and Kurn had gone into the trade area of the port for resources.

'By my elders, where am I?'

The childlike voice that came from the cot framed the first words spoken coherently by Sheldrak for seven days. Inside Shel's head, Isthmus gave a little cheer.

Menth answered. 'You are in the river port of Seathon, in the house of Dee, mother of Kurn, the healer who has kept you alive this past five days and apparently got you back to some semblance of health. My name is Menth and I have nursed you, along with your good friend Marggitte, since you arrived.'

Shel lifted his head to look around but not for very long,

as even this small movement was still too much effort. His body needed to recuperate.

'My Faith, I don't have the strength to sit up. Where are my friends?'

'I will go and awaken Marggitte and she will tell her tale.'

Not a moment later Marggitte was sat on the edge of the cot and, in an unusual show of emotion, harder to see for the lack of facial expression, she hugged Shel to her ample bosom and gave thanks to Faith.

'Oh, am I glad to see you back. I have recently feared the worst. First Hemm and then you. Also, when I went this morning to meet Gregorn and Shade they were not where we said we would meet. If they are not there tomorrow then I have vowed to go back into the flatlands to find them.

'But some good news – Shel is back with us.'

As she said this, a little involuntary gasp spilled from her mouth like the last gust of wind from a storm that had blown itself out. She stood, turned and walked to the outside door, but it was plain to see from the shaking of her shoulders that her relief was expressing itself physically.

Menth said to Shel, 'OK, patient, I'll get some food made for you while you talk with your friend. You are welcome in the house of Dee for as long as you like, but by Marggitte's story I fear you will want to be on the move as soon as you can.'

Shel lay back again as Margg came back to him and spoke of the others and what had happened since he had taken ill. As it was she knew little of Gregorn and Shade or where they were. If she had known, she would now be riding Bold into the flatlands to try to prevent their impending doom.

Dee and Kurn returned and introductions were made. Afterwards the table was set around the bottom of Shel's cot for the main meal of the evening. Dee had traded well and they ate thick fishcakes made at the local market with fresh herbs and roots collected by the fine hand and eye of her son, Kurn. He certainly knew how to use nature to great effect, either for sustenance or, as in the case of Shel, for medicinal purposes.

Shel soon flaked out again and Menth, even though she had been on duty all day, insisted she stayed by his side until she was absolutely sure he was sleeping well and not liable to start wheezing and spluttering as he had been through the night.

Kurn said, 'Will you come for a walk with me when you have finished, my love?'

'Of course,' replied the beautiful Menth, 'as soon as Shel settles.'

Four hours later, when the rest of the house was silent with sleep, Kurn had to waken the sleeping Menth, who had fallen asleep with her head resting on the edge of Shel's cot.

'Come,' he said gently, 'I will walk you home.'

They spoke little that night and Kurn received a perfunctory kiss, one that would not have seemed out of place coming from his own mother. Dee watched, hidden from them both in the undergrowth, before dashing away to get home before Kurn got back.

The next morning Marggitte left for the inn next to the biggest place of worship in the port. She returned an hour later, alone. Sheldrak was awake, and sat up when she arrived back and motioned for her to come and sit next to him. Menth fussed in the background, literally attending to Shel's every need.

'By Faith, Shel, they are not there again and now I truly fear for them. At Gregorn's great pace they should really have arrived yester eve, but even allowing for Shade getting in and out of a couple of scrapes they would undoubtedly have got here today. I must find them.'

Shel said, 'Did you make that agreement?'

'Exactly that. If they did not arrive by today then, by my honour, I told them I would search to my death.'

'Good Faith, what have I got us all into? '

'Shel, you must stop blaming yourself for everything that happens to us all. We know the dangers and accept them as part of the quest. If we are to throw down the Grey One then we know the perils of the journey.'

'Margg, you must go at once. Take Bold and ride. As soon as I am well again I will follow you back into the flatlands.'

'That would be pointless. I can get back to where I left the others in three days, but they must have made ground since then, and I can track. Part of my training as an Inner was to be able to track across the plains, flatlands and forests of our lands. No, if I am not back in ten days then you must go on. Speak to Isthmus, for even without me you have four of the Seven here with you now.

'By my elders, I will be gone. May we meet again, for my love and honour grow for you by the day.'

She left before Shel could speak another word and he heard the thunder of Bold's hooves carry her away into the territory of the Sandpeople.

Later that same day, Shel got out of bed and walked for the first time in well over a week. He looked like old Methon, his tutor, after a particular rambunctious night at the Jolly Farmer back in Jost, the right leg not quite sure the left one knew the way it was going. He held on to the table in the middle of the room, with Menth as his support on the other side.

'Do you think you could get me on to the balcony? It would be wonderful to feel fresh air on my face, even if it is turning cold.'

Menth obliged, chiding Shel that this was not to be for long otherwise Kurn and, especially, Dee would take her to task. The blackness on his chest was still surfacing with the barks that Shel continued to produce. Recently infected lungs did not welcome the cold, pre-winter air.

Shel sat himself down in a low wicker chair, which also supported his legs. Menth went inside to bring out extra throw rugs and a chair so she could sit by the side of Sheldrak to keep him company.

'So,' said Shel, 'tell me about yourself.'

Menth, unusually, turned the colour of spring blossom at the thought of talking about herself to this relative stranger. She had sat by his side for five nights but yet knew so very little about him, apart from what she saw.

'Well, what do you want to know? Life is not very exciting in this port of ours. People come and go and we see all kinds from all races, but it's not the place that people settle in. I'll bet that nine out of ten who live here were born here. It's a quiet, gentle township with very little trouble and not much to set the pulse racing.'

'Well, you've told me about Seathon, but what about you? What sets your pulse racing?'

The cherry blossom of earlier quickly went through the seasons and turned into the deep red of autumn.

'By my Faith, Sheldrak, you put a girl on the spot. What indeed makes my pulse race? Well, I'll tell you.'

The young woman took a deep breath and the pressure put upon the buttons of the blue silk blouson she was wearing did not go unnoticed by Shel, still sickening or not.

'Awaking to a summer's morn and opening the shutters to watch the sun rise over a green meadow.

'Biting into the first red apple of the harvest.

'Sailing across the river in a fast, open boat that cuts through the water and sends the spray over you as the wind streams through your hair.

'Diving into the fresh, clear waters of the Landsplitter and feeling the breath sucked out of you by the cold of the waters on your body.

'Riding my uncle's horse, Rowan, through the copse at the back of his farm.

'At the festival of Faith, exchanging presents with my friends, especially finding that special something for someone and seeing their face light up when they open it.

'A stolen kiss, the first kiss and, of course, first love.'

Shel laughed.

'My Faith, you know exactly what makes your pulse race, and are these things you have experienced or wish to experience?'

Isthmus whispered inside Shel's thoughts, 'I think you will find, Sheldrak, that it is your pulse that quickens.'

'Some I have experienced and some I will do one day. Information that is for my knowledge and for your education. But what I ache for is adventure. I would love to be like you. I am four years senior and have never left my birth town. You are travelling the lands and having battles and seeing cities like Ontrades, meeting giants and emperors, while I sit in Seathon with nothing but a promised marriage to Kurn to look forward to.'

'And nearly not even seeing my seventeenth birthday. Don't forget, when I turned up here I was carried. But for my friends, I would now be the fodder of some scavenging animal in the flatlands.'

'Please take me with you, Sheldrak, as one of your company. I cannot fight but I have been raised on a farm and can hunt and use a bow better than anyone I know. I swim like all the Seathoners – not like a fish, better. I ride, sail, cook, shoot.'

Sheldrak became serious. 'You are a grown woman and will not need me to tell you the dangers on a journey such as the one I have undertaken with my friends, but let me tell you a little more before you make a rash decision.'

Shel then told of Divad and Methon, the Great Race, and how Isthmus came to his aid to carry him over the line.

Menth giggled as Shel told of meeting Shade and gasped at the tale in Ontrades and of Hemm, Marggitte and, of course, Joice.

Menth shed tears for Marggitte's sorrow and Shel swore her to secrecy until Margg was ready to tell the story herself.

He continued with the loss of Northstar and the journey, what he remembered of it, to Seathon. When he was finished they both looked around, to realise they were sat in the dark, only able to see each other's teeth in the dusk, flashing like rows of firebugs standing to attention.

'Please help me back inside now, for it grows cold and my chest starts to pain me.'

Once more the two struggled back across the main room of the wooden house before Shel flopped on to his cot. The way they staggered across the room, one imagined them both in seventy years and how they would go out for an afternoon stroll, arm in arm with only each other for support.

Menth tucked the covers in around Shel and asked, 'Would you like your chest rubbed with ointment before I start the evening meal for Dee and Kurn?'

It's just as well that Shade isn't here because he would surely have some ready quip for that question, thought Shel.

'Yes, please, if it's not too much trouble.'

Menth got the thick rub on her hands and gently massaged the ointment into the muscular chest of Shel and down to the taut stomach muscles. She looked up at Shel but his eyes were closed.

The door opened and Kurn walked in.

'By my elders, it is getting closer to the Faith festival with every turn of the sun. Good evening, Menth, and how is the patient?'

Menth jumped from the bed as though a mild shock had passed through her arms and she thrust them out at her husband-to-be, covered as they were in black goo.

It didn't stop Kurn from hugging her and planting a deep kiss on her red lips.

Across the room, Shel looked on from heavily hooded eyes and a sharp pain shot across his chest. The rub would ease most pains, but not this one.

It took Sheldrak another week to fully recover his health. Most of it was spent in the company of Menth, as Kurn had a small healing practice in the centre of town, and his mother, Dee, was his nurse and administrator. Kurn was oblivious to the chance that he might be losing his loved one to another, but Dee was not. In fact, she had been dreading the day it would happen since Kurn had been a young boy. A mother knew these things, especially a mother who had connections, connections that gave her eyes a distance of sight far beyond normal vision.

Kurn trusted Menth completely; his love for her blinded him to the possibility that she might not feel the same for him.

Shel and Menth had nothing to be ashamed of, but both felt pangs of pleasure intermingled with the pain of guilt. They were both innocent, two young people becoming friends, but everything they did was in the shadow of Kurn. Shel knew that Kurn and Menth were the final pieces to the human jigsaw that had become his life, the two final members of the Seven. He was concerned that his relationship with them both would break the group beyond repair.

Isthmus kept in the background and only spoke to Shel when he was alone, which wasn't very often. His counsel was guarded, as he knew the danger of telling a young man of the pitfalls of falling in love with someone's betrothed.

Sheldrak and Menth were falling in love and Kurn watched on innocently, encouraging them to spend more time together, as 'It would be good for Shel's recovery to get out as much as possible.'

It was the seventh day after Marggitte had left the port in her search for Gregorn and Shade, and Shel, the leader of the quest, had hardly given them a second thought. The patient and his nurse were out on the boat that they had hired from the old hermit who lived on pier twelve. Menth had not been misleading anyone when she had said she could sail and she moved about the listing small sailboat with all the ease of a dancer on a stage.

'My Faith, you're a natural in a boat. Who taught you?' queried Shel.

'My uncle, of course, the man who has taught me everything in life.'

Menth tied the mainsail off and came and squashed her warm body in next to Shel so she could speak to him without shouting over the rush and swell of the Landsplitter.

'My parents both died when I was very young. My mother, who had never learnt to swim, was swept overboard when my father took the boat out to fish and a storm swept in off the distant mountains. Father tried to save Mother and at the age of four I was an orphan. My father's brother, Defhert, brought me up, as his own wife could not have children. I vowed I would learn to swim, fish, and of course sail, so that the river would never take me as it had my parents.

'It was my uncle who also taught me to ride and hunt. I wanted my independence. Luckily for me, my uncle also wanted me to have it.

'I met Kurn on my first day at lessons. He has been my best friend ever since.'

'But have you been his lover?' shot back Sheldrak.

'No, although it has not been through Kurn's lack of trying. Everyone has always expected us to be wed one day. I don't believe I have ever been asked, it has simply been assumed by everyone, including Kurn.'

Shel took a deep breath.

'And is it the assumption that you do not like, or the betrothal itself?'

'I love Kurn very much and, for someone who would like to spend the rest of their days in Seathon, he will make a wonderful husband – but I want more.'

Shel was torn: love or bravery? He would be the bravest man alive, to walk away from someone he knew was meant for him. At this moment he could have told Menth that he knew Kurn was destined to leave Seathon with him, as was Menth herself, but he didn't. He kept it to himself and, with that choice, cost Menth everything.

He turned to her and pulled her mouth to him, kissing tenderly, softly at first but then becoming enraged with passion. As he pulled her into him, Menth felt the hardness of his love and gave a small involuntary gasp. She had certainly found someone who made her pulse race.

Shel pulled away and said, 'Let's take the boat in and go back to the house.'

Twenty minutes later they lay naked on Shel's cot and, if his breathing had felt laboured with his illness, it was nothing compared with the shortness of breath he now experienced. He cupped the full breasts of Menth, urgently kissing them, feeling her body move into his, fitting perfectly. Shel entered a woman for the first time in his young life and, as much as he would have liked it to last a little longer, his youth got ahead of him and he erupted within his lover in seconds.

'Was that OK?'

'It was OK, but I think if we practise a little we can get past ten seconds next time,' laughed Menth.

Shel wasn't overjoyed to hear the comment but if he needed practice, then practice he would have. They fell asleep in each other's arms after a hard training session.

Shel awoke to find himself in his room alone. He was now sleeping downstairs in the room that Marggitte had occupied and heard banging from the room above. He dressed and climbed the staircase to find Dee, Kurn and Menth preparing the meal.

'Hello, sleepyhead,' greeted Kurn. 'You are not as well as you seem to think if you need to spend all afternoon in your cot. Did the fresh air out on the river make you tired?'

'Yes, yes, of course. Fresh air. Tired.' Shel did not seem capable of putting full sentences together and so didn't try. He sat down at the table, thinking of polite conversation but acutely aware that anything he thought to say had a double meaning. Kurn rattled on about his day and whom he had treated, every now and again putting an arm around Menth or planting a little kiss on her cheek.

For Faith's sake, leave her alone, thought Shel, but only smiled weakly. The plates and utensils were laid on the table and they sat down to eat. Shel had his first spoonful raised to his lips when the door crashed open.

Stood framed in the light thrown from the homestead stood the large physique of Marggitte. In her arms she held the limp, lifeless body of Shade.

'By my Faith, help me,' she implored, before crashing to the floor.

Sacrifice or Loyalty?

Marggitte had left Sheldrak on his cot, knowing he was in good hands, jumped on to the back of Bold and sped off into the night, riding back towards the flatlands. Gregorn and Shade had not been at their intended meeting place and she guessed that something was wrong. She only hoped they had got lost and not something worse, but Gregorn was an experienced traveller who could navigate by the stars. No, something must be wrong, and she had promised she would return.

By Faith, she thought, my rear end is getting sore. It's spending too much time in the saddle recently. She afforded herself a grim smile as she patted the neck of Bold, who was proving one of the most useful presents she had ever received. Marggitte had joined this expedition led by Shel for one reason only, revenge. Her heart ached, she was empty, but because of the plain, white mask the exterior world detected little.

Yet she had grown in a short time to love Shel. Not the kind of love that she had held for Hemm – that could never be duplicated – but the kind of love reserved for a son. His goodness was obvious, and he believed in Strepsay and the Faiths more strongly than many elders did. His passion drew people to him, people of many races who grew to love him for his honesty, and his willingness to trust that honesty and to put it before everything else.

If Shel represented good, then Essdark was evil and the Seven would hunt him down.

She rode on through the darkness, not really sure how she was going to find Shade and Gregorn. Where were they and why had they not managed to get to the port? A voice in her head spoke. It was Isthmus.

'By my elders, Marggitte. I cannot tell you where they are but they have moved on from where we left them. Head north now, not west. They no longer have control of their own direction. Be careful, danger lies ahead and it will find you before you find them. Farewell.'

Before Marggitte had time to answer, he was gone and she was once more alone riding through the flatland dunes.

Gregorn and Shade were being bodily dragged behind the last kamer, the preferred mode of transport of the Sand-people. Joice was thrown over the back of the same beast, her breathing so laboured that it was a wonder her lungs could continue to move the hot air in and out.

It was not like the Sandpeople to pass on a fresh meal but at the minute their 'larder' was well stocked with salted meat. It was unwise to consider the origin of the meat, but some was definitely human. Other sources were cattle, kamer, horse and, if Gregorn wasn't mistaken, there were also a couple of Sandpeople in there. The Sandpeople could afford to keep Shade and Gregorn 'fresh'. As for Joice, the Sandpeople thought she was poisoned within or Offwal, so for the moment there was no rush to kill any of their captives.

Shade had kept his mouth firmly shut. The longer the Sandies, as he referred to them, thought he was a normal lupine the better chance of escape. He and Greg were afforded the bare minimum of water, to stop them from hindering the Sandies while also keeping them both alive. The caravan stopped when one of the Sandpeople outriders returned with news for the leader of the nomadic tribe.

Rizzer, the scout, spoke to Qwant. 'Give me ten men and I will bring more meat. It is the one we saw several moons ago. She rides in our direction but I do not think that she has seen us.'

Qwant answered. 'I have a better idea. We will camp just over that rise. Day draws to a close and it is time to eat. I will try a piece of that animal tonight, the wolflike creature. You take five men and make tracks that she cannot miss, then let her ride straight to us. We will set the nets as we did before. More meat for the tough days ahead. It will not be long before we enter the caves and sleep through the cold months. The extra fat will be welcome.'

The two Sandies spoke in front of the captive Shade and Greg, but did not worry about being overheard as their language came out like hyenas yapping at each other and not even the lupine form of Shade could understand their feral screeches.

They stopped and set up the camp as discussed. In Seathon, Shel had been up and about for the third day.

Dinner was served in the most horrendous manner possible, sixty or seventy of the small flesh-eaters whooping and screaming, gathered around a large fire. Chunks of meat were taken from the cache; some thrown on to the fire while some younger Sandpeople ate raw, screaming and gibbering as they did so. They chanted together and walked around the fire in a mad, bastardised version of a bonfire party but, instead of jacket potatoes in the embers, hands, feet, lumps of human flesh and even a head were smouldering in the flames.

Shade whispered to Gregorn, 'Listen mate, whatever happens, we cannot die like this. I am not going to be burned piece by piece and fed to these screaming gibbons. Even I can't find the humour in this situation.'

The two friends were bound totally, from just below their necks to their ankles, with thick pieces of cord. The only part of Gregorn you could see was his huge head sticking out of the top of the ropes. He looked like the biggest caterpillar in the world. Next to them lay Joice, an empty husk. The Sandies didn't waste any food and drink on her and her body lay twitching, no binding necessary as she would never walk again.

Gregorn answered. 'I don't know how, but if one of us gets the chance, we must take it. Sheldrak needs to know that the Sandpeople have the sword. We must not forget why we are here and Northstar is crucial to the quest.'

'With all due respect, me big mucker, the last thing I am thinking of is the bloody sword. Save ourselves – we can fight for the sword on another day,'

Shade quietened down as a Sandperson came over to him and shackled all his paws together. He then applied a gag, tying the muzzle of the lupine so that he could not howl or yelp. He was dragged into the circle of light thrown out by the sparking fire.

Qwant, the leader of this troop of inhuman carnivores, walked over to the quivering hound that was Shade. A squirt of urine shot out of the beleaguered lupine. A whoop went up from the hostile Sandies, who in a few minutes had degenerated thousands of years. Qwant grabbed Shade by his ear. The crowd yapped, louder and louder, screaming, shouting, jabbering.

Next to Gregorn, Joice stirred, closed her eyes and twitched.

The noise from the Sandpeople grew. Shade's eyes widened, the pupils tiny pinpricks in an ocean of white flecked with the orange from the fire.

Qwant dipped his head and with his bare teeth ripped Shade's left ear completely off. The bloody prize was raised into the air like a proud trophy, blood dripping from Qwant's teeth as Shade fell over in a dead faint.

Gregorn's shout of fear and anger could be heard by a group of people stood waiting for a train at Leicester Square Tube station. They looked at each other before scampering for the exit.

It was precisely then that Bold flew over the sandy ridge and all hell broke loose.

Marggitte had been searching for eighteen hours out of every twenty-four, for three days since leaving Seathon. She feared that the Sandpeople had Shade and Gregorn and if so, she might well be chasing ghosts. She shivered. It was almost nightfall and she was exhausted. The past two weeks had been a nightmare; in fact, the past two months had been a nightmare. The young man, Sheldrak, son of Whinst, had certainly changed her life. But at least I still have one, she reminded herself.

The tracks running parallel to her but a hundred yards to her left had gone unnoticed by Marggitte until they veered right and went straight across the line she was taking. She was now in line with a set of tracks that looked to her like four or five kamers, fully loaded, from the depth of the marks.

Marggitte stopped Bold and dismounted. She trailed back, examining the path, and could not come up with any reason why five kamers had veered at right angles across to where Bold stood patiently, before continuing north again. It made no sense. She had to be a little more cautious and, after climbing back on to Bold, she proceeded at a careful trot.

As darkness fell the tracks became increasingly difficult to follow, fading in and out of her vision in the wavering gloom as high clouds passed periodically in front of the silvery half moon. She heard something and then sighted, about a mile away, a large campfire. Even from this distance she could clearly make out the cries and shrieks of Sandpeople preparing a meal.

She picked up the pace, closing the gap very quickly. The fire was just on the northern side of a deep sand ridge, so it disappeared from view as Bold struggled up the southern side. There was to be no refinement about this attack. Bold was going to explode over the top of the ridge and charge into the waiting hordes of Sandpeople.

On the other side of the ridge, six long nets had been set, one behind each other. Shade would have recognised it as the same principle used for jet fighters landing on an aircraft carrier. Each net would slow down anyone entangled in them, net by net, until they were dragged to a halt. On the final ones, Sandpeople were stationed to grab the ropes tied to the nets for extra weight.

Bold came crashing over the top of the ridge, hitting the first net.

'Shhh, don't say a word. Shade is in trouble and we must help him. Here, take my sword, I have a thick spear to fight with.'

The voice was that of Marggitte, whispering into the thankful ear of Gregorn. She knew the tracks had been deliberately laid and had sent Bold over the top without her. It pained her to do so, but it would have pained her more if Greg or Shade had been killed. Using her knife, she quickly cut all the bonds pinning Greg's arms to his body. He stood, flexing, trying to get blood into his numb limbs while the Sandpeople struggled with the bucking horse.

Bold was more intelligent than most horses and, after hitting the first net, had applied the brakes sharply so that he slid into the second but never reached the third. He was kicking and lashing out on all sides as the Sandies tried to get their teeth into him.

By the fire lay the bloody figure of Shade. He was still breathing but Gregorn knew they would have to stop that bleeding quickly if he was to live. He turned to the pale visage of Marggitte and said, 'Let us fight as kindred. We are the Seven and tales will be told for centuries of our deeds. Come, let us make history.'

Gregorn ran down to Shade with a roar of defiance that stopped all. Marggitte was by his side. Their blade and spear flashed in front of the firelight and the night turned red. They were merciless. Gregorn was a renowned warrior among the giants of Arbrain and Marggitte was one of the best-trained guards of the Inners of Ontrades. Never before had they fought with such passion and fervour.

Sandpeople dropped to their knees as arms, legs, heads went missing under the sword of Greg and the spear of Marggitte. By their feet lay the heavily breathing man-wolf called Shade. In the fracas, Bold broke free of his potential captors and sprinted away; not too far, as he would not leave his mistress, but out of immediate danger.

The Sandpeople dropped back to regroup and the fight paused for breath like a wounded animal waiting to gain strength. Marggitte stooped and tended to Shade. The ragged hole in his head had bits of flesh hanging from it and was still bleeding profusely. Marggitte took a thick wooden log from the fire built from the wood carried on the backs of the kamers.

She spoke quietly to Shade but her voice carried, 'Forgive me, my friend, but I do this for your good.'

She thrust the glowing red wood deep into the flesh, sealing the raw wound and stopping the bleeding. Shade howled but then passed out again. The smell of burning meat, burning live meat, drifted in the night air. While Marggitte was on her haunches, the Sandies took their opportunity and she was knocked flat on to her back. Some of them had circled behind and Margg was on the floor without her weapon.

The battle renewed but Marggitte could not get to her feet. The smaller bodies hit her, sending her tumbling, and teeth started to bite. She was now covered in the snarling, screaming bodies and Greg, turning to help, had gone down on his knees as razor-sharp needles of pain ripped off chunks of his leg. Been here before, thought Greg, grabbing a Sandie by his neck and twisting hard. The crack was as final as it was pleasurable.

Marggitte scrambled to her feet as the blade of her short knife stabbed and cut. She was one of the best close-quarter fighters the Inners had ever produced, but she still could not regain her feet. The sheer numbers were too great and her blood loss was reaching alarming proportions, although none of the bites or cuts were yet fatal. They needed a change of fortune.

It was supplied from the most unusual of sources.

The zombie-like walk of the woman that had once been Joice frightened the Sandpeople to a standstill. They pulled away from Margg and Gregorn, gathering in fear around their leader. Qwant gave an order to one of his people and moments later he reappeared with what looked like a bundle of rags in his arms. He struggled under the weight.

Joice was a walking skeleton. Virtually all of her hair had fallen out and the thin rag that she still wore covered little of her body. The veins in her pitiful covering of skin stood out like tendons and the fire blazing behind her shone through the grey old wrinkled parchment that had become her skin. She looked like an Egyptian mummy that had managed to walk.

She held her arms out in front of her as if awaiting a gift. Qwant walked forward with undoubted worship in his eyes. What did he think she was, some kind of god? What did the leader of the Sandpeople know that Marggitte and Gregorn didn't? Greg and Margg looked at each other. They recognised that they might not get another opportunity to escape with their lives, but seemed transfixed with the events unfolding in front of them.

Qwant gave back to Joice the bundle of rags, as the grey man in his dreams had told him to – the Grey One who one day would rule all and who had a special place for Qwant in his kingdom. Joice took the bundle and from it pulled the blade of Northstar. Once more the smell of burning flesh filled the night air, but Joice was oblivious to it all. She somehow used the last of her energy to raise the sword above her head.

The Sandpeople cheered in their doglike way.

Joice took one last look at Marggitte, whom she had known from childhood, and, thus, knew even behind the mask. For one final second Marggitte saw the woman who had once existed as a nanny, who had loved children before the greyness had invaded her. Joice's eyes held a smile for the final time before glazing over. She turned and, with one last effort, held the sword aloft as she walked into the middle of the fire.

Qwant screeched. This was not supposed to happen. The woman was important to Essdark. She could not kill herself. Essdark was keeping her alive for greater duties. The old woman literally burst with the pressure of the heat and the sword fell into the fire.

Marggitte whistled and Bold galloped towards her. Snatching Shade up in her arms, she mounted Bold quickly. Gregorn looked at her forlornly.

'It is a fine horse but it cannot carry a giant as well. Get him safe. I will find my way to Seathon and I will bring the sword.'

Gregorn thrust out a huge arm into the centre of the fire, and as his arm blackened he triumphantly pulled out Northstar.

'Do not fear for me, I can outrun them.'

He ran out into the flatlands, not realising he was headed east towards the Landsplitter. Bold took Marggitte and Shade back towards Seathon while the Sandpeople took a toll of their losses. Qwant sent a party after Gregorn but, if they knew what was good for them, they would make no real effort to catch the giant that night.

The Seven Faiths of Strepsay

Kurn was the first to react. Shouting at Shel to help him, he managed to lift Marggitte, placing her on the cot on which Shel had spent so much of his recent history. Dee and Menth lifted Shade and placed him on the table, sweeping everything off it on to the floor.

It was obvious that Marggitte was bleeding from several wounds scattered about her body and quickly Kurn realised that most of them were bites. He was skilled and soon had the situation under control, even though Margg had lost plenty of blood.

He carefully washed every single cut and gash on the woman's body. He then applied a very fine white powder to each of them, binding some with gauze and bandages; others he left open to the elements. Finally he gave her seeds from poppies and arzemia, which helped her sleep and sent some of the pain away.

He then turned his attention to Shade. It was intensely disconcerting to be attending to a lupine that muttered and cried out in pain in a human voice. One side of Shade's head was blackened with dried blood and where the ear had come away was a deep rip that needed stitching. Kurn gave Shade a sedative that he administered with a dropper in milk before cleaning the ripped hole. He chipped away at the charred flesh, reopening the wound gently so that he could seal it permanently with catgut.

The whole procedure took about two hours, after which Marggitte was taken down into the room that Shel was sleeping in and Shade was moved off the table and into the upstairs cot.

Menth said, 'Sheldrak, you will have to sleep in my uncle's barn. It may be a little smelly but I'm sure we can find enough covers to keep you warm and cosy.'

Kurn agreed. 'That's the best solution for the moment. Shel, you are almost well again, while these two new patients may well need my help again before the night is through. The barn at Whistle Farm will be good enough tonight.'

Sheldrak had remained tight-lipped throughout the night's events but now spoke. 'You must get them well again as soon as you can, for one of my friends is still missing, and if I can go to help him then I must. I don't think I'm coping very well as a leader. Am I fit to lead so many people of different races? All I seem to do is put everyone into danger and get them hurt.'

'Come,' said Kurn, 'I will walk Menth home and we will talk on the way.'

As the three friends walked the short distance to Whistle Farm, Sheldrak wondered about his honour. He was, without any doubt, in love with the beautiful young woman who walked arm in arm with the man next to him. The man who had saved his life and made him well again; the man who had saved his friends also; the man who was to join Shel in his quest and to be the final piece in the jigsaw, one of the Seven as sure as honour was one of the Seven Faiths of Strepsay. Shel's mind was in a whirl. He would have to finish this and he would do it tonight.

He chose this moment to invite Kurn and Menth into the Seven. 'Come into the barn, please, for I have a tale to tell you both.'

Menth had heard most of Shel's story but listened as though for the first time. She knew what she wanted to do but, sure as she was of herself and her love of Sheldrak, she was also sure that Kurn would not be prepared to go. Kurn, to his credit, never said so, saying instead that he would need to discuss things in private with both his mother and Menth.

Menth, for her part, was true to herself, disregarding the fact that she had fallen in love with Shel. 'We should go. We must go. We are part of an adventure that will change the lands in which we live in. We are part of a bigger story, not one which is born and dies in Seathon. I will go, Kurn, if you go or not.'

Kurn smiled and nodded. 'I know, my love, I would not have expected any other reaction from you. And if that is your final choice then I believe that I also will be left with no option.'

Sheldrak stepped in. 'There are no decisions to be made this evening. As Kurn rightly points out, there are discussions to be had with his mother, and you two must talk in private. We will wait here in Seathon until Shade and Margg are fit to travel, but we also wait for Gregorn. Without him there is no Seven. We need what he brings to the Seven, humility, wisdom and loyalty.'

Kurn walked Menth over to the farm and then returned with blankets for Sheldrak.

'Menth sent these for you. I hope that we make the right decision, for I could not be without her. I have loved her since the day I met her. We were aged five and I loved her then and still love her now.

'I have one consolation, Sheldrak, son of Whinst.'

'And what is that, my friend?'

'That if I choose to stay in Seathon but Menth does indeed follow her strong will and join your adventure, at least I will leave her in safe hands. By my elders, Shel.'

Kurn walked away, the light mist soon hiding him from Shel's gaze.

Within the hour Menth was indeed in safe hands, and they made love again and again, into the night.

The next morning Sheldrak and Menth walked the short distance to Kurn's home. The weather was getting colder by the day and it was a brisk, cold wind from the North that whisked into Seathon, reminding all that winter was not long in coming. Shel was quiet; guilt had taken his tongue, not for the first time since he had left Jost. In ten days time he would have seen three full moons on his journey. Menth also found it difficult to make conversation. Living their lives as a lie was not easy, especially as they saw Kurn's smiling, gullible face every day.

He was waiting for them when they arrived. Menth offered a weak smile followed by her cheek. It was not the sort of kiss that Kurn either expected or desired. He nevertheless kept his cheery disposition. My Faith, thought Shel, does nothing ever upset him or make him miserable?

'Come, you two, Marggitte is awake and wishes us all to be present before she tells her story.'

'Is Shade awake?' asked Sheldrak.

'No, not yet, but I would not have expected him to be. He will be in a state of shock when he comes round and I have given him a very strong sleeping draught. I have to say I find it very strange treating an animal that mutters to me in my own tongue.'

'Is there any sign of Gregorn?'

'I'm sorry, but no giant has been seen in the town. I was up early and spoke to the guards to ask them to keep an eye out for a stranger.'

'You need not worry,' said Shel, 'they will know it's Gregorn when he arrives. He doesn't normally need any introduction.'

They entered the sleeping quarters of Margg, who was sat up, drinking a hot brew in her cot, the one that Shel had occupied the previous week. He ran across the room and hugged Margg for all he was worth. It seemed that neither would let go until at last Shel relaxed and sat by her side.

Dee, Kurn, Menth and then Isthmus appeared and listened as Margg told of the horrors that had befallen Shade and Gregorn and ultimately herself.

Kurn actually cheered when Margg told how she had tricked the Sandpeople into thinking she was astride the magnificent Bold when she had in fact crept into their camp to cut Gregorn loose.

Shel paled when confronted with the demise of Joice and was saddened at the loss of Randeed, his furze. Shel asked the question he had thought of first but had waited to ask.

'What of Northstar? Do we have to face the Sandpeople once more to retrieve it?'

'The last I saw of Northstar, it was heading off into the desert, clutched in the mighty hand of Gregorn. Woe betide anyone who tried to take it from him that night.'

Dee did not know the full story and was puzzled by elements of it, so she quizzed each of them until she grasped the full tale.

Dee spoke. 'And, Sheldrak, young boy, you intend to take this hastily thrown-together bunch of people and face the might of the Grey One. Are you completely mad? You have a magic sword and a talking wolf and you believe that will beat Isintress the Grey, Millghrew the Child-Taker, Essdark, whichever malevolent title he chooses to use.

'You will all be killed. He will take the sword from you like a toy from babies and rule the lands once more. Your deaths will be slow and torturous. The sun will set and never rise again.'

'Mother, please do not talk that way. I have not said yet whether I go or not and Shel knows this.'

'Not go! You cannot fool your mother.' Dee flung out an accusing finger as though she were naming the killer in a whodunit.

'If *she* goes, you will follow. She has you and you don't know it.'

'Please, Mother, not in front of our guests. And Menth does not "have me", as you so unkindly put it. We have each other.'

Kurn looked at Menth for any form of acknowledgement but was greeted with naught but a pregnant pause. Menth turned her eyes to the floor.

'See, she knows it,' continued Dee. 'She uses you, please see this, Kurn. Do not go to your death. Essdark wants you. You are special to him. He will take so much pleasure in killing you all.'

Isthmus spoke for the first time. 'Dee, you speak as though you know him.'

'Don't be so bloody stupid.' She started to rant. 'I'm surrounded by spirits and talking wolves while we sit and wait for a giant to arrive. This is not some game you are playing, and you are *not* taking my son to his DEATH!' She shouted the last word and walked out of the room, stomping up the steps so that everyone was well aware of her position.

Marggitte spoke. 'Sheldrak, we must be careful. Everything Dee said is true. We must be sure for all our sakes. She was very upset but it could be what we all needed to hear.'

Sheldrak replied, 'I am sure. I am so sure that if no one chose to accompany me then I would go alone. But you are correct, Marggitte, each must be true to his or her heart. I do not make anyone follow me, it is each individual's choice.'

Isthmus added the words of experience – experience gained from living once but having the chance to put right the mistakes he had made first time. 'I am not so sure of choice. If it is already written, then we are merely pawns. I am not yet convinced we are the Seven.

'Sheldrak, Shade, Marggitte, Menth, Kurn, Gregorn and myself, Isthmus. We are the chosen Seven, who represent the Faiths of this land, to do battle with the evil that is Essdark. Yes, we can all refuse, but I think it will be a braver act to stay than it will be to go.

'Kurn, I have a worry. Your mother is not one of the Seven and as such should not be with us. The next stage of our journey draws nigh and we must not tempt Faith. Once Gregorn arrives, for arrive he will, the Seven will set forth and Northstar once more will lead us onward.'

Isthmus faded out of view and a welcome voice said from the stairs, 'He knows more than he bloody well says, that see-through bugger. All right, Shel, me old mucker. That phone has started to ring again, but only on one side.'

Shade howled with laughter before jumping on to them all and providing some much-needed mirth. He had looked better, but the large linen dressing covering one side of Shade's head hid most of the damage.

'What a babe,' offered Shade, seeing Menth for the first time.

'I'm actually twenty summers old, but somehow I think that where you come from it may mean something else.'

'God. I can't wait to get rid of this body. I feel like a wolf in wolf's clothing.' He howled again before asking, 'Where's the big man?'

Marggitte answered, 'My wager says he will be in the inn by the biggest place of worship when he does arrive. That was our meeting place, and as far as I know it still is.'

And of course she was right. Within five days the Seven were one. They all needed patching up a little; Shade actually needed patching up a lot. Their spirit had got them this far and the only thing that could upset the harmony was disloyalty.

Love or bravery?

Wisdom or sacrifice?

Sacrifice or loyalty?

There were choices to be made. Every one of the Seven

had options, and if they were to remain seven, then they had to choose the right ones.

Comeuppance

Gregorn was sat in the inn called the Scales, propped up in the corner and entertaining all who would listen with his stories of derring-do. Most giants can tell a good story and Gregorn was no exception. He also looked as though he had been well paid in ale for his efforts and his bushy brown beard was fringed by the froth of the beer he had consumed. The white surrounding to his beard, alongside his haggard expression, made him look further advanced in years than he was, giving onlookers a brief look into the future (should Greg be lucky enough to reach an age when his beard would be grey-flecked).

His eyes might have been tired but they sparkled with joy and relief when Marggitte, Shel and Shade walked into the dusty bar.

Shade bounded across the inn, diving into the out-stretched arms of the giant. Everyone turned to watch the reunion as backs were slapped and kisses and hugs were exchanged, before they all sat down together, with Gregorn's new-found audience banished to the other side of the bar, favours sadly already forgotten.

The room was lighter than most inns Shel had frequented – not that he had been in many. The light-coloured wood used to make the tables and chairs, plus the full-wall bay window gave the place a feel of an afternoon tea parlour rather than a hard-drinking establishment.

Shade kept his voice down so as not to attract too much attention, but couldn't help howling loudly at seeing his old friend well again. It was strange for all of them but the bonds between the Seven, especially those who had been in

Ontrades together, was remarkably strong. They hadn't known each other that long but something was drawing them together in a shorter time than normal relationships would take to develop. Shade felt as though he had been raised with Gregorn, had known him all his life and then had been separated from him for five years, not just five days.

As far as Shel was concerned, it was simply explained. It was Faith, and that was that.

Gregorn tried to speak softly to his comrades, which was difficult for him at the best of times but, after the twelve ales he had already put away, impossible.

'By my elders, am I glad to see you all. I have been here since eleven thirty this morning, hence the few drinks I have quaffed. What time is it now?'

'It is three,' said Shel. 'We have been calling in at eleven every day, but we were just coming back from the Seathon market and thought we would check on the off chance. It was a chance worth taking. So, Gregorn where have you been?'

'Nowhere in particular. I headed across the flatlands, east until I came upon the Landsplitter. I met up with a band of giants on their way back to Arbrain and travelled down the river with them. I arrived here this morning, found the inn and drank until you came.

'And, Sheldrak, I have something for you.'

With an arm that had been roughly bandaged for Gregorn, undoubtedly by the kinfolk he had met up with, he pulled from beneath the table a sheath. From the new sheath, bought from the market earlier that day, Gregorn withdrew Northstar. Shel held it low, beneath the level of the table, and it seemed to sing like a bird returned to the wild after being cooped in a cage.

Sheldrak re-sheathed Northstar and then hugged the great giant once more.

'Well,' said Shade, 'we are whole once more. And Greggy, old bean, we have found six and seven, and seven is very tasty. Well, would be if I were still a man. Isn't she, Shel?'

Marggitte stepped in. 'You speak very rudely, Shade, about Menth. Physical attraction isn't everything and, anyway, you are a lupine and she is a young woman – a young woman promised.'

'Sorry, sorry, didn't mean anything by it. Anyway, Greg, we are now seven and the quest is back on track.'

Shel said, 'And now you have returned Northstar, in five days' time we have the next full moon and the direction we must take.'

Gregorn laughed and then stopped abruptly as he remembered something.

'Sheldrak, I will stay with you as it is my destiny, but my kinfolk warned me of trouble deep in the South. They were heading back to Arbrain for a reason. The cave dwellers of the Mountains of Mina have been roused from their sleep and all giants are being called back to Arbrain, ready for any impending war. Plus, the massive trolls of Zani are assembling armies. It seems that all evil in our lands is gathering to try to overthrow the peace-loving communities such as Arbrain.

'The giants I travelled the Landsplitter with could not believe that I, Gregorn, one of the greatest warrior in giants' history, was not to go back to defend our lands. It saddened me to say nay to them, but I believe by all my Faith that to stand with you is equally as important as to stand in Arbrain.

'Come, let us drink to this.'

They stayed in the inn until long after dark when they literally all staggered back to Whistle Farm to sleep the ale off in the barn.

For the next five days, Sheldrak, Gregorn, Marggitte, Shade and of course Isthmus slept in the barn belonging to

Menth's family and worked the farm for their keep. Shel, whenever he could, tried to snatch moments with Menth and used excuses like 'going for a solitary walk' when in fact he was sneaking brief liaisons with her.

In his heart he knew that what he was doing to Kurn was wrong. He also wondered what Faith had in store for him, as this could only upset the alliance that the Seven had forged.

Dee was hardly seen during this time as she worked on Kurn to try to get him to stay. Kurn was more worried about why Menth seemed to have grown cold towards him, but put it down to his inability to make his mind up about whether to go with Shel or not. The truth was, he *had* to go. The difficulty was getting his mother to accept that this was the right life choice to make.

The day of the full moon came around and everyone had gone down to the Landsplitter to sail. Everyone but Shel. He wanted to see Menth and made some excuse about being too tense, waiting to see where Northstar would lead them next. Menth was helping Dee and Kurn at the surgery in the centre of Seathon but had made a pact to meet later at Kurn's home. Menth's uncle was working the farm and could walk into the farmstead or barn at any time.

Shel waited, sat upon the cot in the room Marggitte had taken from him on returning from the flatlands, his heart pounding and his head light. Love was one of the seven Faiths of Strepsay but no one had warned Shel that this Faith could overshadow all the others to the extent that you forgot the rest.

Forgot them all except love – or was that lust?

Sheldrak held Menth close to his body as he kissed her neck. He moved his mouth to her ear, cheek, eyes before moving back to her mouth and feeling the flick of her tongue against his. She moved beneath him, waiting for him. His body ached with the expectation, his breath coming in short gasps. Neither of them heard the footfalls coming down the wooden stairs until a voice screamed at them, 'I knew it. You bitch. Do you two know what you have done to him? This will kill him. Get out of my home, both of you.'

Dee looked as though she could kill. The lovers never moved until another shriek from Dee got them off the cot.

'Where's your precious Faith now, Sheldrak?' Dee's voice was heavy with sarcasm, mocking. 'I thought Strepsay was everything to you. Your Seven have to take on Essdark. Well, who will follow you now? You have lied to everyone. And betrayed one of your precious Seven. He is my son!'

This last word came out as a sob. Sheldrak and Menth tried to retain some dignity as they pulled their strewn garments back on, collected from all parts of the room where they had been discarded in passion and were now collected in shame.

Menth was the first of the two to speak.

'You cannot tell him, Dee. He never need know. Shel can go on his quest and I will stay and marry Kurn as I am betrothed to do.'

Dee did not agree.

'If you think I am having a bitch on heat as my daughter then you are wrong. That jak can go on his quest and you with him, but you must tell my son first. I will not tell him, for he will hate me for the knowledge. Don't think you can trick me, you witch.'

Dee walked over to Menth and spat hard into her face. Menth wiped it away with the frill of her blouson and, as Shel put his hand out to help her, pulled away.

'Gone off you already,' said Dee. She then hit Shel with the biggest roundhouse, knocking him off balance but not off his feet. He gasped in pain and shock. His eye would be the colour of a summer plum by morning. Menth ran up the steps and out of the house, but Shel stayed. He needed to understand exactly what Dee meant to do. This could be the end of them all if he didn't work it out quickly. The thing that hurt the most was that everything that Dee had said was true. He had known it for days but had felt helpless to control his feelings.

He was about to find out what 'helpless' really meant.

Dee was crying hysterically. She had known her son's love for Menth was off kilter, his love greater than hers, but Dee had never believed it would come to this. She did think that one day Menth would walk away from Kurn, but not because she had been behaving like an animal off the farm. This was too much to take.

Sheldrak spoke. 'The quest is bigger than all of us. I will tell Kurn, but I will tell him when the time is right. Tonight the moon is full and tomorrow we will leave in the direction indicated to us by Northstar. You have said you cannot tell him for he will blame you. I do not want to hurt anyone any more than I have already, but I love Menth and she will come with me, as well as Kurn. Interfere and you will have to tell Kurn yourself. I will not stop you but the consequences are great.'

Dee laughed. 'You conniving bastard. Your mistake, your dishonour and now you follow it with a veiled blackmail attempt. I don't know what powers rule these lands of ours, but whoever picked you as a representative of the good of mankind did not use their Faith of Wisdom very well.'

Shel walked past Dee and up the flight of stairs, turning back at the top.

'I now go to fulfil the ritual with Northstar. You must do as you will.'

Dee shouted at the retreating back, now slightly stooped, of the young man, 'If you don't tell him, you'll get your comeuppance, mark my words. I haven't finished with all of this. You have ruined my son's life and I will not rest easy until I am avenged.'

Shel felt like a young child being scolded by his friend's mother for stealing his best toy; then, after taking the toy without asking permission, he finds he has to return it, broken.

Sheldrak headed back to the barn that he and his companions called home and lay on his cot, concocting a story to explain the black eye he already had. The others returned from the sailing trip a little later than scheduled. Shade was starting to become more like his old self, but the ringing had restarted in his head. He didn't continually refer to it as 'bloody phones' any more but at times his concentration wandered and Greg would have to shout to bring him back into the conversation.

Gregorn and Marggitte were repairing their bodies and minds much quicker than Shade, as they had been through numerous situations in their military careers that had required fighting and bloodshed. They had found the mental aspect of battle easier to cope with. Isthmus appeared less and less. He was struggling with holding the secret of Menth and Sheldrak, and wondered if the whole campaign could still be held together with the added pressure Sheldrak had unwittingly brought to the group.

Kurn was going about his healing business in the same cheery manner that he always had done. He had made his decision; it was sharing it with his mother that would be the difficult part. He loved Menth with every fibre of his being but had decided to go with Sheldrak, not for Menth but for himself. This was very important for his mother to recognise; he was doing this for Kurn and hopefully it would be the correct decision for Menth also.

Approaching midnight, the group of friends collected together in the potato fields at the back of the main farmhouse. Everyone was there, with the ghostly glow of Isthmus hovering unsettlingly in the background. Everyone, excepting Menth. She had not been seen that afternoon or evening. Shel was a little worried but not overly. He thought Menth would have decided to lie low with her own thoughts until they decided how to tell Kurn, should that occasion ever arise.

Kurn himself was more concerned. Having known Menth from childhood, he knew that this disappearance was totally out of character. Her uncle knew not where she was or for what reason she might have decided to spend time alone.

Sheldrak asked them to focus on the task in hand. Menth would return, he knew it. He looked to Isthmus for support, who added words of encouragement that she was fine, but the words lacked assurance.

Sheldrak lay the sword down upon the damp earth of the farmer's field, pointing south-west, back towards Jost where he had started just over three months ago.

He took a deep breath, puffing his chest up proudly, and then started the ancient incantation taught to him by Isthmus.

> Northstar, Northstar, this is whence I came.
> If you be true, then turn and lead the way.
> If you be false, then die and be no more.
> Northstar, Northstar, by Faith, where is Tremain?

The sword quivered where it lay. A soft glow emanated from the tip and from the end of the handle. It trembled a little harder, as though a troop of riders had ridden past, but then it left the earth. It rose higher off the ground and, as before, began to rotate, spinning faster and faster while sending out the best firework display any of the six watchers had ever seen. The powerful blue light flickered on and off, sparkling in the reflection of the bright full moon.

The sword stopped dead, three feet from the earth, pointing back south-west whence Sheldrak had started his journey. It then rotated clockwise, slowly, until it pointed due south, straight down the Landsplitter, before falling dully, all lights extinguished, to wet earth below.

'Twice I've seen that now,' said Shade, 'and it's still bloody amazing.'

'So,' said Gregorn,' we head off down the Landsplitter and, if my geography has not deserted me, towards Arbrain. I may well join my folk in the southern fight against evil yet.'

Sheldrak asserted his authority. 'Let us go back to the barn and discuss our plan of action. I wish to leave tomorrow at first light which means, my healing friend, you will have to decide if you come or not.'

'I have decided, Sheldrak. I will come with you, but I need time with my mother to tell her my decision. When we have finished making our plans, I will return home to tell her my actions. I hope she is there as I have not seen her since midday either.'

But he never did.

Dee was distraught. That snake of a girl had promised herself for fifteen years, only to snatch away the promise at the last second, or at the first chance. Whichever, it amounted to the same thing and she wasn't going to sit tight and allow it to happen. She had secrets of her own. Secrets that no one knew about, not even her beloved son. Why did she know so much? Was it because of her powers to entrance? She had traded once and had her son, but what was the trade she had had to give in return? Someone was going to call in an old favour, one she was helpless to resist.

She hurriedly packed some belongings into a jambuli – a waterproof leather drawstring bag. She didn't know how long she would be gone but she had to take Menth from here, away from Sheldrak-Spawn, away from the pain of her son. Whatever it took, she would do it. She had not been able to have children and so Kurn was a special child.

Most secrets are dark. This one was grey.

She scuttled along, her jambuli thrown over her back as if she were a phantom Mother Christmas with gifts of destruction, not pleasure. She went to the farmhouse where Menth lived. Menth had run out of Dee's house and gone straight home to her room. No one else was there. They were either in the fields or on the water. She had the farm to herself, or so she thought.

Dee hammered on the back door that led into the cook-house for minutes, before the bolt was thrown back and Menth stood before her. She was still crying but no matter how unhappy or upset she was, her beauty still managed to shine through the sadness.

Dee forced her way in, relocking the door behind her.

Menth shouted, 'What are you doing here? What are you going to do?'

Dee, keeping her emotions corralled like a wild stallion waiting to be broken, dug into her jambuli and extracted an amulet. The stone was a dull grey in hue, totally flat and approximately the size of a large sovereign coin. Cut into the middle of it was the shape of an eye.

Dee, sticking to her plan like a fly to a spider's web, held the amulet up at eye level, swinging it back and forth while chanting unintelligible words. Menth pulled her eyes away but the chanting was mystical. It told her to look into the eye; the eye would solve her problems, and her worries would be gone. Let the eye take her.

Time passed and Menth fell under the power of Dee, who spoke words of English for the first time since entering the farmhouse.

'Do not worry, pretty Menth, for I have no intention of hurting you, but I am going to take you somewhere, to a place where the sun never shines and Sheldrak will never see you again.'

It was an hour after the ceremony with Northstar when, breathless with running, Kurn arrived back at the barn.

'I can't find Mother anywhere. She left this afternoon to collect food for the evening meal and is nowhere to be found. What's more, one of her sacks has gone and many of her clothes.'

Sheldrak tried not to show any panic. He also had not seen Menth since the showdown with Dee. What had she said? 'You will get your comeuppance.'

'Marggitte, go to the farmhouse and see if Menth is there. If not, check around the farm and down at the pier where her boat is docked.

'Shade and Gregorn, you two follow all the paths around the farm. Check the woods and fields.

'Kurn, you and I will go down to the surgery and see if we can trace either Dee's or Menth's tracks after they left you this afternoon.

'I want everyone back here in sixty minutes with no exception. Two people are missing and if we don't keep our heads we'll all go running off in different directions and spend the rest of the night trying to find each other. Now go.'

He might have had only sixteen summers under his belt but he spoke with such authority that, crisis or not, people listened and followed.

Marggitte woke Menth's uncle and aunt from their slumber by banging loudly on the door with the handle of her sword, sheathing it as a light went on, so as not to cause any more concern than was necessary.

'By my elders. I am sorry for the late hour, but has Menth retired for the evening?'

The large, ruddy-faced farmer shrugged his shoulders and, turning to his wife, motioned that she should look in Menth's room. Only on her return did he deem it necessary to speak.

'Wait there. I'll get my coat.'

He wasn't one for using ten words when a shrug of the shoulders would do. A second later, Marggitte and Defhert were walking towards the Landsplitter and specifically pier three. The rain had started to come in off the river and the swirling wind had it flowing in every conceivable direction. It was one of those nights that, no matter what you wore or however tightly it was fastened, a few drops of rain managed to find their way into your undergarments.

The pier was fifty yards long with numerous different sailing and rowing vessels tied by thick ropes to the bollards. The wind had them bobbing up and down like eager young birds trying to attract the hen's attention for the last worm in her beak. When they got to the second-last mooring point, Defhert stopped.

'My boat. It's gone.'

'And so,' said Marggitte, 'we got to the end of the pier and Defhert's boat had gone.'

'Were any of Menth's clothes missing?' asked Kurn.

'Not according to her aunt, but one thing had gone, her bow and quiver of arrows. According to Defhert, brilliant though she may be as a sailor, no one could have taken a boat up river in today's intermittent rain, especially with that wind blowing as it is. It has been blowing strongly since early afternoon.'

Sheldrak looked at Kurn. 'Has Dee ever headed south before? Does she know anyone, a relative or friend?'

Kurn shook his head. 'It's not the fact that she has gone but the fact that she has not told anyone. During my lifetime we have not been separated for more than a day, so for her to go off with not a word is very strange. And why would she go with Menth?'

Sheldrak was ripping himself into two distinct pieces. In one he pretended to tell Kurn and the rest of his colleagues everything that he knew and left the rest to Faith. As the other piece he maintained the silence that hid his secret, but somehow tried to lighten the problem for the others, especially Kurn. Then he had an idea.

He stopped and had a one-sided conversation with Isthmus. The truth was, this conversation was not taking place, but the others thought it was. Shel fabricated one half of a conversation.

'So what do you say, Isthmus? They were running away from something. They needed our help but could not wait to tell us and by going quickly they got out of danger. They want us to catch up with them downriver. But why didn't you tell us this earlier?' Shel paused for dramatic effect before giving the answer everyone wanted to hear. 'You had to read the signs correctly and be sure, but now you are sure and they are both safe.'

Kurn actually cheered, hugging everyone and grabbing their forearms in an act of friendship.

Inside Shel's head, Isthmus strongly disapproved.

'Sheldrak, you once aspired to be an elder and held every Faith sacred. Now you seem intent on breaking every one of them. What will the cost of this be, I wonder? Never forget the Faith of Humility. We are Seven because Seven can when one cannot.'

Shel tried to answer but Isthmus had obviously heard enough.

Shel spoke one last time, 'Tomorrow we obtain boats and we follow our friends down the river. Get as much sleep as you can. We must be up at dawn and on the water as soon after that as we can. Not only are our friends, and loved ones, heading south, but that is the direction that Northstar would have us take. By my elders, sleep well.' Shel moved upstairs in the barn to sleep on his own and to take his own counsel.

Shade whispered to the others. 'Don't know what's up

with old Shelly, but he's not quite himself and I'm not too sure he walked into a door to get that shiner, either. Keep your eye on him, Margg, he's shutting the rest of us out. And I don't know about you, guys, but I didn't think that was part of the game plan.'

Part Four
The Landsplitter

Pursuit

Dee did not like the water as much as many of the people of Seathon; subsequently, she had rarely been on deck in the past twenty years of her life. One of the rare occasions she had done so was to make this same trip many years ago. Those were the days when she used to travel extensively, before the birth of Kurn. The difference this time was that she had company although, looking at the blank eyes of the girl controlling the small sailing vessel, the company was not compelling. Nevertheless, she knew where she was on board a boat, which was exactly what Dee needed.

The storm was quietening the further south on the river they went, but Dee still intended stopping at nightfall. She hoped she could remember the exact part of the river, as the twenty years had helped to erase her memory. She recalled that she had also been terrified. But he had been worth it, which meant he was worth the trip again. She wondered if either of them had been missed yet, and what jakface Sheldrak would do about it when he found out.

She thought it would take them a while to work out where it was she was heading; well, they could never know that. But with the missing boat it wouldn't be hard to reason that, with the weather, she could have only headed in one direction. Pity about the storm, as she would have headed south down the Landsplitter even if it meant swimming. She shivered at the thought.

She had intended killing Menth. Bewitching her, as she had done, but then running a knife along her pretty throat. Something had changed her mind. Where it came from she knew not, for she had wiped it from her history as well as she had been able. Resurfacing from the sewer of her memory like a bloated rat floating to the surface full of gas, her past had been dredged up.

It was a long journey ahead but it was the right one. Would Kurn chase after her? Probably, but it was for him that she did this. Once Kurn knew the extent of the betrayal of Menth and Sheldrak, he would realise that this was her only option.

She spoke to Menth, or the empty shell that had been Menth. 'Stop by that large willow on our left. We'll tie up here for the night. You may be able to navigate this boat, but I'm taking no chances in the dark with this weather. We'll sleep on board, it's too wet out there.'

Menth steered the small yacht over to the right bank, the sign gaily painted in large red letters, *High Spirits*, at odds with the mood on the ship. Menth sat quietly while Dee prepared some food.

On the outside Menth looked calm, but inside the battle for supremacy raged.

After they had eaten, Dee told Menth to sleep while she sat, singing a nursery rhyme to herself, rocking her body back and forth. It was approaching midnight and, back in Seathon, Northstar was just about to point the way south.

The next morning the rain had blown over and the wind had dropped slightly when Dee awoke from her drowsiness. She hadn't slept well but she never felt comfortable on board a boat and sleeping seemed out of the question. Too many thoughts were running through her head. She thought that by singing a lullaby that had always got Kurn to sleep as a babe, she could have solved her insomnia, but it was not to be. Mr Sandman decided that ladies who kidnapped young girls and spirited them off in the dead of night didn't deserve to sleep.

Dee thought this fair.

She clapped her hands three times and Menth woke and

stood. There had been more signs of life when she had slept, for when she opened her eyes only her body woke. Her mind slept on.

'Come, child, let us wash. Just because we are not sleeping in our nice warm cots back in Seathon, doesn't mean we have to behave like dirty pirates. After that you can cook us some breakfast. There is plenty of dry kindling under the branches of this large willow.'

Menth nodded, her only sign of understanding. Behind her eyes she screamed silently, not even able to weep tears of sadness.

Within the hour they were sailing again, virtually at the same time as the two giant kayaks left Seathon.

Gregorn led the way, striking a hard rhythm for Kurn and Marggitte to duplicate in the second boat. Behind Greg sat Shade and, behind him, Sheldrak. The old boats had belonged to Defhert. They had been in the barn for years, lying under a tarpaulin, but every year without fail he had given each a new coat of resin.

'Never know when they might be needed,' he said. They were large kayaks, designed for four or five men or, alternatively, a giant, a talking lupine and a young lad.

Marggitte had been forced to leave Bold with Defhert as collateral, which grieved her greatly, but her heart couldn't have ached any more and nobody saw the daily pain she went through. Missing Hemm was etching lines on to her face, hidden behind the white mask, leaving scars as surely as a piece of chalk leaves marks on a blackboard.

In these great boats, the first filled with provisions because Greg would have little trouble paddling it up the river, the six companions (five visible) left Seathon, not knowing that some of them would never see it again. They were approximately six hours behind the sailing vessel, but gaining with every stroke of Greg's large forearms. Marggitte and Kurn were working much harder to keep up with Greg's power.

'This is no good,' shouted Kurn from twenty yards back, 'we have no chance of keeping up with you.'

Gregorn slowed his pace, allowing the boat behind to draw level.

Sheldrak said, 'We will go as fast as our slowest. We are one and I have no intention of losing anyone else on this chase.'

'Let's face it,' said Shade, 'we don't even know what we're bloody chasing or if someone is chasing us. Something forced Dee and Menth to make a run for it, and I can't think what. Sandpeople don't sail boats, do they? And Morgs certainly don't, so it's a new enemy. Well, zippiddee-doo-daa, that's just what I need, someone new to rip my other ear off.'

'Pardon?' said Gregorn.

'I said, all I need is someone new to— Oh, very funny, ha, ha. Let's all laugh at the one-eared wolf.'

That set them all laughing, which shook off some of the uncertainty ahead of them and helped to forget some of the pain left behind.

'Stop! Leave the boat over there or we'll end up down the rapids.' Dee shouted at Menth, straining to be heard over the noise of the white water disappearing over the falls in front of them. Kayaks might have a chance going over there with skilled oarsmen, but a sailing vessel didn't have the manoeuvrability and would end up as firewood.

Dee's memories came pouring back with the water pouring over the edge. She knew where she was and it would be an hour's walk from here before they had to re-enter the water.

'Come, bitch, and carry my jambuli.'

They got out on to the west bank and then, as an after-thought, Dee untied the boat and pushed with all she was worth, sending the small ship back out into the strong currents. It was snatched away like a cloud in a puff of wind, spiralling its way towards the first set of rocks before moving out of sight. The river did its best to drown out the sound of the breaking wood but the crunch and groan was like an animal's last defiant roar as it went into its death throes.

'Let our band of merry followers work that one out when they find the remains of *High Spirits*. My, doesn't that sound appropriate.

'Come along, there's a path here somewhere. Everyone has to carry their boats down the Pike's Teeth. Come on, hurry up child, we really haven't got all day.'

Dee's voice had the air of a Sunday school teacher taking her class on a nature ramble, when in truth she was leading Menth to her death. They found the path almost immediately but it was very overgrown. If people had walked down here with their boats then they had not done so for a long time.

Dee led the way, using a large oak branch to break her way through the brambles, cruelly letting them flick back at Menth, knowing that she wouldn't duck to get out of the way. After half an hour of this treatment, Menth's once pretty dress was torn in several places and her face had numerous superficial scratches.

The path did not hug the riverbank but meandered down its own valley, taking them away from the river on occasion. The route was strenuous and the previous rains had left many muddy patches of ground to drag through. The hour turned into two before the roar of the rapids started to dwindle and became an echo of their recent past.

'I think this is it,' said Dee. Her face was flushed and she seemed to be excited. 'This is the difficult part, so wait here. If I never come back, sit down and starve to death.' Dee chuckled to herself, 'I can be nastier than I thought.'

She left the path and pushed her way through the dense

undergrowth, struggling with the worst of it and at times having to detour further out of her way than she would really have wanted. Eventually she came back to the water's edge. Walking south, she looked at each of the trees as she passed, looking for some sign she recognised. After several hundred yards she stopped and went back, her search of the trees becoming ever more earnest. Then she found what she had been looking for.

At the base of a large tree was a T-shaped stone, about two feet in length. It was unusual both in shape and texture and had been buried in the fork of two prominent roots that had burrowed their way out of the earth, stopping anything else from growing in the area. Dee had buried the rock over twenty years ago for this very reason. She had never expected to need the sign, but need it she did, and she cried out in relief.

Running back to the path, she found Menth where she had left her. Obviously not hungry yet, thought Dee maliciously, or she would have sat down by now. Looking at the gaunt face of the still-striking girl frightened Dee a little. The untreated scratches on her face had given her an unearthly look, as though she had been crying, but blood instead of tears.

'Follow me. We are going for a swim, and I know you swim better than I so you will have to pull me along, too.'

Dee took herself and Menth back to the T-tree and walked them both right to the edge of the bank. They hadn't realised that they had gone down quite a steep hill as they had followed the riverbank, but the river itself had cut into the hillside much deeper, leaving them stood about forty foot above the swirling waters of the Landsplitter. The day was drawing to a close as Dee whispered some instructions to Menth and they both stepped off the cliff into the freezing cold water below.

Menth swam straight down to the riverbed, pulling Dee

behind her, tied on with a piece of rope salvaged from the boat. The water was dark at this depth and it became very difficult to see, especially as the daylight was fading. They swam underwater back to the riverbank, which at this depth was hard slate bedrock. Using touch, they felt along the bank, looking for something before, desperate for air, Dee pulled Menth bodily to the surface.

Spluttering, Dee screamed at Menth, 'By Faith, you stupid girl, we need to breathe.' Menth was hardly breathing, as years of swimming and diving had made her lungs strong, and she could hold her breath for well over a minute and a half. Dee did well to reach thirty seconds.

This is never going to work, thought Dee. She grabbed on to a piece of overhanging rock to stop herself being swept downriver, untied the rope and sent Menth diving down again. On the third occasion she was absent for over five minutes before returning. The light was gone.

'You must have found it or you'd be dead by now. Take me.'

This time, Menth knew where she was going. Swimming about twenty yards upriver, then diving to the base of the rock bank, she swam into a tunnel that they had not previously been able to see. The tunnel went directly west, taking them back under the path they had been walking on about an hour ago. Dee was starting to panic when the tunnel turned upwards and opened out into a large underwater pool and cave.

As they pulled themselves out of the water, Dee turned and hit Menth hard across the face,

'Were you trying to kill me?' Blood spilled from Menth's busted nose and pattered on to the rock like tiny footsteps. The walls of the cave had some kind of fluorescent lichen totally covering them, giving the cave an eerie blue glow, and the blood shone unnaturally.

Dee recovered her poise. Almost whispering, she said,

'I'm sorry, I shouldn't have hit you. I've known you since you were a child. Why did you spoil everything? You were my son's, nobody else's.'

Menth stood silently, blood running down her face and forming a little pool on the floor of the cave. Dee, now crying, tended to the girl's face with a dry cloth from her jambuli before hugging the girl and sobbing into her tresses.

'It's too late to go back now. We've come too far. Underworld awaits. Come, let's go. I promise I will look after you until he has you. After that, who knows?'

They walked down the left-hand tunnel, barely big enough for them to fit through without crouching, leaving droplets of drying blood behind them.

Gregorn had set a strong pace. Eating as they went, without need for break, meant they made good ground on the *High Spirits* even though none of them was absolutely sure that they were following Dee and Menth. Sheldrak wasn't even sure that Dee and Menth were together, but at least he hoped they were. The thought had not been lost on him that they could be pursuing Dee only. He shuddered at the thought.

This chase was testing his Faith to the full. If they did not detect some sign that Dee and Menth had headed this way, would he consider turning back? The flow of the river meant it would take three times as long to get back to Seathon than it had taken them to get this far down the Landsplitter. He put the idea out of his head; his feelings told him Menth was ahead of him, somewhere, and he would trust them.

Poor Kurn sat behind Marggitte, wondering what had caused his mother and lover to go charging off in the middle of a storm at night. He knew that Isthmus had said they were fine, but how did he know? Isthmus certainly knew things the rest of them didn't, but did he know what had happened to Menth and to his mother? He didn't wish to doubt one of his companions, but he was very uneasy.

On they went during the day and into the night, taking turns to steal a couple of hours' sleep. Shade slept first as he wasn't helping a great deal with the rowing or the navigation. He slept soundly, dreaming of a nightclub in Soho.

At the same time, Dee swung the flat of her hand into the expressionless face of Menth in the blue, glowing cave.

The pursuers had made good time and were about three hours away from the Pike's Teeth rapids. The river was getting choppier and the only one who had sailed here before was Gregorn and, even though Kurn was a good sailor, progress became hindered.

Marggitte was following the light at the back of the kayak in front but her mind was elsewhere. She gave the impression that she was recovering from the loss of Hemm but nothing could be further from reality. She was becoming more and more dependent on the causes of the group, and in particular Sheldrak, to maintain a reason to live. She was a pale imitation of the woman she had been as a member of the Ontradean society; her friends back in the Inners would wonder where the Marggitte they had known had gone. The mask helped her to hide, but her grief would have to find a way out or it would kill her, as sure as Hemm's love for Marggitte had killed him.

It was Sheldrak's turn to paddle the front kayak through the night and a chance for Greg to pick up some well-earned rest. Shade had woken up and was prattling on about something called a lap dancer when the noise and speed of the water changed.

Shel turned to Shade. 'Can you hear the roar? With your keen hearing, can you tell where it comes from?'

'Are you taking the piss, Shel? All I can hear out of this black mess is a ringing bloody phone.'

Kurn shouted from the boat behind. 'Sheldrak, it's the

sound of the water. Look how it flows. It must be going over a fall. Wake Gregorn, he will know.'

The shouting had woken the giant and he swore under his breath. 'I am sorry, Sheldrak, this is my fault. I slept for too long or misjudged the speed of the river. We are entering the Pike's Teeth. Hold on, it is too late to turn back now.'

The kayak dipped and fell a couple of feet, narrowly missing the first outcrop of rock while water was thrown at them from the splash created by the fall. Behind them they heard Kurn shout something, but they had no chance of hearing him. The noise was almost more frightening than the ride. The roar of the water was so loud it was like holding your head in a drum while someone banged as hard as they could on the side.

The two boats were tossed and turned, spinning back and forth so that they went back to front, then sideways, as their belongings toppled overboard. The front kayak was not being moved about as much, owing to the weight of Gregorn sat in front, but that was their undoing.

The kayak sat deeper because of Greg's weight and, while travelling sideways, hit a boulder low in the water but high enough to rip the bottom out of the boat. It split down the middle, sending Greg, Shade and Sheldrak spinning off in different directions.

The three were dragged down the river, bouncing off rocks and boulders as they went, with their only hope of survival to keep upright and let their bodies rather than their heads hit things. Marggitte and Kurn were managing a little better, in that they had kept their kayak afloat, but the final part of the rapids was a waterfall of over fifty feet.

The three who had been in the leading boat went shooting over the top without a vessel, but Marggitte and Kurn had to jump from their boat as the front fell forward, shooting them like stones from a catapult. My Faith, I'm flying, thought Marggitte as she spun through the air. She landed in the water and hit her head on a sharp edge of flint. She sank with the weight of her armour, passing out from the blow. She had five minutes to live.

Isthmus had left Sheldrak's mind and appeared, hovering over the comparatively still pool of water at the base of the falls. The natural light of his body at least gave them all chance to see. Shel, barely able to breathe, let alone speak with the weight of Northstar pulling him under, shouted, 'Shade, where are you?'

A howl came from somewhere to his left.

Gregorn spoke: 'I'm here also, Sheldrak.'

Kurn said, 'I'm over here, but I can't see Marggitte.'

Isthmus rose into the air, lighting the pool from a greater height, but still no sign of Marggitte. Shade dragged himself to the side of the river and pulled himself from the water and on to the sandy bank.

Sheldrak was panicking. At least a minute had passed and Marggitte was nowhere to be seen.

'Dive everyone, try to find her.'

They all went under the water, including Isthmus, whose life light was Marggitte's only chance of survival. The weeds at the bottom of the river were thick, and even with a little light it was almost impossible to see. Kurn caught something out of the corner of his eye that, had he not been under the water, would have made him scream.

From within the weeds and rushes, the white shape of a face stared out. Faith, it was the mask of Marggitte and she was still attached to it. Kurn surfaced and, taking Gregorn back down with him, they got Marggitte to the side and on to the bank. Applying pressure to her stomach and chest, Kurn got her breathing again and, moments later, she threw up a lungful of water.

Kurn rolled on to his back and looked at the stars as the others dragged themselves over to the prostrate figures of Marggitte and Kurn.

'It was the mask,' he said. 'Without that I'd never have found her.' He turned to Marggitte. 'Your mask saved your life.'

Marggitte managed to speak. 'If it was the mask, then it was Hemm who saved me. His love from beyond the grave is still strong enough to keep me alive.'

She was still sobbing some thirty minutes later.

Daylight came as comfort to the weary travellers. Still damp and cold from the drenching they had taken during the night, they had huddled together to try to generate some heat from the closeness of each other's bodies. They hadn't managed to find too many of their belongings in the dark but no one particularly wanted to venture back into the river until light. The only thing that Gregorn had been prepared to do was pull out the one remaining kayak, still sound even after its fifty-foot fall.

They snuggled together in the light of Isthmus until his energy levels fell and he went out like a wet candle.

As the sun rose, hope came with it, and the optimism of the group rose as brightly as the winter morning's sun.

'So,' said Shade, 'where do we go from here?'

The four followers turned to Sheldrak, awaiting a decision from the youngest among them.

'Well, the good news is that I had Northstar strapped to me, so when the new moon rises we will once again be pointed in the right direction. Also, we still have a boat that we can all squeeze into if we need, but first I want to take a look around. Let us salvage everything we can. I know it will mean getting wet again, but then we will build a large fire, get some food if we can, and decide how to go forward.'

It wasn't a great plan, but it motivated them all to get up, get moving and stop feeling sorry for themselves. Gregorn and Kurn, the two best swimmers of the group, volunteered to go back into the water, and found two of the large, waterproof sacks they had been carrying in the first kayak.

One was full of supplies while the other had dry clothes, flints for starting fires and Sheldrak's bow. He used it to good effect to kill a couple of pheasants out of the forests skirting the west coast of the river. They also found a large piece of blue timber, the same colour as *High Spirits*.

Before long they had a roaring fire burning, bellies full of warm breakfast, clean dry clothes and a hot brew in their hands. Marggitte was feeling much better and gave her opinion as to what they should do next.

'If Dee and Menth came down here in the boat, which the wood you found would suggest, they could only have struggled out of the water to this same bit of beach that we did. But there is no sign of them. We would have seen footprints in the wet earth or some sign of them breaking twigs or flattening grasses. We are the first people here in a long time.'

Kurn followed the line of thought.

'But, Marggitte, you only got out of the water because we pulled you out.' The last word came out a little choked.

'They could not be that far ahead of us,' boomed Gregorn, 'and look how our belongings were thrown everywhere. There is no sign of any clothes or bags.'

'But,' said Shel, 'we don't even know what they took, if anything. Besides, if that is a piece of Defhert's boat we found, then the rest of it has disappeared downriver pretty quickly. What could we reasonably expect to find still here, or would the flotsam have gone downriver?'

Marggitte continued with her theory. 'They would have approached the rapids in the light. I don't think they would have battled to the last minute and gone over the falls as we did. They would have got out beforehand.'

'OK,' said Shel, 'I wanted to look around, but now we have justification to do so. We will hide the kayak and clear up so that no one knows we have been here. Then we will let our wonderful tracker, Marggitte, see if she can find any signs that others have been in this area.'

In his chest, Shel's heart ached. He had not known Dee very long but he didn't think she was capable of hurting Menth. So what in Faith's name was she doing?

It wasn't long before they had the small beach cleaned up; the fire was put out and the ashes buried in the trees. The kayak was dragged out of the river and hidden in the undergrowth. It took Marggitte less than five minutes to find the recently trodden-down path and two seconds more for her to decide which way the tracks were heading. She also confirmed that they were behind two people, once more causing Kurn to hug each of them in turn.

Sheldrak became more urgent with this news and pressed them forward. They followed the tracks up to the river's edge where, twelve hours earlier, Dee and Menth had jumped into the water.

'By my Faith, are we to go into the water again?' asked Kurn.

Shade responded as only he could. 'Bollocks. I'm not going back in there. I'm only just dry, and I was a better swimmer as a bloke than a lupine. Plus I've only got one ear now, and that's full of water.'

The others laughed, but not heartily. Every time they seemed to be getting somewhere, another mystery was thrown at them.

'If they jumped in, then I too will jump in. It's my mother and my love down there and, whether you want to go or not, Shade, I will.'

'Come on, Kurn, I didn't mean anything by it. If that's the way we have to go, then of course I'll go, but are we sure? Are we all just going to jump off this bloody cliff back into the water?'

Shel replied, 'No, of course we are not, Shade, but Kurn and myself will. If they jumped in here, it is for a reason. We know they were not pursued, or Marggitte would be able to tell from the tracks. Therefore they jumped in to get to something or somewhere, unless they intend to swim 200 miles to Arbrain.'

Shel took off Northstar and handed it to Gregorn.

'Guard this well, my friend. If I do not come back then I leave it to you to take it back to Tremain, and to run Essdark through with it.'

'What are we looking for?' asked Kurn.

'I don't know,' said Shel. 'The river is nearly a mile wide here, so whatever they jumped for must be close to this bank. Let us find out what we can see when we get down there.

'Isthmus, can we use the light of your body if we need to go under the water again?'

The spirit appeared, glistening gently in the weak winter's sun.

'At least you don't get wet,' said Shade.

Kurn and Sheldrak held hands and leapt into the water.

They swam up the river with Isthmus hovering behind them, working north at first before coming back to the place they had started. They repeated the exercise south, with their friends shouting encouragement from the cliff above. It was hard work swimming back upriver afterwards, and after thirty minutes they were getting tired and the cold was seeping into their bones. They held on to the very same outcrop of rock that Dee herself had held on to the previous day.

'We must try under the water,' said Kurn, frightening himself with the thought of what he might find. 'We'll take it in turns.'

There were no turns to take. With Isthmus glowing by his side, he found the tunnel at the base of the bank on his first dive. He came up and told Shel what he had found. Five minutes later they were standing in the blue, glowing cave. The chase was back on.

Truth

Isthmus went back to the others and they too jumped, even Shade. Soon all remaining six of the original Seven were stood with blue faces from the strange-coloured lichen growing on the walls of the damp cave. This time they were wet but with no way to get dry.

It was Shade, sniffing around on the floor of the cave, who came across the pool of dried blood.

'I don't want to worry any of you guys, but I think I've found something that you ain't going to like.'

'What is it?' Numerous voices spoke at once.

'It smells like blood to me, tastes like it too. Human blood. And it leads off down that tunnel, which doesn't look very inviting.'

'More to the point,' said Gregorn, 'it doesn't look very big. If we need to go down there, I am finished. Within three strides I will be jammed tight and no one will be able to move forward or backward.'

Sheldrak needed advice and, as always, turned to Isthmus. 'Can you help us, Isthmus? Do you know if the blood belongs to Menth?'

'Or Dee?' added Kurn, looking sharply at Sheldrak.

Isthmus shook his head. 'Unfortunately I cannot tell. If you were to ask me my opinion, then I trust we have made right decisions since leaving Seathon and this is where we are supposed to be. Sheldrak, take out Northstar.'

Shel did as he was asked and the tip of the sword glowed softly with a golden hue.

Isthmus continued. 'The blade tells us we are on the correct route, but if this is where I think it is then there should be a sign. Check the walls of the cave around the tunnel.'

They all frantically moved the lichen about until a shout from Margg took them over to a point to the right of the tunnel at shoulder height. There was a crevice in the rock, not a big one, barely more than a crack, but Isthmus said to Sheldrak, 'Hold the tip of the blade to that gap in the cave wall.'

Shel had barely got Northstar raised when it flew from his hand, settling into the hole in the wall perfectly. The hilt was raised like a handle to a door. The wall seemed to throb and then ancient runes appeared next to the sword. The runes changed and moved on the wall, like small insects scurrying for cover when an old flagstone is raised.

They merged to form one word, 'truth'.

The throbbing stopped and Shel pulled the sword easily from the wall and then the cave was as before, a gentle blue with water lapping against the stone floor behind them.

Sheldrak spoke to them all, growing in stature with every word that left his lips.

'This is the way to Tremain. The path to glory or death. The evil that awaits us at the end of this journey is great. My heart tells me that Dee and Menth have also taken this route and we must follow. It is our destiny, and our lands rely on our strength.

'Get our things. We must waste no more time, we must find Menth and bring her back to the Seven.'

Gregorn's raised voice boomed around the cave. 'Listen to me, Sheldrak. I cannot fit down that tunnel. It is a physical impossibility. How can I be part of the Seven if I cannot continue the path to Tremain?'

Isthmus spoke for Sheldrak. 'You are not meant to make this part of the journey. Your services to the cause must lie elsewhere. This is meant to be, Gregorn. You have a role to play, but it must be back in your birthplace. A war is starting in Arbrain – go and save your people. It is Faith.'

'Then Faith it is. I shall go to Arbrain, alone.'

'Not a hope in hell, Greggy old bean. You and I are a team. A double act. Shel, I love you mate, but I can't let Gregorn go on his own.'

'Wait, please,' said Sheldrak. 'This is happening too fast. Is this right, Isthmus? Are Gregorn and Shade to walk a different path from the rest of us?'

'It is Faith, Sheldrak. Remember why we are all here. This is how it is meant to be, or Gregorn could walk freely down that tunnel. He cannot go. Sheldrak, we must not delay, for if Menth and Dee are down there we are letting them get a long way ahead of us.'

Sheldrak pulled everyone together quickly and with little sentimentality they said their goodbyes.

'By my elders,' bounced off the walls of the cave so that the words seemed to be surrounding them. With tears in his eyes, Shel sheathed Northstar and picked up his bag. Ahead of him, Marggitte followed the light of Isthmus with Kurn behind her. Shel was the last to walk down the tunnel.

As he was fading from view, he turned and took one last look at Shade and Gregorn, stooping into the frame of the tunnel entrance.

Shel shouted one last farewell. 'We will all be together again one day. Hold that thought on your journey.'

But, of course, he was wrong.

He lifted his hand weakly in one final wave and then turned on his way to Underworld.

The darkness swallowed him whole.

Endgame

Essdark had been recuperating, building his strength. Powers throughout the land were coming together. The cave dwellers of the Mountains of Mina were uniting their armies, thousand of creatures ready to fight for the powers of darkness and evil.

The trolls of Zani, not seen in this land for centuries, were mustering troops. If he could rid the land of giants and take down Arbrain, the ancient city, then he would rule once more. What was Tremain without the legacy of the giants, the ancient people? They had lived the longest of all, men, animals, Morgs. They had all come after the giants.

He had always been there, in some form, before the giants, somewhere, some time. Or so he thought.

This time it was winner take all. He wouldn't be given a second chance. The world that he loved saw him as evil. Did they not know he was as much a puppet as they were? Too stupid. Couldn't see past love and Faith and all that other Strepsay jak.

He walked around his chambers. The old city was starting to take shape around him again. Had to get things ready for when his visitors arrived. The room he was in was fading in and out of existence. The walls were one second seemingly solid and the next transparent. They were getting closer, the Spawn and others, but he would be ready for them when they arrived.

His strength was returning. He had made a mistake,

walking out before he was ready. The stupid Morgs had let him down. Joice had proven stronger than he thought. He would be far better placed if he were ruling Ontrades, but he wasn't. Arbrain was the one. Take Arbrain and move north.

It was all superficial. If he got the Sword of Destiny then it didn't matter. Of course, taking as much good out of the world as possible would aid the final confrontation. If he had the Spawn's friends dead, Ontrades and Arbrain taken, the Spawn would be his also. And then, well, then he would rise to take his birthright.

He paused in his thinking. Sheldrak did worry him. Essdark knew the ancient writings and what they foretold. But he could not be killed by hand of man. They were the rules of the game. So what lay ahead? Why this battle with the Spawn?

There were too many unanswered questions for him. Keep to his game plan and then, when they reached the endgame, all questions would be answered.

And so the bitch was on her way to him. He looked into the wavering wall in front of him and with a pass of his hand he saw Dee and Menth. He waved his hand again but the picture remained unfocused. He still did not have the strength or the power to see what Sheldrak was doing or where he was.

Essdark wondered if he would ever have the power. The thing about the Spawn was that he had no self-awareness. Sheldrak didn't realise how he could grow and, as long as that remained the situation, then Essdark would always have the upper hand.

The Grey One sat back on his throne. Tremain continued to rebuild around him taking up all his strength and energy.

'Let's bring one more pawn into the game,' he said aloud.

In the little village of Jost, life had been moving on as normal, day in, day out. Sheldrak had been missed, but no one knew the bigger story of which he was now such an integral part.

Divad rose from his cot for the first time in several months. His legs gave way but he waited until the blood flowed through them again. He got to his feet and silently got dressed and packed together some possessions for a journey.

In the next room his mother tossed and turned in her sleep, the same way she had since Divad's condition had started. Divad took a flint from the box near the fire and went outside the cottage. Striking the flint, he raised a small flame that he threw immediately on to the thatched roof of his home.

The flames licked into life, spreading quickly like an angry swarm of bees disturbed from the hive. He looked once at the fire but there was no reflection. His eyes were totally grey. No pupils, no whites, just grey.

He hauled his bag over his shoulder and turned away into the woods, never looking back. He had a long walk ahead of him, a long walk to Tremain.

Here ends the first book of the Tremain saga.

Sheldrak and his companions will return in the second book of the series:

Underworld and Overland

Alan J Hill

Lightning Source UK Ltd.
Milton Keynes UK
24 March 2010

151839UK00001B/33/P